STINGRAY™

THE TITANICAN STRATAGEM

PART OF THE

STINGRAY™
DEADLY
UPRISING
SAGA

STINGRAY™

THE TITANICAN STRATAGEM

By Chris Dale

PART OF THE

STINGRAY™
DEADLY
UPRISING
SAGA

ANDERSON
ENTERTAINMENT

Anderson Entertainment Limited
Third Floor, 86–90 Paul Street, London, EC2A 4NE

The Titanican Stratagem by Chris Dale

Hardcover edition published
by Anderson Entertainment in 2024.

http://www.gerryanderson.com

ISBN: 978-1-914522-77-2

Editorial director: Jamie Anderson
Cover design: Marcus Stamps

Typeset by Rajendra Singh Bisht

Table of Contents

CHAPTER 1 7
Casting the Net

CHAPTER 2 21
The Reprieve

CHAPTER 3 35
First Impressions

CHAPTER 4 51
The Paper Trail

CHAPTER 5 67
The Wreck of the Titan

CHAPTER 6 85
The Third Degree

CHAPTER 7 107
The Gilded Cage

CHAPTER 8 127
Very Strange Bedfellows

CHAPTER 9 145
Death From Above

CHAPTER 10 163
Power Mad

CHAPTER 11 187
An Unlikely Hero

CHAPTER 12 209
Fool's Bargain

EPILOGUE.. 221
Tea For Three

Casting the Net

"**S**teady as she goes, Marina. Stand by for all-stop."

From her position in the navigator's chair aboard Stingray, the green-haired girl nodded in response to the words of Captain Troy Tempest as she listened intently to the hydrophones that would be their first indication of trouble.

The journey thus far had been uneventful enough, if not exactly to Troy's taste; escort duty, particularly for a vessel as slow as the remote-controlled freighter submarine currently alongside them, seemed like a waste of Stingray's formidable capabilities. Nevertheless, it was precisely those capabilities that made the super sub the best candidate for the job, as the freighter was on the last leg of a very special assignment that, if successful, would prove vital to Marineville's defences.

Climbing out of his seat, Troy crossed to the portside console a few feet away where Phones was manning the remote-control link to the freighter. "Nearly there, Phones."

"Right, Troy." The navigator threw a switch on the console and turned to face his captain. "Well, we're all set this end. Soon as we're in position I'll set this baby to work and before you know it, we'll have ourselves our very own early warning system between us and Titanica."

Troy leaned back against the handrail that ran along the side of the deck. "Fine. Well, it's been quiet so far – although my guess is if Titan is going to make a move, this'll be the time."

"He may not even know we're in the area," Phones suggested, in a tone of voice that suggested he didn't completely believe his own words. "I mean, we've done pretty much the same trip half a dozen times already installing the other relay devices over the last few days, and we've not seen hide nor hair of a mechanical fish."

"Yeah. And if you buy that, I've got some magic beans I can sell you! This is the closest we've gotten to his territory so far, remember."

Phones laughed. "Well, it's like my old grandpappy used to say; 'can't never could'. Ain't no harm in thinking positive, at least until you see the other guy's cards. And speaking of cards…" He worked the remote controls for the freighter, gradually reducing her speed and manoeuvring her into position over a specific spot on the seabed before bringing her to a dead stop. "I think here's where we're gonna lay our last hand."

"All-stop, Marina," ordered Troy. Marina gave a thumbs-up in acknowledgement, before reducing their speed to zero and matching Stingray's attitude to that of the freighter.

Troy couldn't help smiling at the sight of Marina working the sub's controls as competently and professionally as any aquanaut in Marineville might have handled them, despite not having received such extensive training as that given to commissioned W.A.S.P. officers. It reminded him that there had been some at World Security Patrol Headquarters, and even within Marineville, who had initially regarded Marina's defection to the W.A.S.P.s with extreme suspicion, many presuming she was a spy working for Titan. In time, everyone had come to see what Troy and Phones had seen from the very beginning; that Marina's loyalty was beyond question. Her resolve to do whatever it took to assist in their fight against the enemies of her people had carried her through the gruelling W.A.S.P. training regimen that had ultimately earned her place on the Stingray crew. It may have been an honorary one according to her official file, but in Troy's mind she was as much an officer as any of them who wore the W.A.S.P. uniform.

The sound of Phones working the controls on his console brought Troy back to the present moment, and he watched as his long-time colleague and friend began the next phase of the operation. A monitor on the console showed a view of the underside of the freighter as a hatch slid open and a small spherical device with a drill on one end drifted slowly down towards the seabed.

Over the last few days, Stingray had escorted the freighter as it had installed twelve similar devices in the seabed at various points near and around Titanica. The creation of Marineville scientists, each device was a link in a communications chain that, when activated, would give early warning of the movement of vessels out of the home city of their sworn enemy. Today marked the conclusion of the project, with the device they were now deploying completing the network. Troy only hoped that thirteen wouldn't be the unlucky number.

As the listening device reached the seabed, the drill attached to its underside began to revolve, while thrusters on the topside fired to force it down, and the water around the target area became murky with dislodged rock and debris. A couple of the devices that had been deployed previously had damaged their drill bits attempting to install themselves deep within the seabed and had needed to be replaced, but as the sphere's drill began burrowing in Phones turned to Troy and smiled. "We're in business, Troy."

"How long?"

"Average rock density around these parts, just under four minutes to get her all dug in and hooked up."

"Four minutes it is," agreed Troy, returning to the captain's chair and taking the controls once again. Now it was simply a question of waiting – unless the unexpected occurred.

Marina suddenly raised her hand. "Got something?" Troy asked. Marina didn't respond immediately, her hand remaining raised as she listened intently to her headphones, but he knew that she'd share any further information as soon as she had it.

The sudden shift in mood caught Phones' attention. "You want me back up front, Troy?" he asked quietly.

Troy dared a look in Marina's direction, weighing his duty to Stingray and the mission against keeping Marina where she was. It wasn't her first time manning the navigator's chair, and Troy was keen to give her every opportunity to gain the practical experience she was keen to pursue as part of the Stingray crew, but it was rare to have her at the controls during a combat situation. Nevertheless, she'd had training for just such an eventuality, and her reflexes were good. But in a life-or-death fight for their lives, would they be good enough?

As if sensing he was watching her, Marina gave a short almost imperceptible shake of her head that clearly said *I'm staying put*, before returning her full attention to her work. That was good enough for Troy. "Hold your position, Phones…"

The seconds ticked by, and as they did so Troy's eyes scanned the murky ocean depths outside for any sign of movement; any sign that they might be about to tangle with the enemy. *Come out, come out, wherever you are…*

Suddenly Marina snapped her fingers and Troy gave her his full attention. This was it. "How many?" Marina raised three fingers. "Course?"

Marina grabbed a lock of her hair and shook it, before quickly signing out three more numbers with her fingers. "Green-185?" She nodded.

"Acceleration, rate one. Bringing us about, green-185." Troy operated the controls to bring Stingray to bear on the oncoming vessels – revealing them to be three of the mechanical fish used by Titan and his Aquaphibian soldiers, approaching fast. "How long until the relay device is installed, Phones?"

"Two and a half minutes, Troy!"

Three against one, and one hundred and fifty seconds before they could consider retreating. *And there I was complaining about how uneventful this trip had been.* "Ready Sting missiles, Marina."

Marina prepped the missiles, then visibly tightened her grip on her steering column, mentally bracing herself for what was about to come. "Keep cool, honey. Follow my lead, and we just might get out of this."

Troy's words were as much to reassure himself as Marina, although he knew that whatever happened he could depend on her to remain calm and professional. Nevertheless, he didn't blame Marina when she suddenly drew a sharp breath as the three mechanical fish opened fire on Stingray in near-perfect synchronicity, their missiles now hurtling through the water toward them.

"Stand by for Rate Six, Marina... now!"

Troy's strategy was a desperate gamble but to his mind the only course of action open to them. Stingray accelerated to maximum speed, cruising towards the oncoming missiles as if on a suicide run and then, at the last second, Troy threw the sub into as steep a climb as it could manage, with the enemy torpedoes now following close on their tail, before diving backwards into a loop that would ultimately bring them right into the centre of the mechanical fish shoal.

The enemy fleet scattered, each Aquaphibian crew uncertain how to proceed with the attack after the loss of what had seemed an easy victory. In panic, one crew made the mistake of moving towards Stingray rather than away from her, giving Troy the opening they needed.

"Hold on, Marina!" The three torpedoes were now so close it was only the powerful wake of Stingray's ratemaster propeller that was preventing them from striking home, and Troy's plan involved getting even closer than that to this isolated mechanical fish. Realising that their opponent had singled them out and was heading straight towards them, the Aquaphibian crew attempted to move out of range – but Stingray was faster. At less than ten feet until collision the super sub suddenly banked sharply, forcing the Aquaphibians to take evasive action – and leading them straight into the path of the oncoming missiles. All three impacted with the fish and obliterated it in an instant, giving Stingray valuable time to dive for a rough landing on the seabed amid the flurry of fire and debris, temporarily eluding their remaining two pursuers.

Troy shot a look over his shoulder. "Phones, where's that freighter now?"

Phones glanced down at his controls. "I've got her holding position over the relay sensor, providing cover while it's drilling itself in. Want me to keep her there?"

Troy shook his head. "Let's make some use of her. Steer her course green-150, we'll set her up as a decoy. With any luck, maybe one of those mechanical fish will go after it. Could buy us some time."

"Green-150," Phones repeated, inputting the necessary commands to the freighter. "Setting her running at Rate Two..."

Seconds later Troy and Marina saw the robot ship cruise past the cabin windows, moving away from the battle scene. For a moment it looked as though one of the Aquaphibian crews might be fooled into taking the bait and pursuing it, but to Troy's dismay the two surviving mechanical fish kept their attention firmly focused on Stingray. Moving through the debris cloud of their fallen sister craft, it didn't take the duo long to locate Stingray's new position.

"Let's get moving, Marina!" Troy ordered, and within seconds Stingray was off the seabed and moving through the water once again – just in time to avoid being hit by two more missiles fired from the mechanical fish.

"Change of plan, Phones!" Troy called again. "Buzz them with it. Do anything you can to make that thing a nuisance to them."

But the freighter was already on its way back towards them. "Way ahead of you, Troy!" replied Phones. "She's not as spry as Stingray, but I'll see what I can do."

By now, Stingray was back on the tail of the two surviving mechanical fish, which now peeled off from each other and headed in different directions. "Marina, if you think you can —"

Troy's words were cut off as a Sting missile erupted from Stingray and tore into the nearest mechanical fish, destroying it instantly. Marina looked to Troy, a somewhat apologetic look in her eyes, but Troy just smiled. "As I was about to say; if you think you can get a clear shot, don't wait for me to give the order to fire. Good girl."

Relieved that she hadn't stepped out of line, Marina winked – and then a sudden explosion from somewhere behind Stingray caused both to grip their steering columns tightly to avoid being thrown from their chairs. "Hold on!" Troy called, before swinging Stingray around in a tight arc—

And straight towards the gaping maw of the third mechanical fish.

"Ready Sting missile three!" Troy barked. Marina's hand was already working the controls, but they both knew it was too late. Troy could have sworn he could see the torpedo with their name on it, waiting inside that horrible fish mouth, preparing to launch…

Suddenly, the mechanical fish erupted in flame, and Stingray was rocked by the shockwave of the detonation as she hurtled through it. Both Troy and Marina covered their eyes with their hands at the brilliance of the unexpected explosion, an explosion far larger than the destruction of the previous two fish had created. A split second before this fish's destruction, Troy had had the distinct impression of a large dark shape looming into view just slightly to port. Daring to open his eyes, his suspicions were confirmed as he brought Stingray around for a second look; debris from the robot freighter mingled with that of the mechanical fish in the water ahead of them.

Troy clapped his hands in delight. "Phones, that was terrific!"

Phones shrugged. "Well, like you said Troy, I figured we'd make some use of her. Be a shame if she'd survived but we'd all been blown sky high."

"It would at that…" Troy nodded slowly, watching the debris from the robot freighter and the last mechanical fish drifting toward the seabed, stunned at just how close they'd come to meeting the same fate themselves. "Still, I don't think Commander Shore's gonna approve of using her for a suicide run…"

Phones nodded. "Completing the mission, defeating an enemy aggressor, and saving Stingray and all our lives in the process?" He sighed. "He's gonna be furious."

As calm returned to the undersea world around Stingray, Troy allowed himself a moment to breathe. Any victory celebration would be premature – and perhaps fatal – if this were only the prelude to a larger attack. "Any more out there, Marina?"

Marina was already listening intently to her hydrophones once again. The seconds ticked lengthily away… before she finally shook her head and gave a thumbs-up. "All clear, huh? Well, let's hope it stays that way."

A green light suddenly began flashing on Phones' console. "And whaddya know? Our new surveillance network concurs."

"Up and running already?" Troy asked, as he heard Phones get to his feet and move towards the front of the cabin.

"Yep," Phones confirmed, leaning against the backs of Troy and Marina's chairs. "Now if Titan so much as chucks a pebble in our direction, we'll know about it ahead of time."

These were the moments that made Troy Tempest proudest to serve as captain of Stingray. The vessel was a triumph of engineering and technical precision, but it was all for nothing without a good crew to man her – and he knew his ship had the finest crew in the world. "Nice work, Phones. You too, Marina."

"Yeah Marina," agreed Phones. "Much more of this and you'll have done me out of a job!"

Smiling, Marina shook her head, before holding up her hand up to him for a high-five. Phones responded eagerly, slapping his hand against hers with considerable gusto and laughing, before making his way back to his chair.

Troy watched their exchange with amusement. Marina had grown so used to human customs and idiosyncrasies by now that sometimes it was easy to forget that she came from another world entirely. Noticing him watching her, Marina smiled warmly before saluting at her captain. Troy couldn't resist saluting her in turn.

"Okay then Marina, let's head back." He reached for the radio controls. "Tower from Stingray. Operation complete. Final sounding device positioned and activated. Surveillance network is now fully installed and operational. Returning to Marineville."

Stingray banked to port before accelerating to Rate Six and setting sail for home...

A few hours later, not too far from the scene of Stingray's triumph over the mechanical fish fleet, a small slim metallic green and red vessel cut through the ocean depths, heading in the opposite direction. Its single occupant surveyed the wreckage of the mechanical fish scattered around the ocean floor and sighed to himself, before reaching out a green reptilian hand to operate a control.

"Surface agent X-20 to Titanica. Approaching from the south. ETA two marine minutes."

No immediate reply was forthcoming, but he could picture the scene in Titanica's traffic control room right now; the two Aquaphibians on duty were no doubt squabbling over which would be the one to pick up the microphone to answer the call, and whomever had won that battle would now need to carefully plan their response to make sure all their words were in the right order.

Sure enough, after a few moments more, the gurgling and halting reply finally came. "This is Titanican traffic control. Airlock and travel tube are ready to receive you."

"Acknowledged, Titanica. X-20 out." Closing the channel, X-20 slowed his craft and gradually pitched her towards the seabed, into the vast ocean trench which held the domain of his master. The view through the portholes began to darken, almost to utter blackness... until finally pinpoints of light began to show on the seabed. The lights gradually grew larger, illuminating the vast underwater complex that was the city of Titanica, sprawling on the seabed seven miles beneath the ocean surface.

X-20 had always loved this view of the city as it offered a chance for him to admire the skill and ingenuity of its construction that had seen it endure for so many marine decades. It was perhaps the greatest engineering feat that the underwater races had ever accomplished, although

X-20 ever so slightly preferred the more elegant design aesthetic of the city of Pacifica – not that he would ever have dared to admit it, of course. The view was also one he cherished because it was often his final solace of the day before Titan unleashed another plot, scheme or master plan, that he would then expect X-20 to put into operation no matter how impractical or foolhardy it might prove to be.

After docking his vessel at one of the perimeter stations, X-20 took a moment to ensure all systems were powered down and that the airlock seal was secure before boarding the travel tube that would carry him directly to the throne room. The travel tube journey took less than two minutes before X-20 found himself in the outer chamber of Titan's throne room and faced by two Aquaphibian guards. Gesturing at them to move aside, the two guards glanced nervously at each other before stepping sideways, allowing X-20 access to the throne room of Titanica – and King Titan himself.

It took X-20 a moment to locate his master, standing in front of the tank containing the fish Teufel. Aware that Titan may have been in some form of communication with the fish god, X-20 waited a few moments before clearing his throat and announcing in his most servile tone of voice, "I am here as you requested, Great Titan…"

Titan turned at X-20's voice and nodded, albeit only a half-nod that was less a greeting and more an acknowledgement of his presence, before returning his attention to Teufel.

X-20 had never been comfortable around Teufel. He wasn't entirely sure why, although the fact that the large fish was the only being in Titanica who was entirely safe from Titan's wrath possibly had something to do with it. Worshipped as a god by Titan, for reasons X-20 had never quite managed to get to the bottom of, he had yet to see any true sign of the fish's supposed deity. Had Teufel been a sentient being, X-20 might have suspected him to be some kind of master con artist playing a cunning long game for free food and lodging. As it was, it was more likely that the fish was an overpampered pet who had simply grown too fat on snails and seaweed to be safely removed from the confines of his tank.

"I take it this has something to do with the incident along our border earlier today…" X-20 began, as he finally dared to approach his master.

"You would be correct, X-20." Titan's powerful voice echoed impressively around the chamber. "The W.A.S.P.s are growing ever bolder… and I believe that we must meet their challenge in kind."

Sounds like yet another job I'm not going to like, thought X-20. "I take it you have some kind of scheme in mind by which we achieve this, Mighty Titan?"

"Indeed." Titan now turned away from Teufel and strode across the room towards his throne – X-20 close on his heels all the way. "Since we have failed to dispose of the accursed Troy Tempest and Stingray by ourselves, I feel the time is right to open negotiations with other races willing to aid in our cause."

As Titan climbed the steps to his throne, X-20 stopped and replayed his master's words in his mind. *Negotiations?* It sounded a bold strategy to be sure, but before he offered any sort of opinion, X-20 wanted to be precisely clear about what was under discussion here. "Surely you speak of… an alliance, Majesty?"

"Indeed I do!" Titan agreed triumphantly as he reached the top of the steps and lowered himself onto his throne, grandly running his hands along its arms. "Perhaps several, should it prove necessary."

Always ready to appear supportive where his master's plans were concerned regardless of his personal feelings – which in this case were somewhat mixed – X-20 clapped his hands enthusiastically and applied his most fawning tone of voice. "Oh, a masterful strategy to be sure, Great Titan…"

Titan nodded sagely. "Of this there can be no doubt, X-20." He gestured towards the tank. "It came from Teufel, after all."

X-20's face froze in mid-smile. His eyes darted over toward the tank where the vacant-eyed piscine stared back at him, as if daring the surface agent to find fault with the scheme. X-20 managed to bow in reverence to the alleged fish god, although it took a little longer for any words to come. *Say something, you fool, anything!* "I… marvel at the boundless wisdom of the all-powerful Teufel…"

Titan shot a reverential look towards Teufel, giving X-20 a narrow window of opportunity to stand upright again before he did his back an injury. "As do we all."

Relieved that he'd apparently managed to dig himself out of that particular hole, X-20 took a moment to consider this idea of an alliance. Wherever it had really come from, the notion was certainly an interesting one, particularly since there were many other underwater races who had just as little time for the terraineans as did the people of Titanica… although Titan's reputation had long been one of conquest rather than co-existence. Was he really capable of navigating the choppy waters of diplomacy and successfully forging a lasting alliance with another civilisation? It seemed to X-20 as though this was potentially a proposal with a very short lifespan. "Have you a specific potential ally in mind, Great Titan?" he asked tentatively.

"I have." An air of smug satisfaction appeared on Titan's features, a look that X-20 had seen many times before – and one that usually meant X-20 was about to be made to feel very small indeed. "Has it never occurred to you, X-20, that we have a ready-made army within our own territory, just waiting to be let loose on the terraineans?"

X-20 gave the question some thought, but whatever answer Titan had in mind eluded him for the moment. "The Aquaphibians?"

Titan snorted. "Of course not! I need hardly seek an alliance with my own servants." He leaned forward on his throne and steepled his fingers. "No, the army I speak of is elsewhere within our borders. We shall enlist their service immediately! And so X-20, for the first step in this great plan to rid ourselves of the terrainean scourge once and for all..."

X-20 knelt at the base of Titan's throne, trying as hard as he could to appear outwardly excited while at the same time mentally preparing himself for the worst. "Yes, Mighty Titan?"

A thin smile crept across Titan's lips, and X-20 felt his blood freeze at the sight of it. "I'm finally going to do what I should have done years ago – and send you to the underwater prison of Aquatraz!"

X-20 fainted dead away. Only Teufel, and the Aquaphibian guards, heard the cruel laughter that echoed mercilessly around the room...

CHAPTER 2

The Reprieve

One marine hour later, a small fleet consisting of three mechanical fish and Titan's personal yacht departed the city of Titanica, heading deeper into Titan's domain.

Seated on a plush sofa aboard his master's craft, X-20 was still recovering from his earlier shock, and an even greater one now greeted him as Titan handed him a mug of steaming hot seaweed tea. It was the first time the surface agent could remember seeing genuine concern on that imperious face, and it did nothing to reassure him. "You should know by now when I am joking and when I am serious, X-20," said Titan, sitting down beside him.

X-20 took a grateful sip of his unexpected drink. "You have threatened to imprison me in Aquatraz on several prior occasions, Great Titan…"

Titan scoffed. "Oh, but only to give you an incentive to succeed in your assignments. I would never really condemn you to life imprisonment in such a place for failing in a mission."

"You wouldn't?"

"No. I suspect I would be more likely to have you permanently exiled to the surface." He gazed casually out of the window. "Or simply put to death…"

X-20 glanced down in sudden horror at the seaweed tea, wondering if such a death lay waiting within the mug via one of the underwater poisons Titan had at his disposal. "You are too kind to your humble servant, majesty," he managed to reply through gritted teeth, as he set the mug down on a nearby table.

Titan grinned. "Remember that, X-20. Always."

Desperate to change the subject to anything else except his own potential fate, X-20 brought the conversation back to the purpose of their mission. "This idea of an alliance, your majesty..."

Titan nodded gravely. "You may speak freely, my friend. I would welcome an honest opinion."

Oh, I bet you would, X-20 thought to himself. The use of the word 'friend' was another particularly unsettling development. Nevertheless, the journey from Titanica had provided X-20 with the opportunity to reflect on his master's latest scheme; if nothing else, it had been a useful way to distract himself from the relentless churning of his anxious stomach.

He had to admit that the idea had merit, as it represented the kind of unconventional thinking that many of their operations against the terraineans so often lacked. Should an alliance be forged with members of another underwater race, it would also mean that there would then be other people around to suffer Titan's wrath should things go wrong – and that was always a good thing in X-20's eyes.

"I see the wisdom of it most clearly now," he began. "The Titanican people are strong but were we to be allied to another race of equal power—"

"*Almost* equal power," Titan cut in firmly.

X-20 raised a hand in a gesture of contrition. "Forgive me; *almost* equal power, then the W.A.S.P.s would not dare to oppose us. It is a bold, courageous move, to be sure..."

Titan nodded. "And it is one that the W.A.S.P.s will not be expecting!"

"Oh, of course, great Titan. But it seems to me that the plan lives or dies by the quality of allies that you obtain." He stood, and moved to gaze out from the forward windows at the vast underwater complex their vessel was currently approaching. "Do you really believe you will find such quality in this place?"

Titan moved to join X-20, and together the two men took in the view of their imminent destination, the underwater prison of Aquatraz – the place where those who were decreed by Teufel to be enemies of the Titanican people were sentenced to spend the rest of their natural lives. Including, Titan reflected, the accursed Tempest... had the traitress Marina not helped him to escape!

Aquatraz was legendary among the water-dwelling peoples, with even its name striking fear into the hearts of the most formidable of Titan's foes. Founded many marine years ago, the prison complex was an example of the underwater races making use of items discarded by the terraineans; in this case, a number of vessels that had sunk (or been encouraged to sink) over the decades. From nineteenth-century sailing ships to late twentieth-century naval destroyers, the wrecks had then been chemically treated to prevent deterioration before being permanently installed on the seabed in a secret location not too far from Titanica itself – and guarded by a dangerous whirlpool. Gutted of their original interiors and outfitted with the very latest security technology, these abandoned ships now served new roles as a prison compound for the enemies of Titan – somewhere where they were unable to do any further damage to him or his reputation.

Titan considered X-20's words carefully. "I do take your point... but nevertheless, I believe this to be a logical place to start. Within the walls of Aquatraz are some two thousand prisoners; perhaps more, I don't keep count! But I do know that it's about time they were put to some use!"

X-20 dared to voice the obvious flaw in the plan. "But surely those prisoners are here because they hate you? Why would they choose to side with you now?"

He winced as Titan suddenly gripped his shoulder – but the gesture was oddly not one of anger, but exuberance. "Ah, but think of it, X-20! This place is packed to the gills with the downtrodden, the defeated, long-forgotten souls starved of food and freedom. You think any of them would refuse an opportunity to leave this place if I were to offer them a chance to serve me in a final massive offensive against the W.A.S.P.s?"

He's clearly committed to going through with this, thought X-20. *Nothing I say is going to change his mind, so I may as well agree with him.* "Well, when you put it like that..."

Titan nodded, basking in his own brilliance. "You will see, X-20. They shall join me. And when they do, I shall have a fighting force with which to crush the W.A.S.P.s once and for all!"

I hope you're right, X-20 thought, as the yacht commenced its final approach to the docking tube. *I'm dreading the trip back to Titanica if they don't...*

X-20 had never visited Aquatraz before, but its interior lived down to all the nightmares he had ever had about it. Overcrowded cells crammed with the dregs of the underwater world met his eyes as he walked with Titan along the central corridor of one of the main prison ships, and alien faces twisted in rage shouted angry epithets (including some in languages he had never heard before) in the direction of the underwater despot as he marched proudly past them.

X-20 tried not to make eye contact with any of the prisoners lest he too become a target for their anger... but he was surprised to see Titan regarding them with expressions of amusement and contempt. His master was clearly enjoying parading past cells packed with enemies he (well, Teufel) had condemned to this awful place, although X-20 was starting to get a horrible feeling that if any prisoner here actually agreed to serve Titan, they'd be too psychotic to be of any real use.

Perhaps Titan spoke the truth when he said he would do me a kindness to kill me rather than send me here, X-20 thought to himself, quickening his pace as Titan mounted stairs leading to a footbridge overlooking the corridor and a communications station from which he could address the entire facility.

"Prepare the intercom, X-20!" Titan ordered grandly. "I wish to speak to the entire prison!"

"At once, great Titan!" X-20 hurriedly worked the communications station, all while two columns of Aquaphibian guards marched into the corridor and took up position along the doors of the cells. "All is ready, Titan!" X-20 confirmed after a few moments of work, before handing Titan a microphone. "Speak, and every prisoner in Aquatraz shall hear."

Titan nodded, before holding the microphone to his mouth. "Prisoners of Aquatraz!"

The corridor erupted in noise, as the prisoners began shouting and yelling to drown out the words of the man responsible for their incarceration. Without waiting for orders, an Aquaphibian guard stepped forward and fired his rifle into the air. The sudden ring of shots echoed around the interior of the ancient hulk, and – much to X-20's surprise – the prisoners fell silent. Satisfied that he had done a good job, the guard lowered his weapon – and tried his best to ignore the seawater now dripping onto his head from the minute hole he had just created in the ceiling.

Titan's voice boomed loud and clear from every speaker across the Aquatraz prison complex. "You all know who I am; I am Titan, leader of the underwater city of Titanica! Each and every one of you is imprisoned here because, at some time or other, you dared to oppose me, and were found to be an enemy of Titanica! Now I come to you with an offer you would be wise to accept. I am offering you... your freedom...!"

A murmur of interest rippled around the prison cells before Titan continued. "I am plotting a massive offensive against the terraineans – beginning with the complete and utter destruction of the World Aquanaut Security Patrol! But I require men. Loyal soldiers who will aid me in this great and noble cause. Serve me well in my new army, and when the terraineans are no more, you shall be free to depart my service to resume your old lives once again."

Titan turned and nodded to X-20, who now operated a control on his console. As the heavy metal doors of every cell throughout Aquatraz suddenly rolled open, Aquaphibian guards raised their weapons and aimed them at the prisoners, prepared to quell any sudden attempts to escape en masse.

Titan's voice now built to a rousing crescendo. "Those who would be part of this great mission step forward now and join me in a bold new future for the underwater peoples!" He raised his arms triumphantly and stared down from the footbridge, eager to greet his new army of loyal cannon fodder.

Nothing happened. The Aquaphibian guards looked first at each other, then to Titan in disbelief, with one or two gurgling in confusion at the unexpected lack of response from their prisoners. Not one of the inmates appeared the least bit impressed with Titan's sales pitch.

"It's the same all across the complex, great Titan!" cried X-20. "None of them are leaving their cells!"

Titan stalked over to X-20's side and stared into the monitor displaying video feed from other sections of Aquatraz, as if willing the images on it to change. "What is wrong with these fools, X-20? Why do they not volunteer to join our noble cause?"

"Perhaps, your majesty, they do not believe victory against the terraineans is possible for you…"

At the sound of the vaguely familiar voice Titan whirled around and glared down from the bridge with a fury in his eyes that X-20 had seldom seen before. "Who spoke!?!"

A solitary fishman had stepped from his cell into the corridor below, and now raised a guilty hand. "I did, your Majesty…"

A flash of recognition crossed Titan's face; the creature's build, posture and fawning tone of voice were all very familiar. He pointed at the malcontent. "X-20, who is that man?"

X-20 squinted as he attempted to identify the prisoner in question. "I believe it to be Sculpin, your majesty."

Titan rubbed his chin thoughtfully. "Sculpin, eh?" Then the memories came flooding back to him. "Ah yes – the incident with the echo sounder and the giant Gargan…"

"Indeed." It had been many months since Titan had found himself an unwitting prisoner aboard his own personal yacht when a scheme to destroy Troy Tempest and Stingray had backfired horribly. Sculpin had constructed an echo sounder, a device capable of attracting the powerful sea creature known as the Gargan and driving it into a destructive frenzy. Titan had then used the sounder to turn the Gargan against a deep sea bathescape under the protection of the W.A.S.P.s, but the intervention of the devious Troy Tempest had seen the Gargan tricked into attacking Titan's yacht instead. Once the sounder's power had finally run down and the Gargan had given up its attack, Titan had had no hesitation in sentencing Sculpin to life imprisonment in Aquatraz for the failure of the project. It was bad enough that the device had proved catastrophically unreliable on its very first deployment in the field – but putting the life of Titan himself at risk? Unforgivable.

Still, the fact that Sculpin had spoken up now made Titan wonder if perhaps there was more to this snivelling little creature than he had previously suspected. He pointed directly at the cowering engineer. "Bring him to me!"

Two Aquaphibian guards grabbed Sculpin, dragging him along the corridor and hauling him up the stairs, before throwing him at Titan's feet. Sculpin staggered as he struggled to stand, rubbing his bloodied palms that had been injured when he had fallen.

Titan loomed over him. "So Sculpin, you feel that victory over the terraineans is impossible, do you?"

Sculpin shook his head. "Oh no, not I majesty. I merely voice the opinion of the majority. Many of those incarcerated here believe that they shall not regain their freedom until Titanica falls to the might of the World Aquanaut Security Patrol…"

Titan looked down towards the cells and into the angry desperate eyes of those who had wronged him in the past. It was clear from the expressions on their faces that they agreed with every word that Sculpin said… and it was also clear what they felt towards Titan himself.

X-20 was right, Titan thought ruefully. *There is no army here.* He made a fist, and pounded it against the handrail in frustration. "I offer them their lives and this is how they repay me?"

"As they see it, you are offering them a chance to throw away their lives, great Titan! How many times have your mechanical fish engaged Stingray… and how many of their crews have ever returned to Titanica to tell the tale of a glorious victory over her crew?" Sculpin gestured down towards the prisoners. "These people may be your enemies but they're not fools. They know that participating in an attack on the terraineans would merely be a somewhat quicker death than the one they are experiencing here."

Sculpin's words infuriated Titan and for a moment he considered grabbing the man and hurling him from the bridge just to make a point to all the inmates of Aquatraz, but the awful thing was he couldn't deny the truth of what he was saying. If he were in their place, would he feel any differently? "If your incarceration has proven so arduous Sculpin, why should you wish to help me now?"

"Oh, but I do, majesty! You see, I have had ample opportunity to reflect on my failure in the many months since you sentenced me to this hellish place... and now I wish to revenge myself upon the man responsible for my incarceration!"

A nearby Aquaphibian guard immediately stepped forward, quickly raising his weapon and placing himself between Titan and Sculpin. The engineer quickly took a pace backwards, raising his hands in surrender. "No, my friend, you misunderstand! My grievance is with the accursed terrainean, Troy Tempest! It was he who placed the echo sounder on the mighty Titan's craft, thereby setting in motion the chain of events that led to my fall from grace. It is *he* that I seek vengeance against. Your majesty, I wish only to serve you once again..."

Titan maintained eye contact with Sculpin, trying to decide the man's fate. Did he speak the truth? Was he merely trying to save his own skin? And was it better to save face by leaving this place with a single ally, albeit one as useless as Sculpin, rather than none at all? "Seal the other prisoners back in their cells, X-20."

"At once, mighty Titan." X-20 pressed a button on the console, and the low heavy sound of multiple cell doors closing in unison reverberated around the prison. The Aquaphibian guards relaxed, albeit with one or two clearly disappointed that they wouldn't be getting to indulge in any brutality against their prisoners today.

X-20 stepped forward to advise Titan. "Sculpin was one of the finest engineers ever to serve you, your majesty. His technical genius is spoken of in hushed tones throughout Titanica even now. It may perhaps be advisable to grant him a reprieve..." He visibly wilted under a sudden glare from Titan. "O-or not."

Titan came to a decision. It was true that Sculpin's engineering prowess had brought considerable benefits to Titanica over the years, the incident with the Gargan notwithstanding. Perhaps he truly had learned from his incarceration in Aquatraz, and if not... well, he could always kill him later. "Very well, Sculpin. I shall indeed grant you a reprieve..."

Sculpin smiled gratefully – although the smile vanished as Titan held up a marine stopwatch and pressed the button on top of it. "Providing you can convince me of your value. You have thirty marine seconds!"

In panic, Sculpin looked first to X-20, who merely looked away, then back to Titan – and then to the stopwatch. Five seconds had already elapsed. "W-well, your majesty... you came here seeking allies for an attack against the terraineans, correct?"

Titan rolled his eyes. "This I know. Your time grows short..."

"Of course... well, it occurs to me that there is somewhere you could find complete details on possible candidates for an alliance. Powerful candidates indeed, whose hatred of the terraineans rivals even ours!" Sculpin's words began to come faster as he watched the seconds on Titan's watch tick relentlessly away. "Er, exact locations of their home bases, their military capabilities, their strengths and their weaknesses. All this valuable information, and more is yours for the taking!"

Titan raised the stopwatch as its hands crept into the final seconds. "And where might I obtain this information? Speak!"

Sculpin dropped to his knees in terror and closed his eyes. "In the stronghold of your most hated enemies!" he gasped, now resigned to whatever fate his insolence had brought upon him.

The idea was so simple that Titan couldn't believe he hadn't thought of it before. Yes... the accursed terraineans were sure to keep extensive records of their past missions. If he could get his hands on those... "The enemy of my enemy is my friend..." he muttered.

"Beg pardon, your majesty?"

Titan blinked, not realising he had said the words out loud. "Nothing, X-20." He looked down at the pitiful figure of Sculpin. Perhaps there was potential here after all.

Titan knelt down, took hold of the man, and eased him back to his feet. When Sculpin opened his eyes, he saw on Titan's face... what was that? Gratitude? Appreciation? Respect, even? Whatever it was, he couldn't remember seeing it there before. It scared him.

Titan nodded slowly, as he pocketed his stopwatch. "Very good, Sculpin. Come, X-20. You and I – and of course our friend here – shall return to Titanica at once to plan our campaign!" He wrinkled his nose. "And perhaps to find this fellow some clean clothes too..."

"And something to eat, majesty?"

Titan laughed, and placed an arm around Sculpin's shoulder. "But of course, my friend! Tonight, you eat like a king!"

X-20 watched indignantly as Titan and Sculpin walked away, Titan heaping praise on Sculpin, and Sculpin cravenly making all sorts of promises and suggestions to aid their master in his great cause.

Crawler, he thought to himself, before following the pair back to Titan's yacht...

The following afternoon Sergeants Hank Waterman and Stan Seaver, the two security guards who manned Marineville's main entrance security checkpoint during the day, looked up from the paperwork in their security hut as a refuse collection truck rolled up to the gate. Grabbing his clipboard and pencil, Hank headed out to meet it – but the small man seated in the truck's cab was not the one he was familiar with. "Say, what's going on here? You're not the usual driver!"

The driver's unnaturally large eyes went a little distant for a moment, before he replied "He's, er... he's sick! Yeah, yeah, real sick..."

"Aww gee, I'm sorry to hear that. What's wrong with him?"

A strange smile crossed the driver's face, beneath his crooked moustache. "Let's just say he's a little... *tied up* at the moment..."

"Oh, caught that flu that's been going around, huh? Yeah, I had a bout of that last month. I was in bed for three days. Nasty stuff." Consulting the schedule on his clipboard, Hank added "But you know you're a day early?"

The driver shrugged. "Alas, it could not be helped. Staff shortages. It is either today, or not at all."

"Fair enough." Hank logged the truck's arrival on his clipboard, then slipped his pencil behind his ear. "Say, er, give the other guy my regards, will ya?"

"I shall. I am certain you will see him again."

"Thanks, buddy." Hank slapped the side of the truck twice. "Okay Stan. Raise the gate!"

From the security hut Stan gave Hank a thumbs-up, and the security gate swung upwards to allow the truck access. The driver nodded gratefully as he restarted the engine. "Thank you, officer..."

Hank watched the truck drive into Marineville until it turned a corner and headed out of sight, then looked towards his partner as he approached. "Say Hank, do you ever wonder if maybe we don't check these delivery and collection guys as thoroughly as we oughta?" Stan asked.

Hank laughed, shaking his head. "You didn't catch the stench, Stan. Titan and his crew would think twice before stowing away aboard a truck that smells as bad as that!" He rubbed his chin thoughtfully. "Still, I can't help feeling that I've seen that driver somewhere before..."

Aboard the truck, X-20 cackled with delight at the ease with which he had once again infiltrated Marineville. "The fools! I don't know why they don't just issue me with a permanent pass! I'm here often enough!"

As the truck winded its way around the buildings that made up the Marineville administrative section, X-20 suddenly put his foot on the accelerator and swung the garbage truck sharply into the next turning – then slammed a button on the dashboard with precision timing. He heard a loud clattering sound from the rear of the truck, as one of the trash cans suddenly tumbled out and onto the road – urged on by a hidden prod activated by the button.

"Oh dear," he said quietly, watching the can roll away in his wing mirror. "I seem to have lost something..."

But the truck drove on without stopping.

Unnoticed by anyone else the trash can rolled at speed along the road – then abruptly slowed to a stop, took a moment to ascertain which direction it wanted to go in next, and then resumed rolling. It apparently had a very specific target in mind. Bouncing over a grass verge, it finally came to a stop when it crashed into a group of fellow trash cans standing at the rear of the building that housed the Marineville records archive.

Had anyone been around to observe the can's arrival, they might have heard it emit one or two muffled grunts of discomfort – almost as if someone were inside it. After a moment, the grunts died down– replaced by an odd electronic hum, and the sound of buttons being pressed from within.

Trying valiantly to ignore the unfortunate spasms of cramp in his left leg, Sculpin chuckled to himself as he activated the banks of sophisticated surveillance equipment that lined the inside of the can... and waited for nightfall.

CHAPTER 3

First Impressions

As dawn broke over Marineville the following morning, the shrill sound of the alert klaxons echoed around the base, followed by the voice of Commander Shore over the loudspeakers. *"Attention Marineville! Security alert, all stations! All personnel are ordered to remain clear of administrative block until further notice! That is all."*

The main security vault of the Marineville records archive, ordinarily one of the tidiest and most well-ordered rooms on the base, had been torn apart. Folders of sensitive documents had apparently been pulled from their shelves, hurriedly searched and then discarded, while every filing cabinet in the room had been pulled open and rifled through. The room had been sealed off pending an investigation, but now stray papers littering the floor were displaced by the jets of his hoverchair as Commander Shore entered the room, followed closely by Captain Troy Tempest. "Boy – what a mess!"

"Yeah Troy. In fact, it's in such a mess that it's too early to tell what's missing."

"How did they get in?" Troy asked. "I thought these vaults were impregnable! What happened to the alarms, the voiceprint checks, and so on?"

"All bypassed. Whoever got in here obviously knows their way around security systems." Then in a quieter voice, Shore added "World Security Patrol Headquarters aren't too happy about this, Troy."

Troy nodded. "I can imagine. We were holding some pretty top-secret material in this archive." Kneeling down, Troy started to gather up some papers, then gave up when he realised just how many of them there were. "Still, I guess there's not much they can do about it..."

"Oh, they can. And they are. They're flying in one of their own people to take charge of the investigation. She should be arriving mid-morning."

Troy blinked in surprise. "She, sir?"

"Yeah, Troy... a Lieutenant Sara Coral." Shore shrugged. "A fine young officer by all accounts; professional, dedicated, driven. Should get to the bottom of this in no time."

With that, Shore turned his chair towards the door and hovered out of the room, his exit once again disturbing the papers scattered across the floor. Troy followed the commander out of the building in silence; it was obvious Shore had more on his mind, and as they headed outside he decided to dare to coax it out of him. "What's wrong then, sir?"

"Oh nothing, Troy. Nothing..."

Shore and Troy looked out across Marineville. The morning sun was now climbing high over the base, and it looked like it was going to be another fine day – despite what had happened in the records archive.

In a quiet voice, Troy said "There was nothing you personally could have done to prevent this, sir."

"I know that, Troy. They shouldn't, but these things do happen after all, even in Marineville." Shore sighed wearily. "No, it's just... oh, I don't know. I've been here so long now that sometimes I feel less like the commander of a military base, and more like... well—"

"The mayor of a town?" Troy suggested.

Shore chuckled. "I guess so... and part of me likes it that way. I know everybody here, everybody here knows everybody else, and we all get along just dandy. The idea of an intruder coming in and tearing up the place, then another total outsider coming in and interfering with the way we do things... well, it doesn't quite sit right with me. I'm sure our own security boys could sort all this just fine."

"Well, maybe that's part of the problem." Troy suggested. "I mean, from Headquarters' point of view, we're all just a little *too* familiar with each other, a little too cosy to get to the bottom of this efficiently. Maybe what's needed here *is* a total outsider to come in and shake things up a bit. Y'know, someone who can be truly objective?"

"Yeah, maybe," Shore agreed. "And it'll only be until this mess is cleared up. If she's as good as they tell me, Lieutenant Coral will have whoever did this behind bars within six hours, and probably earn herself another twelve medals for bravery beyond the call of duty in the process." Shore sighed, rolling his chair away from the building. "Just keep her out of my hair, will you?"

Troy smiled as he watched him go. "I'll do my best, sir."

A few hours later, Stan and Hank's mid-morning coffee break was interrupted as the same garbage truck they had allowed through yesterday backed up to the main gate. Glancing at each other in surprise, the two guards left the security hut and walked out to meet the driver – the same small wide-eyed moustachioed man that had paid them a visit yesterday.

"Say, you can't come in today Mac!" called Hank.

"Oh, not any trouble I hope, officer?" asked the driver, as he stepped down from the cab.

"The whole base is on alert, pal," added Stan. "Ain't nobody coming through this gate until we get the all-clear from Commander Shore."

"I see." The truck driver was wringing his hands and looked decidedly perturbed. "Oh well, I guess that's that then…"

"Anything wrong?" asked Hank.

The truck driver sighed. "Oh, a most unfortunate accident on my part. When I was here yesterday it appears I either mislaid or just didn't collect one of your trash cans. I was one short when I got back to the depot last night."

"So? No big deal. The other guy can pick it up next week."

"Would that that were so," said the truck driver mournfully. "Unfortunately the depot supervisor is a real tyrant about such things. Security, you understand. I have taken full responsibility for the error, but he is inclined to blame the colleague I was covering. Observe." The driver pointed to the cab of his truck, and the pale figure slumped in the passenger seat, apparently unconscious.

"Say, isn't that—"

"Your regular driver, yes. So concerned is he about this matter that he insisted on leaving his sick bed to come and search for the missing can in person." The driver shook his head sadly. "Alas, he was just too unwell to stay awake for the duration of the journey."

"Yeah, he does look real sick," Hank agreed. "Maybe we oughta call the doc out here to take a look at him…"

"Oh, no no no!" The truck driver leaned over the gate and waved his hands frantically. "There's no need for that. If you can just load the missing can onto the truck, that would be more than helpful."

Hank idly scratched the back of his neck as he considered the request. "Well, yeah, I'd love to help you pal, but like I said, ain't nobody getting through here until the alert's over."

The truck driver pointed over Hank's shoulder. "Oh, but surely that's it right over there," he said innocently.

Hank turned, and blinked in surprise. Indeed there was a garbage can parked along the wall just a few feet away from the security hut, where such a can had never stood before. How had he not noticed it was there? Shooting a suspicious glance at the truck driver, Hank walked over to take a closer look at it. The lid of the can bore the same words as were printed on the side of the van; Acme Trash Company Ltd, with Marineville's address also printed on the label. It certainly seemed to be one of theirs. Lifting the lid, he recoiled in disgust at the sight and smell of the trash it contained, and slammed the lid back on again.

"One of the night crew must have found it and brought it up front," suggested Stan, as he approached pushing a hand trolley.

"Yeah... well, seeing as he's here, he may as well take it now. One trash can's not gonna make much difference."

As Stan wheeled the can over to the gate, Hank addressed the driver – all while trying to ignore the bizarre and oddly creepy look of excitement on the man's face. "Okay pal, you got lucky today. My buddy here'll load this onto your truck, then you can be on your way."

"Let me help you with that, officer," insisted the driver, as Stan pushed the can to the back of the truck. "These things are often heavier than they appear..."

Working together the two men soon had the stray can safely lifted onto the truck, and the inordinately happy driver scurried quickly back to the cab. "I can't tell you how grateful I am, gentlemen!" he called back as he turned on the engine.

"Well, happy to help, buddy," said Stan. "Safe journey!"

As the truck drove away, Hank suddenly clicked his fingers as something occurred to him. "Peter Lawford!"

"… what?"

"That's who that weird little driver reminds me of. Y'know, one of them real old-timey movie stars." He paused, suddenly unsure of his movie memories. "Well anyway, I'm *sure* it was a Peter somebody…"

Stan just shrugged. He rarely went to the movies. "Coffee's getting cold," he said, before heading back into the security hut.

Just over a mile south of Marineville the garbage truck pulled off the road and into a layby close to the woods, the driver leaping from the cab and hurrying to the rear of the vehicle. Much to his surprise, X-20 discovered that Sculpin had already managed to free himself from the garbage can he'd been sealed inside, and was now struggling to climb down from the truck. X-20 assisted him, not envying his comrade having spent the last nine or ten hours sealed in a tight space like that. Besides, it was the least he could do after crying off the assignment himself on account of his own (invented) claustrophobia.

"Was our plan successful?" he asked.

"It was indeed!" Despite his ordeal, and the garbage scraps clinging to his clothes and hair, Sculpin was chuckling with excitement as he produced a folder of what looked to X-20 like some 400 pages of W.A.S.P.-branded documentation. "An extensive list of potential candidates for an alliance: names, locations, vehicles, weapons, *everything!*"

X-20 had to admit that for all his doubts about the man, Sculpin had succeeded in his assignment admirably. "Ah, well done my friend! Any problems?"

Sculpin shook his head. "None! My anti-security devices disabled the locks and cameras at the Marineville archive with ease. And, as you suggested, I made sure to make as much of a mess as possible to throw the W.A.S.P.s off the scent that little bit longer!"

"The mighty Titan will be most pleased with your work."

"Thank you, X-20!" Sculpin stretched, then took a few slow steps on stiff legs. "Oh, but my knees may never be the same again..." Blinking under the glare of the midday sun, he looked around at the trees and bushes that surrounded them. "So, this is the surface. It's very... green."

"I wish we had time for you to stretch your legs a little," said X-20, as he grabbed hold of a nearby pile of seemingly ordinary bracken and hauled it aside to reveal a small blue and yellow two-seater hovercar hidden beneath. "However, we must away with all speed!"

Sculpin clutched the folder of documents close to his chest as he slowly but surely plodded over to the car. "What about the human driver?" he asked.

"Forget him," said X-20, producing a key from his pocket. "By the time he comes to, we shall be far from here..."

With that, the two undersea creatures climbed into the hovercar that would take them on a short journey to a disused house on the nearby island of Lemoy; the first step in their journey back to Titanica...

The security clampdown at Marineville had seen Lieutenant Sara Coral's flight diverted to an emergency airstrip a few miles away from the base, meaning that she now had a short drive north in a car she'd been loaned by the staff there. It was an inconvenience, true, but she didn't mind. She enjoyed driving, having always had something of a passion for fast cars, and although this one wasn't going to break any speed records getting to Marineville, it was just nice to be driving along a peaceful country road rather than through the noisy crowded streets she had to navigate every day back in Washington.

As she drove, she replayed what few facts she already knew about the case she'd been assigned to investigate. It sounded like a simple enough break-in, so she wasn't entirely sure why her superiors at World Security Patrol Headquarters had selected her to investigate. Nevertheless, she understood that Marineville often faced situations that were out of the ordinary, and the possibility that underwater creatures were behind all this lent the case an exciting frisson of danger.

Sara had been with the World Security Patrol for almost eleven years now, having risen through the ranks of the organisation's military police division before being singled out for special officer training. Now, in her late twenties, she'd been promoted to junior grade Lieutenant just two months ago, following her successful infiltration and exposing of a Bereznik terror cell operating in the world capital Unity City. Although her work varied from assignment to assignment, her role was generally one of an investigative troubleshooter, getting to the bottom of mysteries faced by the world security services and resolving them with an efficiency that few others were capable of.

It was a role that often brought her into contact with many other security organisations around the world, and sometimes into conflict with those within those organisations who resented the idea of an outsider coming in to sort out their problems for them. Earlier on in her career, Sara had made the mistake of trying to maintain an air of icy detachment during such assignments, concentrating solely on the facts of the case rather than the human beings involved with it. That approach had often backfired on her but now, older and more experienced, she had come to understand that the two were very often intertwined, and she had worked hard in the intervening years to present a more friendly and approachable exterior while on assignment – one that more closely matched her true nature. Unfortunately, it hadn't always worked out. This case would put all that self-improvement to the test – she'd heard such good things about the staff at Marineville that she was desperately keen to make a good first impression. After all, Sara thought to herself, she'd only get to do that once...

Suddenly she slammed on the brakes, as a figure staggered from the trees lining the opposite side of the road, before stumbling forward and collapsing. Thinking quickly, and grateful for the lack of traffic about, Sara pulled her car off the road close to where the man had fallen and leapt out to run to his aid.

By the time she reached him, the man was already up on his feet again, but Sara just managed to catch him as his legs gave out from under him once more. "Easy," she said, struggling to support his weight. "It's alright, I've got you."

There was nothing to do except get him off the road, so Sara hauled the semi-conscious man over to her car and eased him into the passenger seat. "What happened?" she asked. "Is anyone else hurt?"

The man shook his head as if trying to clear it, and Sara got the distinct impression he wasn't entirely aware of his surroundings. "Prisoner..." she heard him moan. "Marineville... garbage... through there..."

He pointed in the direction of the woods, and Sara noticed the garbage truck visible amongst the trees for the first time. The investigator in her couldn't resist taking a quick look, especially since the man's groggy state meant she couldn't trust that there weren't more people hurt back there.

"I'm just gonna take a look," she told him, although she wasn't convinced he had heard her. Drawing her pistol, Sara turned and ran into the woods to investigate the truck, aware that she would only have seconds to make the most cursory of examinations before she would have to find help for her passenger.

As she took her first closeup view of the truck, Sara's investigative senses were on full alert. On the surface, nothing much was wrong – which in her experience meant *everything* was wrong. A check of the cab and the surrounding woodland revealed no other passengers needing medical attention, but a nearby patch of flattened grass and what appeared to be a clump of several branches stuck together suggested that another smaller vehicle had been parked under cover there until very recently.

The truck itself had obviously recently visited Marineville, judging by the Marineville markings on an empty trash can that lay on the ground nearby... so had something simply caused the driver to swerve off the road and crash shortly after leaving the base? Possibly, although the apparent lack of damage to the truck and the man showing no sign of any external injuries led Sara to believe that more had taken place here than met the eye.

First things first; she had a passenger needing medical attention. The truck could wait until later. Leaping back into her car Sara first checked the man was securely seat belted before she revved the engine and soon the vehicle was hurtling once again at top speed in the direction of Marineville...

Three hours later, Commander Shore turned in his hoverchair to face the two new arrivals in the Marineville control tower. "Any injuries, Doc?"

Marineville's chief medical officer shook his head. "None, Commander. I'm confident the driver'll be up and about by the end of tomorrow."

"But there is one other important piece of evidence to consider, Commander," Sara interjected quickly. "The doctor here—" She paused, placing her hand on the doctor's sleeve apologetically. "I'm so sorry, I didn't catch your name?"

The doctor shrugged. "Everyone here just calls me Doc," he replied, as if that fully answered the question.

Sara nodded slowly. "Right... well, 'Doc' here has made a discovery that could possibly help identify our intruder."

"Oh really, Doc?"

"That's correct, Commander. As I said, Mr Watson has no physical injuries... but I did detect traces of an unusual compound in his bloodstream. It appears to act on the human body like a powerful sedative, although it's not one in any medical database I've ever seen."

"So in other words, it could be some kind of underwater drug?" Troy asked.

"Which points to our intruder potentially being a member of an underwater race," Shore mused.

"That's my hypothesis," Doc drawled. "I'll know more when I get the test results back from the lab. For now, I should get back to my patient." He turned to Sara, and added, "I'll let you know when he's well enough for you to take a full statement."

Sara nodded gratefully, while trying to ignore the fact that every word out of this man's mouth sounded like an actor delivering bad news in an even worse hospital soap opera. "Thanks, Doc. Send him my best."

As Doc left the control room, Troy stepped forward to shake Sara's hand. "Well, I guess it's a good thing for Mr Watson you happened to be passing – though I'm sure it's not how you expected your visit with us to start, huh?"

Sara smiled, and shook her head. "No, not quite Captain. I'm just glad I could help."

"Well, we sure do appreciate it," chimed in Commander Shore. "And I can assure you of the cooperation of everyone in Marineville during this investigation. Just ask for any help you may need."

Sara smiled warmly. "Thank you, Commander, that'll make things a lot easier." Deciding to get down to business immediately, she reached into her pocket for a notebook and pencil. "For starters, I'd like to ask more about this truck I found. You say it's your regular trash collection truck?"

"From your description of it, it sounds like it," Troy confirmed. "It stops here once a week every week, without fail. You think our thief at the archive somehow made use of the truck in their escape?"

"Well, the timing just about fits – particularly the unexpected return trip today, and it does seem like a perfect way for an intruder to come and go as they please," Sara observed. "My concern is that this may not have been their first visit. Just so I'm aware, how many civilian vehicles and contractors pass through the main gate in an average week?"

"Well, aside from the refuse collection, there's the laundry collection on Thursdays..." began Troy.

"Supply trucks for the Marineville supermarket most weekdays," added Atlanta.

"Don't forget the bookmobile," chipped in Lieutenant Fisher helpfully.

"Plus special deliveries as and when," Shore said, rounding off the list.

Frowning, Sara noted the information in her pad. "And you don't post guards on these vehicles to prevent hijackings and so on? Not even while the drivers are in Marineville?"

Shore shrugged. "It's never been necessary so far..."

"I see," said Sara, in a tone that suggested she wasn't happy about any of this. "So in other words, a dozen intruders could show up at the main gate dressed as girl scouts selling cookies and the guards would just wave them through?"

"Now hold on, Lieutenant!" Troy interrupted firmly. "We may have had the occasional security breach here at Marineville, but... erm..." His voice trailed off, as he realised he'd been so quick to leap to the Commander's defence that he hadn't actually worked out how he was going to end his sentence before he started it.

"… but? You could have had an enemy agent wandering in and out of here for months, and the way things are at the moment you'd never know it!"

Atlanta stood quickly and moved to put herself between Sara and Troy, attempting to smooth things over as best she could. "I think what Troy's trying to say is that if someone has been gaining entry to Marineville without authorisation, well… no real harm's ever been done. Not until now, anyway."

"That you *know* of," Sara insisted. "But now that you've had an underwater creature break into your archive—"

Troy blinked. "Wait a minute! The Doc's still waiting on the results of those tests. What makes you so sure—"

"That your intruder wasn't human? The *footprints*, Captain. Your intruder left some damp footprints on some of the documents in the archive during their raid. There was enough dirt and grit stuck to their feet to leave reliable outlines of the shape of their feet on those documents, and they're *webbed* footprints. Three-toed, if you were wondering." Producing her notebook, she flipped through the pages, and held up a crude sketch of the shape of the intruder's feet. "See?"

By this point, Commander Shore was rubbing his forehead in exhaustion. "You've already taken a look at the crime scene too?"

"That *is* why I'm here, Commander. And I have to say, based on what I've seen so far, my immediate recommendation is that Marineville needs to tighten up security all round."

"Oh, it does, does it?" Shore's voice was now raised in frustration, and Sara raised hers to match.

"Absolutely, Commander! And furthermore—"

CHRIS DALE

The heated discussion was interrupted as the radio on the large main control console in the centre of the room suddenly crackled into life. *"Main gate here. Pizza delivery guy's looking to make a stop in the residential block. Do I pass him, or…?"*

All eyes were on Shore, who finally nodded to Fisher to approve the request. "That's okay, Sergeant. Let them through…"

Sara looked at Shore with an expression of utter disbelief on her face. *"Pizza delivery?"*

"Well…" Commander Shore looked around the room, first to Troy and then to Atlanta, desperate for an ally who would back him up… but found no one willing to meet his eyes this time. "Marineville's gotta eat!" he finally cried in exasperation.

"Okay, that does it!" Sara cried, as she flipped her notebook closed and thrust it back into her pocket. "You people are *insane!*"

The control room fell silent, with everyone present shocked at the sudden unexpected outburst – and clearly, no one was more shocked than Sara herself. When she finally spoke again, she avoided making eye contact with anyone, and simply said quietly "My apologies, that was… uncalled for." She gestured weakly towards the door as she began moving towards it. "If you'll excuse me, I'd better get on with the investigation…"

After mumbling one final word that might have been a very muffled 'sorry' she hurried from the room, leaving the control staff to reflect on a meeting that could perhaps have gone better. Troy was the first to speak. "Well, what do you make of that?"

"I'll say one thing for her," chimed in Fisher. "She's not afraid to speak her mind. I've never heard anyone talk to the commander like that. Well, except Admiral Denver…"

48

"Oh, she's just not used to how we do things in Marineville," Atlanta suggested. "I'm sure that once she gets a feel for the place, she might..." She fell silent, as a sound she rarely heard filled the air; the sound of Commander Shore chuckling to himself, almost uncontrollably. "Father? What's so funny?"

"Would you like me to get on to Headquarters, sir?" Troy asked. "See if they can send out a replacement officer who might be a bit more—"

But Commander Shore was already waving his suggestion away. "No Troy, no, don't do that," he urged, finally managing to speak through his subsiding laughter. He wiped away a tear from one cheek, and sighed contentedly. "I like her."

CHAPTER 4

The Paper Trail

Sara had spent the rest of the day buried in her work; partly through necessity, and partly through choice. With her usual air of precision efficiency, she'd spent the latter part of the afternoon consulting with the records officer in the archive and the forensic team still working there, while the evening had been taken up with interviews: firstly the guards at the security checkpoint, and then the truck driver in the Marineville hospital. She was grateful to have enough work to keep her from being alone with her thoughts, but every so often her attention would wander and she'd first herself replaying the events in the control tower over in her mind – and every time she did so she became more and more frustrated with how she had behaved.

The sun had long since set over Marineville by the time Sara made her way to the apartment she'd been allocated for her temporary visit to the base, but it wasn't until she turned the key in the lock of the door that it even occurred to her that she hadn't anything to eat since she'd left Washington. The diner might still be open, but did she really want to risk going back to the control tower so soon after her previous humiliating visit? *Maybe I'll try to find the number for that pizza delivery place instead...*

Sighing heavily as she sank onto the sofa in her apartment, Sara winced as the doorbell sounded almost immediately. She considered ignoring it and pretending she wasn't home, but ultimately decided it was worth answering if there was even a chance of salvaging something constructive from today. Hauling herself back to her feet, she trudged dejectedly across the room and opened the front door.

A large bowl of flowers on legs stood on the doorstep. At least, that was the *first* impression Sara had, until the smiling face of a young woman peered expectantly around the technicolour floral arrangement. At any other time the unusual greenish tint of her visitor's hair might have clued Sara in to just who it was that was calling on her – but this late in the day, her brain was just too tired to keep up with the world around her.

"Hi," said Sara. "Um… are those for me?"

The girl nodded, and passed them towards her. Still confused, Sara didn't take them. "But I didn't order flowers…" she mumbled.

Her visitor continued to smile at her with a hopeful look in her eyes, but still didn't speak. Almost as if she wouldn't. *Or couldn't…*

Then it all suddenly fell into place. "You must be Marina!" The visitor nodded happily. "Oh I'm sorry, I'm absolutely hopeless today. Come in, please."

Standing aside to let Marina in before closing the door behind her, Sara followed her visitor into her apartment. "You really shouldn't have gone to all this trouble for me," she said, as Marina placed the bowl on the dining table and adjusted the flowers, but the smile on Marina's face seemed to insist that it was no trouble at all. "Let me at least see if there's another bowl in the kitchen I can find to put them in, to save you losing yours…"

But Marina was already waving her hands to stop her, and Sara got the distinct impression that the flowers and the bowl were being presented as a single package. "A gift?" Marina nodded. "That's really very kind, Marina. Thank you."

Marina waved the compliment away – before pointing again to herself, and then towards the far wall. This time, Sara was quicker to put the pieces together. "You live next door? So we're neighbours?" Marina nodded excitedly. "Well, it's very nice to meet you, Marina. I've never met anyone from under the sea before."

An awkward silence followed, as Sara discovered for the first time the challenges of continuing a conversation with someone who couldn't speak. "I guess you heard what happened today then?" Marina nodded once more.

"I've been trying to avoid them all day," Sara continued, as she flopped down on the sofa and gestured for Marina to join her. "Commander Shore, Troy, the others... I'm not really sure I'm going fit in around here."

She felt Marina's hand close around hers, and she watched her visitor shaking her head gently. "You mean, they're not mad at me?"

Marina shook her head again, this time more firmly, and a smile of recognition slowly crossed Sara's dark face. She'd noticed that when Marina had shaken her head, she had also tapped the arm of the sofa twice with her free hand. "One tap for yes, two for no, right?"

Marina tilted her head in surprise, then beamed with delight and nodded frantically – although there was also a question in her eyes. "How did I know the code? Oh, I've read your file. I mean, not just *your* file, I've read the files of all the Stingray crew, and the Marineville senior staff. I figured knowing something about you all would be useful to help get to the bottom of this break-in sooner. And I..." Her voice trailed off, as the memory of her earlier embarrassing behaviour flooded back. "I also just wanted to make a really good first impression on everyone. Guess I've blown that, huh?"

Marina was once again shaking her head emphatically, and Sara only hoped that her visitor was right. "Marina, you've been here a while now. Was it difficult fitting in when you first arrived?"

Marina pouted, and held her left hand aloft palm down, giving it a gentle shake. "So-so?" Sara elaborated. "I guess it must have been even harder for you than it is for me, suddenly finding yourself in a world so totally alien to you." Marina nodded slowly, and Sara thought she could see just a trace of sadness in her eyes. "How did you get past that?"

Taking hold of Sara's left hand, Marina raised it into the air and pointed to the face of the watch on her wrist. "Time," Sara said. "Right. Thing is, I probably won't be here for long. Not long enough to make friends, anyway."

Marina frowned, then gave a few firm shakes of her head – before pointing to herself and smiling warmly. It was a smile that Sara found it impossible not to return. "You mean... I've already made a friend?"

Rolling her eyes in mock exasperation Marina suddenly opened her arms wide, and Sara found herself on the receiving end of a tight hug. "Okay, I get the message!" Sara laughed, returning the hug just as tightly. "Friends, absolutely! Thank you."

She's paying it forward, Sara realised. *She remembers what it was like to be the new girl, and she wants to repay the kindness Troy and the others showed her when they took her in.* "Really Marina, thank you," she said quietly. "This means more to me than you know."

Marina eventually released her grip, then made an eating gesture and pointed towards her mouth with a questioning look in her eyes. "No, I haven't eaten," Sara admitted. "As a matter of fact, I've not even had a chance to see if there's anything in the fridge yet."

Standing, Marina held out a hand to Sara and pointed her head in the direction of her own apartment. For a moment Sara considered turning her down, not wanting to have to put her new friend to the trouble of cooking for her… but suddenly the idea of spending time with someone she'd actually made a connection with was very appealing, and she couldn't resist the invitation. "I'd love to," she replied, taking Marina's hand and following her towards the front door.

"You know Marina," she said as the two friends stepped out into the night air, "you are real easy to talk to. Did you ever consider becoming a therapist?"

Marina pointed at herself and pulled an expression of disbelief, before gesturing expansively out across Marineville. Although her new friend could not speak a word, Sara understood her meaning perfectly.

What, for all the 'insane' people around here? Are you kidding me?

Some hours later, in the throne room of Titanica, X-20 was engrossed in the Marineville security documents. They made for fascinating reading, particularly the reports of cases that he had personally been involved with; frequent mentions were made of suspicious characters hanging around Marineville who had later disappeared, or of mysterious goings-on connected to the nearby Island of Lemoy, but apparently those working at Marineville had never felt these occurrences significant enough to warrant further investigation. X-20 couldn't help but feel pleased with himself, and took considerable pride in the fact that his disguises really were as convincing as he'd always suspected them to be.

He glanced over at Titan, who had donned his reading glasses and was also reviewing a page of the stolen material on the opposite side of the throne room dining table. "It is indeed a terrific haul of information, is it not, great Titan?"

Engrossed in his reading, Titan inhaled slowly and turned the paper over before replying. "Yeeees... although I confess, I am somewhat disappointed by the number of cases involving a mere two malcontents from a race otherwise on peaceful terms with the terraineans." He suddenly crumpled the piece of paper into a ball and tossed it aside in frustration. "To say nothing of Stingray's various escort missions, exploratory trips and supply runs, the minute details of which are of no use to us whatsoever...!"

X-20 opened his mouth to reply, but fell silent at the sound of rapidly approaching footsteps. "Your majesty! Your majesty!"

Titan and X-20 both looked up as Sculpin hurried into the throne room, clutching a piece of paper and chuckling to himself. He held the page aloft in triumph. "Your majesty, I have it! I *have* it!"

"Calm yourself, fool!" ordered Titan. "What precisely is it that you believe you have found?"

Sculpin took a few quick breaths to steady himself and then pointed to the paper again. "It's all here, your majesty. This mission report details an attack on Marineville by members of a race whose craft was shielded with a new metal that Stingray's Sting missiles were unable to penetrate!"

"Ah, you intrigue me," said Titan, leaning back in his chair and giving the engineer his full attention. "Pray continue!"

"Yes, great Titan! Well, a scientist was brought to Marineville to devise a new metal for the nosecones of the Sting missiles – one that would allow the missiles to pierce the hull of this seemingly indestructible underwater craft. Thanks to the help of this scientist, Stingray was then able to successfully cripple the attacking craft with a single shot!"

X-20 had a sudden urge to leave the room. Sculpin had ended his recap on such a triumphant note so completely at odds with the words he was speaking that the surface agent was almost certain the engineer had just earned himself a one-way trip back to Aquatraz – or possibly instant execution.

Instead, Titan just stared impassively at Sculpin, before slowly and deliberately removing his glasses without taking his eyes off the excited engineer. Turning them over in his hands, he began "Sculpin, perhaps you misunderstood the assignment. Our purpose in obtaining these files is to locate suitable allies for a final decisive attack that will utterly destroy Stingray and Marineville once and for all. I have little need for allies who can be taken down by a single Sting missile." He shot a glance towards the two Aquaphibians standing guard near Teufel's tank. "I have enough of those already..."

"But your majesty – the *formula* for the metal used in the nosecones of the missiles! It's attached to the mission report!"

"What?" Titan hastily donned his glasses once again as Sculpin scurried over to pass him the document, which he skim-read in short order. "And in your opinion, could this civilisation's scientists use this information to create their own defence against the improved Sting missiles?"

Sculpin nodded eagerly. "I believe so, your Majesty! All indications are that this is a society of significant technological development."

X-20 clapped his hands in excitement. "Then at last we have a chance to turn one of the W.A.S.P.'s own weapons against them!"

"More than that, X-20... this formula represents considerable bargaining power in our negotiations with this race." Titan raised a hand for attention, which X-20 and Sculpin were more than happy to give him. "Think of it; we can approach this race in friendship, offering them this information by which they may be able to resume their own campaign against the W.A.S.P.s! What better incentive to join us...?"

X-20 nodded his understanding. "And if they still refuse to ally themselves with us—"

"Then we shall adapt the nosecones of the missiles on our mechanical fish to the same formula as Stingray's, and use those missiles against them... until they change their minds and agree to serve our great cause!" Titan laughed, and slapped the document in triumph. "And it's all thanks to the W.A.S.P.s themselves...! Excellent! Excellent! I cannot believe I am saying this, but... well done, Sculpin."

Sculpin bowed gratefully. "Thank you, Excellency!"

"Your estimate for production time on these new nosecones for the missiles on our own craft?"

"Oh, within the next twelve marine hours, Excellency. Work has already begun."

"Twelve hours... and the W.A.S.P. document gives the probable location of their city as..." Titan checked the piece of paper, and then tapped his chin thoughtfully. "Yes. Just time enough for an exploratory force to make first contact with these beings before reinforcements arrive to close the deal – one way or another." He turned to Sculpin. "Order a mechanical fish fleet prepared to depart Titanica within the next thirty marine minutes! And *I* shall command this fleet myself."

"At once, your majesty!" As Sculpin hurried away to make the preparations, X-20 stood and moved to Titan's side.

"You, your majesty? You're going with the fleet?"

Titan was practically beaming with excitement. "Of course! I make it a policy to handle all first contact duties myself. With the stakes as high as they are it is only fitting that I attend in person to deliver my most benevolent overtures to our new... allies."

"But surely Titan, it would be safer for you to travel with the second fleet? Remember, their vessels are heavily shielded. If they respond unkindly to your benevolent overtures—"

"Then I have faith in the Aquaphibians to defend me from harm. They have pledged to give their lives to save mine if necessary. I shall be in no danger." Titan frowned. "I sense you have concerns other than that of my safety?"

"Oh, merely that... well, things are moving faster than I had anticipated—"

Titan gave X-20 a hearty slap on the back that nearly knocked the surface agent off his feet. "Ah, but this is a good thing, X-20! Think of it; the sooner this alliance is forged, then we can move on to the next!"

X-20 blinked in shock. "The next?"

"Of course! Why settle for allying ourselves with just one race?" Titan pointed triumphantly to the stack of unread papers on the table. "Find me some more suitable candidates to join our cause, X-20! I wish to present the W.A.S.P.s with an overwhelming confederation of enemies, all united in the cause of their destruction!"

X-20 nodded eagerly. "Oh, I shall, your majesty, I shall..."

He flinched as Titan suddenly grasped him tightly by the shoulders and whispered into his ear. "Think of it, X-20! Marineville in flames, crushed by the sheer power of our mighty alliance! Ah, but the glory... the *glory* shall remain ours, X-20, never fear!"

X-20 looked into Titan's eyes and saw in them a kind of manic energy that he couldn't remember seeing there before. He nodded again, not knowing what else to do. Whatever it was that Titan would encounter when he reached the home city of these underwater creatures, X-20 was somewhat glad he wouldn't be there to witness it.

"Titanica is yours until I return!" Titan announced brusquely, marching away from X-20 and striding out of the throne room. Now in an even deeper state of shock, X-20 glanced from the door up towards the throne itself, and felt the great weight of the responsibility he'd just had thrust upon him.

He'd never been left in charge of Titanica before. He'd spent enough time at Titan's side to know that there were enough administrators around the city to keep the place running smoothly until Titan got back, but even so... *he* was the one in charge now. *He* was the one who could tell everyone else what to do. *He* was the one who could berate hapless subjects for the most minor transgressions, with no one to hold him accountable for it. The whole city and everyone in it was his responsibility, and no one else's. It was a new feeling for the surface agent, so used was he to supervising only himself. For the first time in their long association, he felt that Titan truly valued his contribution to their ongoing efforts to crush the terraineans.

Watched by the Aquaphibian guards, X-20 climbed the small curved staircase to the throne itself. Once there, he took a moment to admire the beauty of its construction before he slowly began to ease himself onto it, running his hands along it reverently, imagining how things might be different around here if he really were—

"X-20!"

The shock of Titan's sudden reappearance at the door of the throne room caused X-20's legs to give way beneath him. He fell, landing hard on his posterior in a crumpled heap at the base of the throne. Despite the pain, he struggled to sit up as quickly as he could, desperate to salvage something of his dignity. "Er, yes, yes great Titan?"

The smirk on Titan's face told X-20 that his master had received precisely the reaction he had been hoping for. He waggled a disapproving finger towards the interim ruler of Titanica. "Do not get *too* comfortable."

"Oh, no great Titan…"

Titan's finger now swept towards the far side of the room. "And be sure to feed… *him.*"

X-20 followed the line of Titan's finger – and found himself on the business end of Teufel's dead-eyed stare. The fish gazed blankly up at him, but X-20 could have sworn that he detected a hint of amusement in those swollen orbs. "Oh, er, yes Titan, of course—"

But Titan was already gone.

Staggering to his feet, X-20 looked down at the throne and briefly considered attempting to sit on it again… but the moment had been lost. Sighing, he trudged back down the steps and made his way over to the table to continue reviewing the Stingray mission reports. As he sat down and picked up a piece of paper, he attempted to focus all his attention on the secrets it might contain… but all the while he was aware of Teufel's constant gaze, and the slight trace of an expression that hinted at what the fish was thinking; *I'm glad I was here to see that.*

X-20 had never felt so humiliated.

Commander Shore had called for a briefing on the latest developments in Sara's investigation to be held at 8 am in the conference room the following morning. While he, Troy and Phones picked at a plate of light breakfast fare she'd brought in from the tower diner, Sara took a moment to compose herself and prepare to share her findings – good and bad. She'd decided to forgo breakfast herself in case she was humiliated still further by any food or beverage accidents, although thankfully she wasn't all that hungry. Marina's cooking had proven to be the best meal Sara had had in quite some time, and having someone to talk to had left her feeling better than she had since she'd first arrived at Marineville.

"Good morning gentlemen," she began, when it appeared that the men were ready to start listening to her.

"I'll kick things off with the good news. Mr Watson the truck driver regained consciousness early yesterday afternoon and Doc's confident he'll be able to discharge him this afternoon."

"Hey, I heard about that," Phones cut in. "Good on you for finding him and bringing him in the way you did."

Sara gave a grateful nod towards Phones before continuing. "Well, unfortunately, he couldn't tell me much about the man who attacked him and took his truck. Said he stopped for a car that seemed to have broken down. When he got out to help the driver, he got a hypo jabbed in his neck and that's all he remembers until waking up in the hospital."

"Whatever that underwater sedative is, it must be powerful stuff," Troy mused.

"Exactly. But I've still got a team combing every inch of the garbage truck and its contents, which is what I'll be getting back to after this briefing..."

"Why does she get all the best jobs?" asked Phones, as he poured himself a cup of coffee.

"Any time you wanna transfer to waste management, just say the word," grumbled Shore, as he finished buttering a slice of toast before raising it to his lips. "Go on, Lieutenant."

"Well sir, the main issue is the archive. We've now got a precise picture of what was taken in the raid, but I'm afraid it's not good news."

"It already wasn't Lieutenant," retorted Shore, removing the toast from his mouth a split-second before he could bite into it, "so just spit it out!"

"Yes sir." Consulting her notes, Sara took a deep breath before announcing, "The records officer estimates that four hundred and fifteen pages of material have been removed. Specifically, all Stingray mission reports filed over the last eighteen months."

Phones whistled. "Well, if that don't beat all. Now why would someone go to such lengths to get their hands on Stingray mission reports?"

"Well, obviously somebody felt they needed to refer to them for some reason..." Shore replied.

"Would they contain any technical data on Stingray itself?" Sara suggested, keen to help if she possibly could.

"Nothing that springs to mind," Troy replied. "Phones? That's more your line of country."

Phones shook his head. "Well, there might be the odd mention of random technical issues that cropped up during missions; breakdowns, battle damage, that kind of thing. But it wouldn't go into any great detail."

"Ah, there must be something in there, some common factor..."

"I wonder..." Phones said quietly. Then, realising that he'd spoken aloud and all eyes were now on him, he added "Eighteen months... does that strike you as the anniversary of something, Troy?"

"Yeah... that's roughly when we discovered that there were civilisations living under the sea," Troy mused. "Our first tangle with Titan..."

Shore considered the possibility of Titan's involvement. "Yeah. Well, we're already reasonably confident that it was an underwater creature that broke into the archive. No reason it shouldn't be one of Titan's crew, I guess. Gentlemen – and Lieutenant Coral – it seems to me that the only way to find out what might be in those documents is to take a look at them ourselves." He turned to face Sara. "Lieutenant, call up Headquarters, see how fast they can have copies of their copies sent out to us."

"I already have, sir, first thing. They're being flown in by special courier as we speak."

Shore nodded, trying and failing to disguise an impressed smile. "Quick thinking, Lieutenant. Well done."

Sara herself smiled gratefully in return. "Thank you, sir. Which does bring me to another point I'd like to discuss with all of you. I just wanted to ap—"

Her words were cut short as the sound of a pounding drumbeat suddenly filled the air, and Troy and Phones leapt to their feet in a flash. "Battlestations!" cried Troy, helpfully negating the need for Sara to ask what was going on.

"*Control tower calling Commander Shore!*"

It was Atlanta's voice that emanated from Shore's wrist radio. "Go ahead, Lieutenant!"

"*The Titanican early warning network raised the alarm, sir. Multiple mechanical fish are departing Titanica as we speak!*"

"Okay Atlanta, keep monitoring. We'll be up as fast as we can." Without waiting for an affirmative from his daughter, Shore pressed his watch to close the channel and immediately turned towards the door. "Let's go, Troy."

"Right sir." Troy moved quickly to hold the door open for Shore as his hoverchair slid from the room. "Phones, better get Stingray prepped for launch. I'll join you in the standby lounge as soon as we know the score."

"Okay, Troy."

"Yes, but sir, I was hoping to...!" Sara fell silent as the doors to the conference room swung shut behind the departing Shore and Troy. "I guess it can wait..."

Suddenly a friendly hand patted her on the shoulder. "Word of advice if you wanna fit in around here," Phones explained cheerfully. "We all make mistakes. It's part of life. But the trick is to not make a mistake *today*. And even if you do, it's still not the end of the world – well, provided nothing explodes, that is. The Commander's really not one to hold a grudge. Heck, nobody here is. So you shouldn't hold one against yourself either."

"But yesterday, I—"

But Phones was quick to cut her off. "Uh uh. The Commander don't give no mind about yesterday. What matters is you've impressed him *today*. That's what he'll remember. Now if you can impress him today, *every day*, why you'll be sittin' pretty, and that first mistake'll be nothing more than a distant memory."

Realising that Phones was attempting to make her feel welcome just as Marina had done, Sara smiled gratefully and tried to engage with Phones on his own playful level. "And is that how you do it, Lieutenant?"

"Me?" Phones laughed. "Shucks girl, I just keep my head down and do what I'm told. And what I've been told is to get Stingray prepped for launch, so if you'll excuse me..." He dived towards the table to grab a bagel from the breakfast tray, then headed for the door. "Duty calls!"

Sara smiled as she watched him go, and then picked up the breakfast tray to take it back to the diner. "Yeah, duty calls," she sighed, mentally preparing herself for a date with a garbage truck...

"Attention! Marineville tracking station calling..."

All eyes in the control tower looked up towards the speaker hanging from the ceiling, as the tracking station officer conveyed his report. *"Relay network detecting enemy fleet departing Titanica. Eight – repeat, eight – Mechanical Fish and one smaller craft on course 318 mark 297."*

Troy and Commander Shore had arrived in the tower just in time to hear the report. Speeding over to Lieutenant Fisher at the radar scanner, Shore asked, "Heading this way?"

"No sir, that course puts them out to open sea. Nothing for miles. But wherever they're heading, they're sure in a hurry."

"Any ideas on that smaller vessel that's travelling with them?" Atlanta asked, as she and Troy joined them at the radar scanner.

"That could be Titan's personal craft," Troy suggested. "The mechanical fish do seem to be in a defensive formation."

"Which rather suggests that Phones was right," Shore announced. "I don't think it's any coincidence that our buddy Titan starts making moves like this just a day or so after the break-in at our archive."

"You want Stingray to shadow them, sir?"

"Right Troy. Keep a safe distance, stay out of sight, and report back the moment you work out where they're going. Do *not* engage the fleet unless absolutely necessary. Understood?"

Troy was already moving towards the door. "Yes sir!"

"Good luck, Troy!" Atlanta called after him.

"Safe travels, Cap'n!" added Fisher.

"Okay, okay, he knows we want him back in one piece," Shore retorted, just loudly enough for the departing Troy to hear. "They still maintaining course?"

"Yes sir," replied Fisher. "But Stingray should be able to keep pace with them just fine, if they set off in the next ten minutes or so."

Shore nodded to his daughter. "Okay Atlanta – give Troy thirty seconds to get to the standby lounge, then sound launch stations!"

CHAPTER 5

The Wreck of the Titan

The ten-mile journey from Stingray's pen through the underground launch tunnel leading to the ocean door was always a matter of uneventful routine for her crew. In fact, much of the launch procedure was handled by others; Atlanta was presently supervising the operation from the control tower, and at any moment she'd pass orders to the team at the Marineville power plant to open the ocean door itself. All Troy and Phones really had to do was keep Stingray on course, which they'd each remarked on more than one occasion they could probably manage with their eyes closed. But for both men, the highlight of launching Stingray was never about the journey through the launch tunnel itself; it was about what awaited them at the other end.

A light on a nearby console began to flash, as up ahead of them the tiny but rapidly growing speck that was the ocean door began to move. "Ocean door opening now, Troy."

"Thanks Phones," Troy replied, before speaking into the radio. "Tower from Stingray. Are we clear to leave Marineville?"

Atlanta's voice sounded loud and clear in reply. *"Clear to go, Stingray!"*

With the ocean door now open Stingray accelerated, as if the ship itself were yearning for its freedom. The super sub surged through the doorway, a great blast of bubbles billowing in her wake, and Troy and Phones looked around in awe at the murky vista that greeted her entrance into the great wide ocean.

There was always something oddly satisfying about that moment, thought Troy. This was where his ship belonged, after all. Not docked in her pen, waiting for a call to action, but free to roam the underwater world where she was truly in her element. A world of near-infinite possibilities, wonders... and dangers.

"Tower from Stingray, seaborne! Any new information, Commander?"

Commander Shore's voice filled the air. *"Nothing as yet, Troy. Proceed to position eighteen hundred miles, west-north-west, twenty-four hundred, reference four. We'll relay further information about the fleet's ultimate destination as and when we have it."*

"P.W.O.R.!" Troy didn't need to repeat those precise coordinates to Phones; it was a region the two of them knew all too well. "Rate Six to Titanica region, Phones. We'll pick up the fleet's trail from there."

"Right, Troy." As Phones adjusted Stingray's speed to maximum, Marina stepped forward and stood between the two men.

"What do you make of all this, Marina?" Troy asked as she looked out at the underwater world that she was better acquainted with than either of them. Troy had already briefed Marina and Phones on the departure of the mechanical fish fleet while they were preparing to launch, so now they knew as much as he did. "Does Titan often take trips outside Titanica?"

Marina shook her head. "So if that smaller craft was his, he must be up to something pretty important. At least, from his point of view..."

"Eight mechanical fish is a lot of firepower," Phones noted. "Could just be there's something big he's got his sights set on blowing up."

"Yeah... though Titan's not the one to show up in person just to watch the Aquaphibians destroy something..."

"Unless it's us, of course."

Phones' remark made Troy smile. It was true that when there was fighting to be done, Titan always made sure to issue orders to his troops from the safety of Titanica – but he could certainly imagine the underwater despot making an exception to that rule in the case of Stingray. "Well, we could be wrong. That smaller craft might not be his. Could be some new weapon, or a visitor they're escorting home, or half a dozen other things."

Troy looked up at Marina, who was once again shaking her head. She at least clearly believed that Titan was aboard that smaller craft.

"I guess we won't know much more until we catch up with them," Phones observed.

"Yeah – and that won't be for a few more hours yet," added Troy. "We'd better keep well out of their sight as we get closer. Though if I'm right, it sounds like Titan will have other things on his mind than keeping track of us just now..."

"Curses! The fool has eluded death once again...!"

Titan's muttering of disgust did not go unnoticed by his Aquaphibian guard or the pilot who manned the controls of his personal craft, although the pair merely shot each other a blank look before returning to their work. They knew his ire was not aimed at them – for a change – but was instead directed at the characters in the book he was currently reading.

Titan had long been a firm believer in the value of obtaining information on your enemy from whatever sources you had at your disposal, hence his decision to establish a network of surface agents on the land. Titan would never admit it to his face, but X-20 had proven to be the best of these surface agents partly because he took the time to truly explore the cultures of the terrainean peoples, immersing himself in their art, their music... and their literature. It was in fact one of their own books that Titan was reading now. At first resistant to the idea of filling his own head with terrainean nonsense, Titan had grudgingly bowed to the wisdom of doing so when X-20 had informed him of an entire genre of terrainean literature dealing with the sea, and so the surface agent had been sending him books as and when he could acquire them.

Titan's latest read, *20,000 Leagues Under The Sea*, was proving a fascinating and frustrating one indeed. Although well-written, to the point of Titan feeling this Jules Verne fellow had some dangerously radical ideas for a terrainean and should perhaps be considered a target for kidnapping or assassination, the book's main character was one of the most insufferable protagonists he had yet come across in one of these works. Seemingly convinced that he had no place on the surface land, this Captain Nemo had built an advanced submarine and set out to explore the ocean – apparently labouring under the mistaken belief that the underwater world would welcome him. Not only that but Nemo was predictably courageous and resourceful in that very un-terrainean-like way that the leads in these books so often were.

So, when a giant squid had attacked Nemo's ship in the passage he was currently reading, Titan had dared to hope that the fool was finally about to get his comeuppance – only for those hopes to be dashed when a nameless lackey had gotten between a tentacle and his captain, and been dragged to his doom instead. Still, Titan mused, better an unnamed terrainean died than no terrainean at all – and the book was fine for what it was. It had helped pass the long hours on this journey, if nothing else. It was certainly no *Moby-Dick* though; now there was a character he could identify with.

"We are approaching the location you requested, your excellency."

The voice of the Aquaphibian pilot made Titan look up from his reading. He carefully placed the bookmark on the current page, before closing the large hardback volume and getting to his feet.

"Very well." He strode forward and picked up the radio microphone. "Attention fleet! Fish one and fish two shall remain on guard here. Fish three to eight; disperse to your assigned search zones! Report back here in thirty minutes with your findings."

As he replaced the microphone on the main console, Titan grinned to himself. "Let's see if we can entice our new allies to come to us!"

"Tower from *Philippine station 178!"*

The control tower staff looked up as the radio crackled into life. *"Titanican fleet has halted their advance in our area and is appearing to disperse. As yet, still no sign of aggressive action."*

Commander Shore spoke into his radio mic. "Okay station 178," he replied, "keep us posted if there are any further developments. Stingray will be in your area soon."

"P.W.O.R.!"

"Sounds like they could be searching for something," Atlanta mused.

"Yeah. Now, the Philippines; what could they be hunting for there...?" Commander Shore turned his chair to face the wall map, tapping his chin with his pencil as he considered the next course of action. It was true that there were any number of targets that Titan could make for in that region – but which of them related to the stolen files?

Shore suddenly whirled back around. "Lieutenant, I want a complete check made on all past instances of trouble Stingray's had to deal with relating to that area."

Fisher stood up, facing the commander with an apologetic look. "Begging your pardon sir, but after the break-in at the records store, we don't have any way to check—"

Shore waved Fisher silent. "There are duplicates of the stolen records being flown in from World Security Patrol Headquarters at this moment, Lieutenant. Get on to Lieutenant Coral about that right away."

"Yes, sir."

As Fisher hurried from the room, Atlanta looked anxiously at her father. "Should I alert Stingray, sir?"

"Yeah, do that Atlanta. They should only be half an hour behind the fleet at most by now. If Titan is after something in that area that we've come up against before, it's only fair to let Troy know he could be in for some trouble, even if we're not sure what it might be yet."

As Atlanta called up Stingray to relay the message, Shore turned his hoverchair back towards the radar map and resumed tapping his pencil against his chin. "But the question is… who's going to tell Titan?"

"What's wrong with these creatures?" Titan fumed, as the clock on the wall ticked off the passing of another marine hour without any response to their presence – during which time Captain Nemo had still stubbornly refused to meet the fate he so richly deserved. "They must be aware of our presence in their territory. Why do they not show themselves?"

"Majesty," gurgled the pilot, pointing to something ahead of the craft. Titan moved to stand beside him... and felt a surge of triumph as a hatch opened in the seabed and three silver submarines of comparable size to a mechanical fish slowly emerged and advanced toward them.

"Ah, at last! Let us welcome our allies, shall we?" With supreme confidence, Titan grabbed the radio mic and set it to broadcast to all craft in the immediate area. "Welcome, esteemed representatives of your mighty underwater race. I am Titan, leader of the underwater city of Titanica. Perhaps you have heard of me?"

There was no response. Titan checked the settings on the radio, just to reassure himself that they were correct – which of course they were, since he himself had set them. The three craft were clearly receiving his message. They just weren't answering.

"I come on a goodwill mission to your people," he continued, in the most friendly tone of voice he could manage. It wasn't one he got to use very often. "I would appreciate the opportunity to meet with representatives of your government to discuss an arrangement that will benefit both our peoples!"

The three alien craft had now slowed to a stop and were holding position directly ahead of Titan's own craft. He imagined the creatures aboard those vessels; what were they waiting for? He'd been as cordial as the occasion warranted, hadn't he? Didn't he at least deserve the courtesy of an audience with them? Didn't they know who he was?

He closed the channel and slammed down the mic in frustration. "Why do they not answer me?" he snarled. "Are these fools really going to keep the great Titan waiting like some common peasant?"

Then he noticed something that shouldn't be; several of his own mechanical fish fleet, which had also been holding position awaiting further orders since returning from their exploratory trips, were starting to move. Slowly at first, but then their movements became more pronounced; short bursts of speed, sudden course corrections, their mechanical jaws flapping open and closed seemingly at random.

"Who gave those fools permission to move off station?" Titan grabbed the mic again. "Attention mechanical fish fleet! All stop! I repeat, all vessels—"

Suddenly a red light began to flash on the navigation console. The pilot was the first to notice it. "Excellency—"

But he never completed the sentence. A few moments later, Titan got his answer – as the ocean around his fleet erupted in flames...

Aboard Stingray, which had continued to follow Titan's fleet over the last few hours and was now keeping just out of their radar range, Phones frowned as the soundings he had been picking up over his headphones for the last ten minutes or so abruptly ceased. "Troy, I've lost them!"

"But you just said the soundings were coming through loud and clear?"

Phones nodded. "That's right, they were... then all of a sudden, they started cutting out in quick succession. There's just nothing there anymore."

Troy's brow furrowed. "Any idea what caused it?"

"Well, there's nothing wrong with our equipment. Could be the fleet entered some kind of a shielded area. Or..."

Troy didn't like the sound of what he was hearing. "Or?"

Phones sighed, as if reluctant to say the words that best reflected what he had heard. "Or... could be they were destroyed." He shook his head, not wanting to believe his own theory. "But if they were, it sure happened mighty fast..."

Fisher found Sara working in Marineville's ground transportation workshop where the trash lorry had been relocated for further investigation. The young officer was busily making notes on a clipboard as he approached.

"Excuse me, Lieutenant Coral?"

"Ah, Lieutenant Fisher!" Before he could respond Sara reached behind her, hauled a trash can between them, and leaned against it with a satisfied look on her face. "What would you say this is?"

Fisher gave the question due consideration. "A trash can," he answered hesitantly.

"Ah, but what's *inside*?"

Fisher had the oddest feeling he was being asked a trick question, but decided to stick with the most sensible answer. "Trash?" Sara shook her head. "Not trash?"

Sara raised the lid of the can, and Fisher peered in… to see that the interior of the can was lined with several wall-mounted screens, control panels and other alien-looking technology, all of which appeared to be dormant. "Oh. Well, that was going to be my next guess," Fisher admitted. He gestured towards the truck. "So how many trash cans did you have to sift through before you found this one?"

"Please don't ask. I might cry." Sara gave Fisher a friendly smile, as she added, "Actually, we found this one at the rear of the records building. And our early tests show DNA traces that match the footprints we found in the archive." She frowned, as she peered intently into the can. "Haven't figured out how to turn all this stuff on yet though…"

Fisher looked into the can, trying to put himself in the mindset of whatever unfortunate creature might have snuck into the base this way – then an awful thought occurred to him. "Say, you don't think all this is a bomb or something, do you?"

Sara shook her head. "Rocket disposal squad people have been over every inch of this thing. We've also tested for radiation, toxins, the works. It's just tech. Alien tech, but nothing dangerous so far as we can tell. Surveillance equipment would be my guess, but we'll know more when we turn it over to the lab boys. They'll be here for it shortly."

A thought suddenly struck Fisher. "Say, I thought you were working on the assumption that all that business with the driver collecting the trash can at the main gate was how our perp got out?"

"Interesting, isn't it?" Sara asked, as she placed the lid on the ground next to the can. "We definitely know this can is how our intruder got into Marineville… but we also know it's not how he got out. So, if this isn't some trojan horse that's yet to reveal itself, then the question is – why'd they switch cans?" She blinked, suddenly realising that her visitor might not have come to see her to talk trash all day. "Actually no, sorry, the question is; did you need something?"

Fisher had become so engrossed in the mystery of Sara's trash can that it took him a moment or two to remember what had brought him to see her in the first place. "Oh yes! Commander Shore asked me to chase you up on those replacement Stingray mission files. We need to consult them pretty urgently."

Sara checked her watch. "Yeah, they should be arriving any time. Give me a minute to get out of these overalls and get cleaned up, and I'll let you drive me over to the airfield."

Fisher followed Sara as she headed for the exit. "Not that I mind, but haven't they assigned you a car of your own to get around in?"

"Ah yes, but I hear *you*'ve saved up and got one of those nifty Lugrin 964s that have just come out. You didn't really think I'd come all this way to Marineville and not beg the chance to take a ride in one of those beauties, did you…?"

As the two lieutenants left the lab, excitedly debating their mutual love of fast cars, the suspect trash can was left alone and unattended. Had the pair remained, they would have been present to witness the monitors lining its interior come to life, and they would also have heard a small thin voice calling faintly out from inside...

"Hello? Can anyone hear me?"

"Can you hear anything?"

Phones shook his head. "Not a murmur, Troy."

Stingray was now in the same general region as Titan's fleet had been shortly before their sudden disappearance, and had begun to slowly explore the area with the utmost caution. Marina had moved forward to join Troy and Phones, as the former skimmed the seabed visually while the latter continued to listen out for any signs of life.

Suddenly Phones clamped his left hand firmly to his headset, and listened intently. "Hold it, Troy! Hold it. I've got something..."

Troy gave Phones a few moments to study the noise, before asking, "A sounding?"

"No... it's a signal... a short, strong, steady repeating signal."

"An S.O.S.?"

"That'd be my guess. And it's not too far off, either."

Troy nodded slowly. "Okay... then this may have just become a rescue mission."

"You know Troy, our orders were to follow the fleet and find out what they were up to. If they've been wiped out, Commander Shore might not appreciate us putting Stingray in danger to find out how it happened."

"That's right, Phones... only the commander's not here. We are. And if someone's in trouble, it's our duty to render any assistance we can... regardless of whether they're friend or foe." Troy looked first to Phones, then to Marina. "Are you with me?"

Marina nodded immediately, as did Phones a second later. "Heck Troy, we're with you no matter what." He turned his attention back to the waters ahead of them. "Cos whether Titan's alive or dead, either way, we gotta know."

"Right. Let's move on…"

Stingray continued her progress through the murky waters, her crew keeping their eyes peeled for any signs of life… or otherwise. The lure of the signal led the sub down into a thin deep trench running along the seabed which forced her to decelerate still further to navigate the narrow passageway. As the end of the trench loomed up, the path opened out into a wider but more uneven terrain – and it was there that they made the discovery.

Marina threw her hand over her mouth in shock at the sight that met the eyes of the Stingray crew. "All stop," Troy ordered immediately, and Phones worked quickly to obey the command. The trio looked out at the waters ahead and the seabed below… which was now littered with the debris from at least half a dozen mechanical fish. One or two of the wrecks appeared to be mostly intact, if scarred by explosion damage, but the majority were nothing but fragments, with only the odd fish-like shape here and there to indicate what they had once been.

Troy knew that Marina's eyes would have been drawn immediately to the multiple Aquaphibian bodies visible either in the wrecks or floating in the water around them, and part of him began to wish she had stayed behind at Marineville to have been spared this sight. While it was true Troy and Phones had both destroyed more than their share of mechanical fish (and therefore Aquaphibians) in their time, those were kill-or-be-killed situations on the field of battle – but this was no battlefield.

"They were massacred," Phones murmured. "What could have worked this fast?"

Troy shook his head. "I don't know. Let's see if we can pick up any clues. Steer us past the debris, then steady as she goes Phones… but be ready to gun it back the way we came if I give the word…"

"Right, Troy."

"What about the distress signal? Can you get an exact bearing?"

"We're almost on top of it. I'd say it's approximately—"

Marina suddenly lunged forward, pointing at a spot on the seabed. Troy's eyes followed her finger, down towards where a small blue spherical craft lay at a crooked angle at the base of a jagged rock formation. "Yeah, right about there," Phones concurred.

"Well, that's Titan's craft alright," Troy observed. "She seems to have got off lightly compared to the rest of the fleet. She's still in one piece, at least."

Phones was now running Stingray's searchlights over the wreck, revealing a tear in one side of the hull which had clearly flooded the interior of the small ship. "Yeah, but no signs of life."

"Remember Phones, we're dealing with underwater creatures. Titan can survive underwater, can't he Marina?" Marina nodded, and Troy thought for a moment before asking his next question. "Are you up for going over there with me to see if there's anyone to rescue?"

Given the pain Titan had caused Marina over the years, he would have forgiven her if she had refused – but he knew she wouldn't even have considered it. That was what made her such an invaluable member of Stingray's crew, after all.

A few minutes later the trio were standing by the entrance to Stingray's forward hatch, as Troy squeezed himself into an aqua suit. "We'll be as quick as we can, Phones," he ordered. "But at the slightest hint of trouble, I want you to take Stingray and high tail it back to Marineville, okay?"

"Sure thing, Troy. Oh, but I'll just have to stop off on the way to pick up some of your magic beans for those flying pigs."

Troy smiled at his old friend's unwavering loyalty. "Thanks Phones. All the same, no unnecessary risks, got it?"

"Heck, that goes double for the two of you," Phones retorted as he helped Troy on with his air cylinders. "I'm not the one swimming into a warzone, after all!"

Phones had positioned Stingray as close to the wreck of Titan's craft as he could safely manage to ensure that Troy and Marina's journey there and back could be as brief as possible. As the pair swam towards the small blue sphere, it became obvious that the damage they had seen was largely to the observation portholes on the control deck. The lower section of the craft housing the drive units that powered her seemed to be mostly intact. Marina swam straight into the control deck, while Troy took a moment to check the outside of the ship.

"Doesn't look like Titan's craft was even hit," he observed, aware that Phones would be listening aboard Stingray.

"What about that hole on the front, Troy?"

Troy followed Marina into the ship, and took a look around at the small cabin. "I'm there now Phones. It's not as bad as it seems from where you are. It's the ship's bridge, looks like the porthole windows were shattered… but the pattern of the blast suggests it was done from the inside."

"You mean maybe that's how someone inside got out after the crash?"

"Yeah, could b—"

Suddenly Troy felt someone tackle him from behind, and he found himself hurtling towards the opposite wall. Turning to break his fall, he found Marina pushing against him with a desperate look in her eyes. "Marina, what's—"

Then he saw what she had seen; an Aquaphibian looming over them, the rifle slung over his shoulder drifting up to take aim. Troy instinctively reached for his own pistol, aware that it would be all but useless underwater... but then he realised that there was no one at home in the soldier's bulging sightless eyes. It was only the movement of the water that had appeared to give life to a very dead body.

There was an apologetic expression on Marina's face as she released her grip, but Troy wasn't going to let her feel like she'd let him down just because she'd reacted to a non-existent danger. He reached out and squeezed her arm, grateful that her instincts were so sharp. If that Aquaphibian *had* still been alive, she could have very well lost her own life in trying to save his.

"Troy, what's going on in there? Troy? Troy!"

"We're okay, Phones," Troy replied, as he and Marina swam over to the body. "There's a dead Aquaphibian in here with us. Gave us quite a turn."

"Poor guy. Mind you, they're not the most handsome of fellas to run into at the best of times."

Troy suddenly felt Marina tap his arm. "What is it, Marina?"

Having taken a moment to close the Aquaphibian's eyes, Marina had moved on to examining the body more closely. She pointed to a large wound in the creature's side, where thin trails of green blood still seeped into the water from blackened and charred flesh.

"Say Phones... this Aquaphibian's got a nasty blast wound on his side."

"Could it have happened during the attack, Troy? Looks like there were plenty of blasts to go around..."

"Yeah, maybe... but the rest of the room seems pretty much intact. I don't think this ship was damaged in any attack. The Aquaphibian's injury kinda has the look of something that was done at close range."

He turned towards what he took to be the main control console, where a green light was flashing above a large black switch. "I'm gonna deactivate the distress beacon, Phones. Doesn't look like there's anyone here to save."

"*Right, Troy.*" As Troy threw the switch and the light went dead, Phones added "*You think maybe your friend in there's the one who sent it running before he died?*"

"Could be." Troy glanced around the small room again. It was an elegant yet spartan affair, with only a few comforts of note; a bowl of fruit, a few bottles of coloured liquid, a large hardback book that Marina had picked up and was now skimming through, and a large sofa, presumably for Titan. "Though there's no sign of Titan. I wonder—"

A flash of light from outside the wreck momentarily caught Troy's eye – then Phones' urgent voice over the radio confirmed his worst suspicions. "*Troy, we got incoming, and fast! Get yourselves back here, on the double!*"

"Ready the hatch Phones, we're on our way!" Troy quickly tapped Marina three times on the shoulder, and she swam for the open porthole without even waiting to find out what was wrong.

Many months ago, during another life-or-death situation, the Marineville crew had worked out a system to enable Marina to answer simple questions over the radio should she be left alone on Stingray; one tap on the microphone meant yes, two was no. This crude but effective communication method also worked whenever Troy and Phones needed to communicate with her underwater, where Marina wasn't able to hear her colleagues since she did not need the oxygen masks they used that also included built-in radio receivers. More recently, Troy had suggested introducing a three-tap addition to the code for use underwater, reserved for situations exactly like this. It was an order that Marina had agreed always to obey no matter what.

Swim for your life.

Bursting out of the airlock, Troy took the stairs leading to Stingray's upper deck two at a time. His pulse quickened as he saw three silver vessels closing on their position. The vulture-like wings at the front of the craft seemed vaguely familiar, although he wasn't going to waste time just now thinking about where he might have seen these ships before.

"Phones," Troy snapped as he leapt into his seat, "why aren't we moving already?"

Phones appeared to be working every lever and button within reach, all to no avail. "I-I can't, Troy! I'm trying, but the controls just aren't responding."

Troy tried giving his steering column a sharp turn first to the left, then to the right... but nothing happened. "What's going on? Have we lost power or something?"

Phones consulted a panel showing the reactor levels. "Heck no, we got power alright, just no response to controls..." He made one last effort to move Stingray by suddenly accelerating to Rate Six, but when the ship still refused to move he finally threw up his hands in frustration. "Troy, we're dead in the water."

Ahead of them the three enemy vessels slowed their advance, and Troy noticed the underbelly of each craft was bristling with missiles and gunports. He sensed Marina quietly step up behind them, still holding the book she had picked up on Titan's ship, helplessly watching the drama unfolding outside. He didn't blame her for wanting to be beside them, if this was truly the end of the line...

"Try the Sting missiles!" Troy urged. "If we can get off just one shot—"

Again and again Phones worked the lever to fire a missile, but once more nothing happened. "Nothing doing, skipper," he replied, looking out at the oncoming craft with fear in his eyes. "They got us cold."

"Yeah," Troy nodded grimly, as he pounded his fist against the steering column in frustration. "And there's nothing we can do about it!"

Slowly, purposefully, the three battlecruisers moved in for the kill...

CHAPTER 6

The Third Degree

"*Tower from Philippine station 178...*"
All eyes in the control tower looked towards the radio speaker hanging from the ceiling as the latest report came in. "*Explosions registered near Stingray's last recorded position. All contact lost with Titanican fleet.*"

Shore was quick to raise his radio mic to his lips. "What about Stingray?"

"*Still registering on soundings. Approaching explosion zone.*"

"Well, that's something at least." Shore was about to give the order to call up Stingray and ask what had happened when Lieutenant Fisher interrupted.

"I think we have something, sir," he called from the planning table in the corner of the room. He and Sara had collected the replacement Stingray files from the airfield and returned to the control tower where they had begun reviewing the sub's past missions in chronological order.

"You wanted us to check for any mention of the Philippines specifically," Sara reminded him, as he approached the table. Pointing to a page from the file, she explained, "There's a report here of a sighting of an enemy craft... it came in from Philippine station 178 during the height of the crisis."

"And just which crisis would that be exactly, Lieutenant Coral?" Shore asked. "There have been one or two over the years, y'know."

Sara smiled at the Commander's mildly sarcastic tone of voice and allowed Fisher to take up the explanation. "Well, that's the bad news, Commander," he added. "This file details our first encounter with Grupa and Noctus."

"Those clowns again!" He took the report from Sara and examined it closely. "Yeah, I knew that mention of the Philippines rang a bell somewhere."

Atlanta walked over to join them. "Those are the two who commanded that enemy sub during the incident with Professor Burgoyne, isn't it father?"

"Sure is, Atlanta." The part of Commander Shore that had treated Burgoyne with disdain upon his arrival at Marineville winced at the mention of the name... while the part of him that had remained in touch with the professor via letter ever since wished that they could have had that brilliant mind of his here now, just in case.

"As I understand it," Sara began, "this sub destroyed a World Security Patrol vessel and then attempted to destroy Marineville. Stingray's missiles weren't powerful enough to stop it until Professor Burgoyne made some modifications to their... nose cones, wasn't it?"

"That's right," Fisher agreed. "There was a real flap on about it at the time."

"And once Stingray had disabled their craft," Atlanta added, "Troy and Phones captured Grupa and Noctus and brought them back to Marineville."

Shore flicked through the folder, and found portrait mugshots of the two creatures that he then passed to Sara to examine. She took the photos and stared down at the pair of silver-skinned beings, particularly noting their short green hair and the fins protruding from the sides of their chins.

"Well, those are faces only a mother could love," Sara observed cooly. "Which one's which?"

Fisher pointed first to the slightly shorter creature, then the taller. "Grupa, Noctus."

"So, what happened when you brought them in?"

"They were given a short prison sentence," Shore explained, "and then returned to their people."

"And that did the trick, did it?"

"For about a week," Atlanta laughed. "Then they stole Stingray!"

"What?"

"Oh, that was a whole other affair," Shore explained dismissively, as if it made any difference. "Y'see, Atlanta was staying at an undersea fish farm and this crazy professor who ran the place got it into his head to team up with them to destroy Marineville. They cooked up a fake Stingray, and took the real thing to attack Marineville while Troy and Phones were trapped outside the fish farm."

Atlanta was quick to step in to the defence. "Father, Professor Cordo was a sick man—"

"You don't need to remind me of that, honey, he threatened to kill you!"

"Could we bring this back to our undersea friends, please?" Sara interrupted loudly, keen to avoid a longer trip down memory lane than was absolutely necessary. "I take it you got Stingray back?"

"Yeah; Troy convinced the professor to order them to bring Stingray back to the fish farm. He and the others put Cordo, Noctus and Grupa under arrest and brought 'em back here."

"The professor's still undergoing psychiatric treatment," Atlanta explained. "As for Grupa and Noctus, er, well..."

Sara looked to Shore. "Let me guess; another short incarceration and then allowed to go free again?"

Shore was scratching the back of his neck in a somewhat embarrassed fashion. "Er, no, not quite..."

"No," Fisher concurred. "They got medium incarceration for that one. It's two weeks longer."

"...I see." Sara could feel her early frustrations with Marineville's lax security measures bubbling to the surface again. Such persistent leniency was no way to deter your enemies, and Commander Shore and his staff were clearly smart enough to understand that. However, rather than voice her concerns – and risk humiliating herself the way she had the last time – she opted to put her hands behind her back as she often did when she wanted to keep her cool, and looked towards the ceiling as she rocked on her heels.

"You have to understand, Lieutenant Coral," began Commander Shore, "Marineville's not a prison facility. We're not set up to hold prisoners for any great length of time, and the World Government isn't exactly generous in their grant money for the upkeep of the detention cells we *do* have. Even when our prisoners get shipped off to World Government facilities we still can't be sure we're done with them because they often end up *back* here for trial anyway."

"Now for what it's worth, I agree with you; I feel longer prison sentences could deter some of our more persistent adversaries from trying again. Unfortunately, our hands are tied." Then he added quietly "Plus I hear there's been some complaints from people who aren't happy about their taxes having to go towards the upkeep of prisoners from the underwater world as well..."

Sara nodded; Shore's explanation, although it didn't solve anything, seemed to make sense. "I completely understand your position, sir," she replied earnestly. "And with your permission, I would like to raise this issue with the grant department on my return to Headquarters. I too can be very... persistent. Might be able to help, even if only slightly."

Shore seemed impressed by the offer, and Sara added it to her tally. "Permission granted, Lieutenant. Thank you. Now, the question is; why is Titan paying our old friends Grupa and Noctus a visit?"

"Could be he likes the sound of that super sub of theirs?" Fisher suggested.

"Yeah, maybe... aww heck, there's no way to know what's going on in that waterlogged mind of his until we know for sure what's happened to that fleet." Shore pointed a finger in his daughter's direction. "Better get on to Troy, Atlanta, tell them what we suspect, and see if they have any more information for us."

"Yes, sir." Atlanta returned to her seat at the main console in the centre of the room, and worked the controls in front of her. "Marineville calling Stingray. Come in, Stingray."

But there was no response. Atlanta waited a few moments more, then tried again. "Stingray from tower; are you receiving me?" Then, one last time, with a note of desperation in her voice. "Come in Stingray!"

"Tower from Philippine station 178!" came the urgent voice over the radio speaker. *"All contact with Stingray broken as of ninety seconds ago! Will continue taking soundings."*

Shore's voice was grave as he asked, "Any further explosions registered from that zone?"

"Negative sir. Stingray's just disappeared."

Sara approached the console, placing an arm around the back of Atlanta's chair. "Does that mean—"

"No!" Atlanta responded hastily, as if trying to convince herself more than anyone else. "No, it doesn't necessarily mean that... that something's happened to them. Could be anything; a radio fault, or their soundings are being blocked somehow..."

Sara looked to Commander Shore. "So, what do you normally do at times like this?"

"I'll tell you what we do Lieutenant, we mount a full-scale search of that area!" Shore's face was grim as he immediately began issuing orders. "Atlanta, I want any combat-ready vessels within three hundred miles of Stingray's last recorded position to converge on that area immediately."

"Yes sir!"

"Fisher, search and rescue aircraft to take off within the next ten minutes."

"Okay, sir!"

"Lieutenant Coral—"

"You want an alert to go out to every WSP base in that area, and for more ships to be made available for the search."

Shore was already gliding away from her, satisfied that she knew her role in this operation. "That's the general idea, thank you," he muttered, as he raised his radio mic to his lips once more. "Tower to rescue launch commander..."

As Shore moved towards the wall map to begin outlining search patterns to the launch commander, Sara leaned in close to Atlanta. "It's all very well sending everyone else out to look for them," she asked, "but... what do we do?"

"We wait," Atlanta replied. She looked up at Sara with a pain in her eyes that reflected the fact that this wasn't the first time she had been in this position. "For now, that's all we can do. Troy'll find a way to let us know what's happened, you'll see."

"Yeah. Yeah, sure he will." Sara patted Atlanta twice on the shoulder then walked over to use the wall-mounted radio mic that hung beside the aquascanner unit. "World Security Patrol Headquarters, please," she ordered as she picked up the mic. "Priority A1."

"Connecting you now."

As she waited to be put through to her superiors, Sara looked around the room. Commander Shore, Lieutenant Fisher and Atlanta were all utterly focused on their allotted tasks, but the concern for their missing friends was evident on their faces. The image of the smiling Marina standing on her doorstep with her bowl of flowers suddenly came unbidden to Sara's mind, and she realised that having met the Stingray crew and gotten to like them in the short time she'd been in Marineville she was now feeling the same concerns as everyone in this room.

Sara had never been one for waiting back at Headquarters while others handled the action. What she wanted more than anything was to be out there leading the hunt herself, doing whatever needed to be done to get their people back. She knew making these calls, as important as they were, was a waste of her field talents, and she strongly suspected it was a waste of Atlanta's and Fisher's capabilities too. Surely there were other officers in Marineville who could man the radio and organise the search aircraft?

If I pushed to get out there and join the search, she wondered, *would they back me?*

Knowing it wasn't her place to voice such concerns, at least not while she had her orders to be carried out, she decided to keep quiet.

For now.

For the second time in the last twenty minutes, Troy Tempest felt that he and his crew were facing the end of the line. He wasn't sure if that was a good sign, since having been wrong the first time he could well be wrong again this time, or if they were merely doubly doomed now.

Stingray had eventually begun responding to orders – but not to those of her crew. Troy, Phones and Marina had watched as the ship's controls had suddenly come to life, as if worked by some unseen puppet master, and the sub had proceeded under the escort of the three battlecruisers. No attempt to interrupt the controls met with any success, and when a hatch opened up in the seabed Stingray had glided inside, into a long dark tunnel that reminded Troy of the one that led from her pen in Marineville to the ocean door. This tunnel however only extended for what seemed like a couple of miles, and when Stingray emerged on the far side her crew found themselves in a subterranean sea.

Unlike the other subterranean seas that Stingray had visited previously, however, this one did not seem to extend very far in any direction; it was as if it had been artificially created, cut out of the seabed itself to create just enough room to hold the underwater city that Stingray was now approaching. Although comparable in size to Titanica itself, the city before them consisted of only one building, a metallic egg-like structure that lay atop a series of support columns that appeared to sink into the seabed beneath. Nevertheless, as Stingray got closer, Troy began to discern windows indicating individual rooms within the surface of the structure, although he could see no signs of life from within.

A door on the city's surface had opened and Stingray slid inside, coming to rest on the bottom before powering herself down. As the water around her began to be pumped out, it was obvious that they had reached their destination and were now in some kind of airlock.

Now Troy, Phones and Marina were crouching behind a barricade hastily assembled on the lower deck, using whatever furniture they could get their hands on, while outside Stingray voices and footsteps could be heard on the hull above the main airlock hatch.

"I reckon it'll only take 'em a few minutes to cut through the hatch, Troy," Phones suggested. Then the two friends heard the sound of footsteps coming down the access ladder – their visitors were already aboard. "Course, that's only if they even need to…"

"Everything else around here seems to be working for these guys rather than us," Troy muttered. "Why not the hatch?" It was irrational, he knew, but Troy couldn't help but feel somewhat betrayed by the way Stingray seemed to have suddenly turned against her crew. Rather than dwell on it though, he reached for his pistol and aimed it towards the door from the airlock through which their guests would soon appear. He glanced toward Phones on his right, and saw that his colleague was likewise taking aim at the door.

"Wait for my order to fire, Phones," he said quietly. "Don't shoot to kill... unless you have to. But they're not taking this ship without a fight."

"Got it, Troy."

Glancing to his left, he saw Marina peer over the barricade to see what was going on. "Marina, you just keep your head down."

The door connecting the airlock to the lower deck slowly opened revealing a trio of large green and silver-skinned creatures – all armed. With rifles raised they marched confidently into the room, as if not expecting the least resistance from the Stingray crew.

"Fire!" Troy cried, and both he and Phones pulled the triggers on their pistols.

Nothing happened.

Again and again Troy and Phones attempted to fire, but without success. Their pistols had been disabled as efficiently as Stingray herself had been. They looked at each other in horror, wondering what they could possibly do to repel these boarders without weapons... but with a sinking feeling, Troy knew it was time to accept defeat. These creatures clearly had the upper hand, at least as far as Stingray and her technology were concerned.

From behind the trio, another smaller creature stepped forward – one Troy immediately recognised. "Captain Troy Tempest," said Noctus. "You will now leave Stingray and accompany us into our city. No harm will come to you – if you do as we instruct."

Phones looked over at his captain. "Well, Troy?"

Troy looked first at Phones, then at Marina, each waiting for him to decide their next course of action. There was only one option left to them; the one he swore he'd never take. Surrender. And it tore him up inside to have to admit it.

Slowly Troy got to his feet. "We... have no choice, Phones. Do as they say."

Noctus and his soldiers watched as the Stingray crew stepped over the barricade and moved towards the airlock door. One by one Troy, Phones and Marina were escorted up the ladder onto the hull and then via a connecting bridge onto the dockside. Stingray was still afloat, now resting atop some five fathoms of water, and it pained Troy to walk away from her... but right now she didn't seem to be of much use to any of them.

"I take it you recognise our captors, Phones," Troy said quietly as the Stingray crew were led at gunpoint out of the airlock and into a waiting travel tube.

"Shucks, who could forget 'em?" Phones replied. "We had no idea about any of this though. Did you, Marina?"

Marina shook her head. "They evidently keep themselves well hidden," Troy mused, as the travel tube began to move, speeding through the city and past submarine pens containing more vessels of the same type Stingray had first encountered during the Professor Burgoyne incident. Their journey took them past what appeared to Troy to be construction facilities, factories and machine workshops; but, he noted with interest, there seemed to be very few people about.

"Where are you taking us?" Troy asked. Not expecting a response he was surprised when Noctus actually opened his mouth to reply, but just as he did so the travel tube slowed to a stop.

"We have arrived," he announced. As the doors opened the Stingray crew stood and stepped out of the travel tube, still very aware of the rifles carried by Noctus and his guards – who appeared to be the females of whatever species this was – just behind them. Now finding themselves standing at an intersection connecting three rounded corridors, each one a gleaming silver marked only by a different coloured line on the floor, the sound of approaching footsteps immediately caught the attention of Troy and his friends.

"Ah, Captain Tempest!" The figure that strode forward to greet them was just as familiar as the man who had taken them prisoner. "Welcome to Igneathea! I trust you and your friends are unharmed?"

Troy was momentarily thrown off by the note of genuine concern in Grupa's question, but he wasn't about to be lulled into a false sense of security. The image of the decimated Titanican fleet was still fresh in his memory. "For now at least, yes, we are."

Grupa chuckled. "Yes, I imagine you must have many questions. And they will be answered, in due course." He nodded towards his colleagues. "Noctus, please take Lieutenant Sheridan and Marina to my office. I wish to speak to Captain Tempest alone… in the interrogation chamber."

Marina immediately grabbed Troy's arm but was forcibly separated from him by the muzzle of an Igneathean soldier's rifle. The soldier pushed her towards Phones who looked gravely towards his captain.

"Look after her, Phones," Troy said in a low voice. "I'll be seeing you."

Phones nodded. "You'd better, boy. We came in here together. We're all getting out together, or not at all."

Troy couldn't help smiling at his friend's obvious determination to escape, reinforced by Marina's eager nodding. The soldier again used her rifle to push the pair away from him, and as Troy watched them be ushered away along the corridor he couldn't help wondering if it was the last time he would ever see them – or they him.

Grupa appeared to sense Troy's concern. "You have my personal assurance that no harm shall come to your two friends, Captain," he said chipperly, before adding, "Or to you."

Troy looked down at the man who, for the moment at least, seemed to hold his future in his hands. "That I find difficult to believe."

"Understandable, considering our past history." Grupa gestured towards the opposite corridor from the one Phones and Marina had just disappeared down. "For now at least, would you please accompany me?"

Without a word, Troy followed Grupa down the corridor, ever aware of the imposing figure of the guard at his back. He considered trying to make a break for it but where would he go? He had no idea where exactly Phones and Marina were being taken, and with Stingray out of action escape from the city seemed impossible. For now, it seemed as though the safest course of action was cooperation.

They turned left at the end of the corridor, then left again almost immediately. Grupa pressed his right hand against a palm reader on the wall and a door slid soundlessly upwards. Grupa gestured for Troy to enter the room, then nodded to their escort. "Please wait outside."

The guard stepped back as ordered, and as the door closed behind him Troy looked around at the small, darkly lit, and clinically sterile environment he now found himself in. Even if he hadn't already known that this was the interrogation chamber it was obvious from the single chair in the middle of the room, around which everything else seemed to be oriented. A large monitor was positioned directly behind the chair, with a smaller monitor mounted to a computer bank and control panel connected directly to the chair. Close at hand were several tables lined with rows of what appeared to be surgical instruments – some decidedly otherworldly, others disturbingly old-fashioned – that he would prefer not to have anything to do with. Unfortunately, it seemed as though the choice was no longer his to make.

Troy watched as Grupa moved to the monitor and powered it on. "Before we start, am *I* permitted to ask a question?"

"Please."

Again Grupa's manner was friendly, almost good-natured. *He's trying too hard*, Troy thought to himself. *He must know that I've seen his little collection of torture devices over there and that I could do him a mischief with almost any one of them... and yet he's turned his back on me. Is he that sure of me? Or... sure of himself?* Deciding to go along with the charade, and aware it might be his last chance to ask anything, Troy posed the big question. "How did you manage to take control of Stingray?"

"Ah yes!" As the computer bank now whirred into life Grupa stepped away from it and gave Troy his full attention, adopting a somewhat conciliatory tone of voice. "I imagine it must have been quite disconcerting to watch your vessel develop a mind of her own like that."

"That's putting it mildly."

Grupa smiled. It reminded Troy of a used car salesman. "After our first encounter with Stingray, we were... impressed. Your vessel was obviously a formidable opponent and we needed to formulate a defence against her. You may have observed that our own battlecruiser is one of the most technologically advanced of any underwater civilisation. We pride ourselves on that, Captain... yet Stingray was able to cripple our cruiser with one shot."

"Eventually," Troy reminded him.

"Quite so," Grupa conceded. "It was, as I believe the terrainean phrase goes, 'touch and go' for you for a time.

Now, you of course remember the incident shortly after with Professor Cordo?"

"How could I forget?" Troy recalled only too well being stranded outside the professor's undersea fish farm with Atlanta a helpless prisoner inside and Stingray having been stolen by Grupa and Noctus. "He hired you and your friend to steal Stingray to use her to launch an attack against Marineville."

Grupa raised a finger. "Ah – *partly* correct. The professor was not a well man, Captain, as I am sure you are aware. We allowed him to believe that we were helping with his plan… but really, he was helping *us* with ours."

"Which was?"

There was that disconcerting smile again. "Your ship, Captain! We needed a chance to get aboard, to study it, to understand the technology that made it function, if we were ever going to devise an effective defence against it."

Troy shook his head in disbelief. "So you just took her for a test drive…?"

"Precisely! We could have destroyed it instantly, of course, but we weren't to know that you didn't have an entire army of Stingrays back at Marineville ready to send after us. We needed to learn everything there was to learn about Stingray, study every inch of her. And we did."

Troy had to admire the scope of this plan-within-a-plan; after all, he, Phones and Marina had been so focused on trying to get back into the fish farm that it hadn't even occurred to them what Grupa and Noctus might have been up to aboard Stingray during that time. Nor, it seemed, had it occurred to anyone else. "But you must have known we'd overpower Professor Cordo eventually, and force him to order you to turn back!"

"Of course! We were certain you would. You and your crew are clearly resourceful and the professor's scheme was obviously doomed to failure, but it didn't matter. It gave us our chance! Those hours we spent gathering intelligence aboard Stingray were invaluable. And, upon our return to Igneathea after our incarceration in Marineville, Noctus and I took what we had learned... and began to devise a method of neutralising your vessel should we ever encounter her again."

"I see..." But Troy still wasn't exactly sure how the takeover had been achieved. "Some kind of remote control device?"

"Precisely." Now Grupa suddenly rounded on Troy, with a ruthless gleam in his eyes. "Now Captain, my question... what brought you to our domain?"

Troy considered his answer carefully. He'd been interrogated before and knew the routine, although he wasn't keen to experience it again. Still, in this instance he saw no sense in concealing the truth. "Well, we were following a fleet from the underwater city of Titanica. We had a break-in at Marineville. Vital security documents were taken, we suspected agents of Titanica may be responsible, and then within hours Titanica sent out a fleet to your territory. We wanted to know if there was any connection."

"I see." Grupa approached the chair in the centre of the room, running his hand over the back of it as he circled it. "Are you familiar with this device?"

"Yeah... I've seen something like it before." Troy's mind was cast back to the time he had been held prisoner by the Atlanteans and had inadvertently given away secret information about Marineville after sitting in a chair connected to their brain-reading machine. "The subject sits in this chair and as he's questioned his thoughts are displayed on the big screen for his interrogators... so that even if he doesn't talk, he still gives information away."

Grupa nodded. "Precisely! But of course, this mind sifter is far more... sophisticated than a simple brain-reading machine. Should the subject resist interrogation, the sifter will gradually apply force to extract the truth directly from their minds. The effects can be quite unpleasant should the subject continue to resist further." He patted the back of the chair with something akin to reverence. "It's my own creation, in fact. I'm really rather proud of it."

Troy tensed, preparing himself for the worst. All pretence of a friendly conversation had now been dropped; Grupa was deadly serious and he knew things were about to escalate dramatically. "You've had all the information you're going to get out of me," Troy told him bluntly.

"We shall see." Grupa spoke into a radio watch on his wrist. "Bring in the prisoner."

The door to the interrogation room slid upwards once again and two Igneathean guards entered the room... dragging the dishevelled figure of Titan along with them. The tyrant appeared to be only semi-conscious but on seeing Troy his eyes snapped open and a look of wild fury seized his face. *"Tempest!"* Troy stepped back as Titan lunged forward, his hands reaching out for his throat – but the heavy manacles around his wrists prevented him from doing Troy any harm, and the guards soon had him under control once more.

"Place him in the chair," Grupa ordered them. The two women obeyed, despite Titan's best efforts to overcome them. He strained and snarled but once pairs of clamps locked into place around his wrists and ankles it was obvious that he was going nowhere.

"Very clever, Tempest," Titan said in a low voice heavy with hatred. "Planting false information about these creatures into your own records, luring into a trap anybody who might try to steal them from you. I congratulate you. A cunning strategy indeed."

Before Troy could reply, Grupa interrupted on his behalf. "I have yet to see any evidence that the good Captain had anything to do with your fleet's incursion into our territory," he replied, his voice level and dispassionate. "But you may explain the purpose of your visit to me whenever you are ready."

"Nearly two dozen of my warriors are dead at your hands!" Titan bellowed. "I owe you no explanation whatsoever! For their memories, I will not speak!"

A horrible thought suddenly occurred to Troy. "Your remote-control device at work again?" he asked Grupa quietly.

Grupa looked decidedly pleased with himself. "An unexpected test of its capabilities. When the fleet arrived and our bellicose friend here began making his... overtures... we saw the chance to make use of them. Within seconds, we had accessed their computers and assumed direct control of their vessels; navigation, propulsion... and the weapons. Those mechanical fish are much less advanced than your Stingray, after all." He chuckled, the memory of his creation's first successful test still fresh in his mind. "From there, we simply had the ships blow each other out of the water."

"And you will pay for that!" Titan snarled. "I swear vengeance on you and your kind, from this moment on!"

"The hollow threat of a defeated tyrant," Grupa sighed. "I have heard similar words before. Now, will you tell us what brought you here – or shall I force the information from you using the mind sifter?"

Titan laughed. "A primitive toy! Do your worst, fool... I can withstand it!"

"Very well then," said Grupa tersely. "Your interrogation commences now." He moved to the instrument panel beside the chair and operated the controls. From the ceiling directly overhead a large transparent helmet descended, lowering itself onto Titan's skull. He thrashed and writhed but every time he did so the helmet shocked him, visible bolts of electricity arcing into his head until he learned to remain still. He glared towards Grupa and Troy, and the latter couldn't tell which of them he was more angry with.

An unsettling hum began to fill the air as Grupa increased power to the mind sifter. "The more you resist, the more pain will be administered, until you have told us what we want to know," he explained. "It's really up to you. Tell us what brought you here."

Titan remained tight-lipped but was now clearly fighting the urge to speak even though he didn't want to. Once or twice a word threatened to escape and he almost swallowed it down... but even he could only resist for so long. As the words finally came, he spoke them in a flat dull voice, as if reading them from a piece of paper. Yet as dispassionately as he spoke them, Troy could tell that every word being dragged out of his mouth was agony for the man. As he spoke, images appeared on the screen behind him to support his words.

"I am here," he began, "because I seek allies for a final all-out assault against Marineville. I propose the formation of a great alliance of underwater races to destroy the terraineans..."

So that was it, Troy thought to himself. *And he's got a lot of names and addresses in those stolen documents. Oh boy, are we in trouble now!*

Titan continued, beads of sweat beginning to show on his brow, although the words seemed to come more freely now. "Documents we stole from their archives indicated that your race was of great technological expertise, a prime candidate to join our cause. I desired you to be among our first recruits."

"Hmm..." Grupa was consulting the readings on the console in front of him. "This would seem to be the truth..." He suddenly glared at Titan. "Up to a point. What is it that you are *not* telling us?"

Titan took a breath, as if about to speak... but then appeared to brace himself. There was more to be shared, that much was obvious, but Grupa was going to have to employ stronger measures to get to it. So he did. He gradually turned up the dial that controlled the power to the mind sifter, and as the hum became louder Titan began to shake as he fought to maintain control. Just at the point Troy thought Titan might cry out in pain, a trail of green blood began to trickle from his nose, and he slumped forward.

"Stop it!" Troy lunged forward to attempt to switch off the machine himself, but he was grabbed by the two guards and held firm. In desperation, he looked to Titan himself. "Titan, for heaven's sake man, tell them what they want to know! It's not worth your life!"

Slowly Titan lifted his head to look at Troy... but there was no hint of gratitude in his eyes that someone had attempted to help him. No understanding that his sworn enemy had no desire to see him suffer like this. Only that same hatred that had smouldered in his eyes ever since their first meeting. "I... would rather die... than show any weakness in front of you, Tempest!" he snarled. Then, looking past Troy and directly at Grupa, he bellowed "If you want my secrets, you'll have to go all the way!"

Grupa shrugged. "Oh, very well," he said quietly, before turning the power dial of the mind sifter up to maximum. Now Titan did cry out, a bloodcurdling sound that made Troy wince. As the horrible sound died away, the screen behind Titan showed new images; images of Marineville being obliterated, of Stingray being destroyed, of Marina once again facing life as his slave... and of the prolonged and painful death of Troy Tempest.

"Mental barriers only," Grupa observed quietly to Troy. "A most curious fellow. His hatred for you overrides almost all other concerns. Even self-preservation."

The images of Titan's fantasies now faded from the screen and a new image appeared in greater clarity than any of the previous ones. The screen now showed a mechanical fish fleet approaching an underwater city that Troy took to be a mental representation of what Titan thought Igneathea might look like.

Grupa clapped his hands in delight. "Ah – a subterfuge!" He gestured towards the screen. "You will explain these images to us, please!"

Titan almost appeared to have lost the will to live. When he next spoke, it was in the quiet hollow voice of a broken man. "I... have reinforcements on their way to your city... with orders to subjugate or destroy you... should you refuse to ally yourselves with me..."

The images on the screen now showed the city suffering a devastating assault from a fleet of mechanical fish; her battlecruisers blasted out of the water and the survivors being rounded up to serve in Titan's army. Grupa watched the hypothetical annihilation of his own race with a clinical detachment, then consulted the readings on his monitor. "Accepted as full truth," he said finally, before quickly deactivating the mind sifter.

As the machine went dormant Titan slumped unconscious in the chair. "Take him for medical examination, under guard, and then back to his cell once he is declared fit enough," Grupa ordered the guards as they released him from his bonds. "Oh, but leave Captain Tempest here."

Troy watched as the guards dragged Titan out of the room, leaving him alone with Grupa. He looked with disgust at the chair his sworn enemy had just been removed from. "And now I suppose it's my turn in your little torture machine..." *Or worse still, Phones or Marina's turn...*

"That will not be necessary, Captain." Grupa turned away from the console to face Troy, who saw no deception in his captor's eyes. "You were well within your rights to take an interest in Titan's activities after what he did to you. That the trail happened to bring you to our doorstep is hardly your fault. I accept your explanation without question."

Grateful for that at least, if somewhat surprised once more by the genuine sincerity in Grupa's voice, Troy couldn't condone what he had just witnessed. "Did you have to be so brutal with him?"

"We had to know why he was here," Grupa said disinterestedly. "He *could* have confessed immediately; it was his choice to conceal his intentions. Oh, but do not worry; there will be no lasting effects from the mind sifter." He gave Troy a curious look. "Our methods do not seem to meet with your approval?"

"I have no desire to see any man suffer, no matter how much suffering they've caused others," explained Troy calmly. "It's our hope that one day Titan will stand trial for his crimes, or that we can at least achieve some kind of lasting peace between our peoples."

"A commendable if somewhat misguided attitude... considering how he clearly does not share it." Grupa shook his head in mild amusement. "A most curious specimen indeed..."

Troy saw nothing amusing in the indignity that Titan had just endured. "What will happen to him?"

"We shall hold him here in our city until I have made consultation."

Troy had no idea what exactly that meant, but whatever 'consultation' was, it had to be better than death. At least, he hoped so. "And what about my crew and I?"

"The fate of your party too shall be subject to the result of consultation," Grupa said flatly. Then he smiled his slimy smile once more and Troy fought the urge to look away. "However, twice before you have had the opportunity to destroy myself and my colleague Noctus... and twice before you have shown us mercy. I believe we can extend the same courtesy to you and your friends, at least for now." He gestured towards the door.

"Would the three of you care for a tour of our city?"

CHAPTER 7

The Gilded Cage

"Captain Tempest, Lieutenant Sheridan, Ms Marina... may I present the citizens of Igneathea!"

Phones looked around blankly. "Where?" he asked.

"Why, they are all around you!"

"You mean... in those things?"

The Stingray crew's tour of Igneathea had culminated in a trip beneath the city itself, travelling via an elevator housed inside one of the giant supports that kept the vast structure standing. This elevator shaft extended below the seabed, down several miles, until it had finally emerged onto a catwalk overlooking a vast underground chamber that appeared to stretch as far as the eye could see in every direction. And in every direction rows upon rows of sleek black tubes, each just larger than a person, lay horizontal on the floor.

"Precisely, Captain Tempest!" Grupa stepped towards the safety rail running alongside the edge of the catwalk, and pointed down towards the nearest tubes resting just a few feet below them. "Inside each of these hibernation capsules is a citizen of Igneathea, perfectly healthy and preserved. Each mind is connected to all the others, creating a vast collective intelligence network that is kept alive by the most advanced life support system ever constructed – all of which is powered by geothermal energy from a subterranean magma reservoir." As he spoke, a handful of technicians could be seen walking – or in some cases driving – amongst the capsules making checks and adjustments as necessary.

Grupa looked down proudly at the thousands upon thousands of life support units. "This... is the Igneathean Cooperative."

Troy couldn't quite comprehend the enormity of what he was seeing. "And your people just... stay in these capsules? All the time?"

"Their needs are met by the life support systems," reiterated Grupa. "You may have observed that our city is far too small to accommodate all the members of our race that you can see here."

"But why keep so many of them tucked away?" asked Phones. "Your city may not be the biggest but from what we've seen most of the place seems almost deserted. What gives?"

A slightly pained look crossed Grupa's face. "Our people once lived on the land, Captain Tempest. At least, we tried to. A question of survival drove us to relocate our people to the seabed – but it was obvious living space would be at a premium, and even more obvious that our resources would be extremely limited. A radical solution to the problem was required and, once more as it so often does, our technology provided our salvation." He looked out across the sea of caskets. "This solution ensured our survival, but this... this is not forever. Merely until we can find an alternative."

"What will that alternative be?"

Grupa shrugged. "Who knows? The Cooperative is always thinking, the group mind ever considering new strategies by which we may return to the surface. Some of those schemes work, some do not." He shook his head ruefully. "Our first attack on Marineville was part of an aborted plan by the Cooperative to remove what they considered the primary obstacle in any attempt to retake the surface."

"Why target us?" Troy suggested. "We might have been able to find some mutually acceptable solution to your problems if you'd approached us in peace."

"The Igneathean Cooperative has a tendency to deal in absolutes," Grupa explained, somewhat sheepishly. "The destruction of Marineville was deemed logical based on reported past instances of human aggression towards other underwater races."

"You mean if there was even a 1 per cent chance we might treat you with hostility, you had to treat it as if it were a 100 per cent chance?" Phones asked.

"Precisely." Grupa now looked Troy directly in the eye. "Well, you must admit Captain, you do have something of a reputation for causing destruction among certain underwater communities."

"Only when provoked," Troy insisted firmly. "We don't seek trouble. But we will defend ourselves if we have to."

"Don't they get bored stuck in those tubes all day?" asked Phones as he leaned over the safety rail, attempting to lighten the mood a little. "I mean, I sometimes think I'd like to sleep forever but this is ridiculous!"

"Oh, there is always the possibility of temporary release," Grupa explained. "Whenever we require additional labour for a workforce, a suitable candidate is released from hibernation to assist in the task. When that task is done, they return to stasis."

As they spoke a dozen stasis tubes about twenty feet away opened in unison and their Igneathean occupants climbed out. After taking a moment or two to adjust to being revived, the group of workers slowly made their way towards a nearby travel tube station, ready to be taken up into the city to begin their task. Marina seemed particularly intrigued by the sight, and as she made eye contact with Troy he could tell what she was thinking. He nodded, just slightly, and she smiled in response.

"And what have they been volunteered to work on?" Phones asked.

"One or two special projects," Grupa replied, with an amused emphasis on the word 'special' that didn't go unnoticed by Troy and Phones. "And when they are in stasis, their minds are part of the Igneathean Cooperative, committed to solving the problems faced by our race."

"And this 'consultation' that you mentioned," Troy asked. "Does that involve them too?"

"Ah yes! Come." Grupa beckoned Troy and Phones to a nearby alcove recessed into the wall close to the elevator doors. Stepping into the computer-lined booth, Grupa pointed up. "This is where I make consultation. When I activate this chamber the brain scanner you see above is lowered over my head, linking my mind to those of all the Igneatheans in hibernation. I make my report of the current situation – and I remain here until the Cooperative relays its orders or decision."

"Which you then carry out?" asked Phones.

"Precisely! I may be the administrator of the city but the Cooperative makes all the important decisions – including deciding the fates of both yourselves and Titan. These," he gestured back towards the rows upon rows of hibernating Igneatheans below, "are your judge and jury."

"You mean our fates are gonna be decided by this collection of sleeping beauties?" Phones asked incredulously. "People who've never even met us?"

"Their decision shall be made based on the honest information and experiences drawn from my own mind," Grupa explained. "I assure you I shall present your case fairly and impartially. The entire Cooperative will receive that knowledge and then consider their verdict as one. You call it democracy, do you not?"

"Some trial, huh Troy?" Phones muttered. "I've always said there's no greater jury than a collection of Fishman Winkles."

Grupa considered his words for a moment, then shook his head in confusion. "No, I do not understand your reference."

Noctus suddenly pushed his way past Troy and Phones to address his leader. "Grupa! The girl! Where is she?"

Grupa stepped from the consultation alcove and looked around in alarm; Marina was indeed missing, and the two terrainean males were now trying to look anywhere but in his direction. "Was she here when we came in?" he asked.

Noctus nodded. "She was with us when we arrived. But now, she... she must have slipped away somewhere!"

"Yeah, she'll do that," Phones said cheerfully. "That girl's always sneaking off somewhere, isn't she Troy?"

"Enough!" Noctus raised his pistol and jammed it under Phones' chin. "Tell us where she is!"

"We have no idea where she is!" Troy snapped. "Phones is right. Marina has a tendency to act impulsively at times, usually without consulting us. I'm sure she's around here somewhere. Maybe she just went to look at something?"

Grupa stepped towards Troy, a knowing gleam of doubt in his piercing blue eyes. *He's not buying it*, Troy thought to himself. For a moment he wondered if he might be about to get hauled back upstairs to be thrown to the mind sifter – but then Grupa seemed to relent, lowering Noctus' pistol. "One girl is no match for our security force, Noctus," he said finally. "Tell the guards that she is to be located and taken alive. Meanwhile, have these two taken back up to the city and place them in a cell." Shooting one final slightly disappointed glance back at Troy, he added "I shall proceed at once with consultation."

Troy and Phones watched as Grupa marched into the consultation alcove and closed the transparent door behind him, sealing himself in. He closed his eyes as the brain scanner lowered over his head – and then they were being marched away by Noctus and one of his imposing guards, back towards the elevator that would return them to the city.

As they walked, Troy leaned in close to Phones and asked quietly "You saw where she hid, Phones?"

Phones nodded. "Inside of one o' them empty casket thingies down below, yep."

"And by now all our questions should have given her enough time to sneak out of there and hopefully make it to one of those travel tubes…"

"Troy, I really don't like the thought of her roaming around the city alone," Phones admitted. "Who knows what trouble she might get up to? After all, she was adamant she weren't gonna leave us behind…"

"Maybe she should rethink that," Troy muttered. He knew that Marina would never abandon her friends – or anybody in trouble for that matter – but it was also obvious that out of the three of them, she stood the best chance of escaping to get help. Perhaps that should be their priority now. "If she can get out of the city, and up to the surface—"

"It's a big ocean, skipper," Phones observed. "The chances of her being picked up in time to be of any help to us—"

"You're forgetting Marineville. By now I'm guessing Commander Shore will have half the combined forces of the W.A.S.P.s and the World Navy out searching for us."

"Only half?" Phones shook his head. "Shucks, I thought we were worth more than that."

"Sure we are," Troy agreed, as they reached the elevator. "That's the trouble. He'll be needing the other half to cover Stingray's duties while we're gone…"

From the moment Titan had announced that he was leaving Titanica with the fleet something important had been nagging at the back of X-20's mind. Something that he knew was desperately obvious, if only he could summon it to the *front* of his mind where it could be of practical use.

For many hours after the fleet's departure he had continued to mull it over, in between reviewing the Marineville documents and trying to ignore Teufel's hard stares. It wasn't until just before the distress call came in from Titan's craft that he finally realised what it was that had been troubling him; the weapons and defences of the submarines used by the aliens Titan had gone to make contact with. It was all very well using Titanican missiles reinforced by the terrainean metal alloy to threaten these creatures into allying with him… but that only really worked if he'd taken some of those missiles along with him. Without those to back up his offer, Titan had simply made a target of himself.

That these creatures were a proven threat to Stingray – which itself had a proven track record of defeating mechanical fish in battle – meant that even protected by eight mechanical fish Titan may have found himself overwhelmed by superior firepower. The respective offensive and defensive capabilities of the mechanical fish, Stingray, and the battlecruisers used by these creatures brought to X-20's mind the endlessly fascinating terrainean game of rock paper scissors – except in this case the average mechanical fish was almost guaranteed to be the loser of every outcome. If Stingray's standard Sting missiles couldn't so much as scratch these battlecruisers, what chance did a mechanical fish stand – even with Titan along to command his troops himself?

So when Titanica's traffic control station had suddenly lost all contact with Titan's fleet, it hadn't come as much of a surprise to X-20. Overconfidence had always been one of his master's greatest flaws. It had, however, been most interesting for him to watch the reactions of the Aquaphibians on duty at the time, as they processed the possibility that their leader had been lost; one had roared with anger and pounded his fists against the nearest console, one had fainted and one had burst into tears. For all his obvious flaws, they truly loved him. He had wondered if it was worth reporting the news to Teufel but decided against it.

Leaving the Aquaphibians to their mourning, X-20 had instead headed for the engineering workshop where Sculpin had been assigned to oversee the production of new nosecones for the missiles aboard their mechanical fish. Inside, he found the engineer speaking into a small portable radio, which he hastily deactivated when he saw X-20 enter the room. "Oh! You startled me! I wasn't expecting... um... c-can I help you?"

"I bring grave news," X-20 began. "It would appear that our fleet has encountered difficulties."

"What kind of difficulties?"

"I fear they have been destroyed."

"Destroyed? You mean, Titan... Titan's *dead?*" Sculpin's face underwent a strange convulsive series of expressions, beginning with the closest thing to joy that X-20 could ever remember seeing on that chiselled green and yellow face, which quickly contorted into some forced parody of sorrow that only someone unfamiliar with the emotion would mistake as sincere. "What a tragedy," he finally forced himself to say in a decidedly strained voice.

"Indeed. Certainly the mechanical fish escorts must be presumed lost," X-20 added. "We simply lost all contact with them. We did however receive a signal from the distress beacon on Titan's own ship."

"Then... *he* may have survived..."

"That is my hope," X-20 agreed. "The signal was eventually manually deactivated at the source. But since it had to be activated by someone to begin with, that someone could have been Titan." He shook his head sadly. "Poor Titan. He may well have been captured, or interrogated..."

"Tortured?" asked Sculpin hopefully.

X-20 decided it was best to ignore that last remark. It too closely mirrored his own line of thinking. "What progress on the reinforcement fleet?"

"Oh, excellent progress! I-I was just talking to my, um, construction team." Sculpin waved his radio towards X-20, before adding "Yes, the Burgoyne formula was easily adapted to our own processing capabilities. We now have seven mechanical fish each carrying a dozen retrofitted missiles, and more of those missiles are currently being loaded aboard an eighth now."

"Could they leave immediately?"

"Er... yes, yes, I don't see why not..."

"Very well," X-20 nodded slowly as he made his decision. "Then I shall assume command of the fleet, and proceed at once to investigate what has happened to Titan."

"NO!" Sculpin seemed on the verge of utter panic at X-20's suggestion. "No, i-it would be better for you to remain here! Titan left *you* in charge, after all. I'm merely a humble technician, I would not know what to do if I had to assume command. O-of Titanica, I mean."

"You sit on the throne and try to ignore the stupid fish," X-20 responded flatly. "It's difficult but even you could manage it."

"No no, I... I really feel I would better serve as fleet commander," Sculpin insisted. "Besides, I-I may be needed to deal with any problems that may develop with the torpedoes while en route. H-have you ever attempted to realign an unstable neutroni micro-transfer circuit on a live Aquadex V warhead during the heat of battle?"

X-20 gave a disinterested shrug. "Alas, life has denied me that pleasure."

"Well, there you are then! That's not the sort of work that can be left to amateurs. Or worse, Aquaphibians." Sculpin gestured to an open satchel on the worktable between them. "And, a-as you can see, I have already begun to pack the equipment I shall need, er, should any other emergencies arise."

X-20 leaned against the table and peered into the satchel, which did indeed contain a variety of engineering tools, as well as what looked like a book and one or two other personal items. "Very well then," he agreed. "I suppose you would be of more use at the front than back here. Certainly you will find no shortage of soldiers willing to accompany you; those useless Aquaphibians are practically in hysterics at the thought of Titan having died..."

X-20 trailed off as he realised that Sculpin had frozen. He was now staring with a look of abject horror towards the table, as if he'd spotted a poisonous sea snail or venomous aquacobra. Looking down, X-20 saw nothing there that warranted such concern. "Is there anything else you need before you go?" he asked.

After a moment Sculpin appeared to come to life again, hastily grabbing his bag of tools and stuffing his radio into it. "No!" he squeaked eventually, clutching the bag close to his chest. "No, I... I will go now and, um... prepare the fleet..."

"At once, if you please," X-20 said firmly. "Use the utmost caution. I want to know precisely what has happened. The rescue of Titan by any means is a priority, but if you find evidence that he has been killed, I expect you to avenge him on behalf of Titanica."

"Oh, absolutely!" Sculpin was now stepping backwards out of the lab, still clutching the bag to his chest. "Yes, you can count on me to rain down upon them fire and fury and um, and so forth." With that, he turned and bolted from the room, his footsteps echoing down the corridor as he ran for the nearest travel tube.

Maybe I'll get lucky and he'll get himself killed too, X-20 thought to himself with a wry smile. Then he remembered Titan, and regretted thinking that thought. While it was true that he found some degree of satisfaction in seeing his master directly falling foul of one of his own schemes for a change, he still hoped that he might yet be found and returned to Titanica unharmed. After all, Titan held dominion over territories beyond the city of Titanica alone. X-20 didn't want to remain in charge of all this forever; he found he was missing his quiet life of solitude in his house on Lemoy, and he certainly didn't fancy having to spend the next few marine months consoling a bunch of depressed Aquaphibians over the loss of their revered leader.

Just as he turned to leave, X-20 happened to look down at the table and noticed that his right hand was resting atop the pile of stolen Marineville documents. *When and why did these end up in Sculpin's lab?* he wondered, as he scooped them up and carried them back to the throne room...

With the two terrainean males now safely locked away, Noctus was now taking the elevator back down to the Chamber of the Cooperative. Tempest and Sheridan had remained irritatingly unhelpful regarding the location of the missing Marina, making jokes and wisecracks when it was obvious that they must have noticed her slip away during the tour. He'd ordered the guards to begin a search as instructed but he currently only had a few at his disposal, and Igneathea offered many hiding places for a girl who didn't want to be found. *Perhaps Grupa might suggest to the Cooperative that we require additional females released from hibernation to assist in the search?*

Not for the first time, Noctus reflected on how lucky he was to be serving as the adjutant to such a great man as Grupa. He had been appointed the city administrator in the days leading up to the population's mass exodus from the cramped confines of their submarine fleet and their city down into the underground chamber where the majority of them now resided in hibernation. Noctus remembered catching sight of Grupa supervising operations as he had walked calmly towards his own hibernation capsule all those years ago, and thinking that the man exuded all the qualities that a leader of their civilisation should possess – but then, he had a very personal reason for feeling that way.

It was estimated by their scientists that only one Igneathean in every million would react badly to the hibernation process – and Noctus had proven to be that one in a million. After only a few weeks in operation, the computer system in his capsule had taken against something about his physiology and malfunctioned without raising an alarm, cutting off his life support gases and leaving the suddenly conscious Noctus clawing in vain at the glass window of what he was sure was to be his coffin. It was only a stroke of fate that ensured Grupa had happened to be passing at that very moment and had been able to release Noctus in time to save him from suffocating to death.

Beyond the occasional nightmare of being sealed within that casket once more, Noctus had suffered no lasting effects from his ordeal and, from that day on, he had sworn to remain loyal to Grupa no matter what. Grupa had rewarded him with a place by his side as they worked together to restore their people to their former glory, and Noctus had worked hard over the years to prove himself worthy of that honour.

As the elevator deposited him in the Chamber of the Cooperative, Noctus noticed that Grupa was still standing in the consultation booth. As he stepped towards his friend and mentor the blinking lights inside the booth went dark, and the helmet over Grupa's head raised back into the ceiling as he completed consultation. Grupa's eyes slowly opened, and Noctus watched as he released himself from the booth and took a few unsteady steps on his stiffened legs. Noctus himself had never made consultation, but he had to imagine that being connected to so many thousands of minds at once must be close to overwhelming.

Grupa acknowledged Noctus' presence with a weary nod. "The Cooperative has made its decision regarding Titan and his people," he announced, wiping a hand across his brow. "This plan to destroy us cannot go unpunished. They are to be utterly wiped out."

Noctus hadn't expected any other response; "Our engineers have begun recovering salvage material from the wreckage of Titan's fleet," he reported. "The debris is being taken for analysis in the engineering plant. Soon we shall know all there is to know about how their vessels operate."

That news seemed to perk Grupa up somewhat. "Excellent! Once we have an understanding of their technology, we can fully prepare our forces to wipe out their city." Helping himself to a glass of water from a nearby dispenser, Grupa took a much-needed drink before replacing the glass and asking, "Has Titan recovered from his experience?"

"He has been declared fit by the medical officer and will shortly be taken to a cell."

"Splendid. Titan shall provide us with all the information we require on his city's location and defences… whether he chooses to or not."

Noctus stepped closer, not wishing his next question to be overheard by any other Igneatheans working nearby. "And the terraineans?"

"Temporary incarceration has been ruled, the precise length of which is to be determined by us. I do not wish to keep them here long." Then a disappointed look came over Grupa's face, as he added "However, the Cooperative recommends that they too are to be punished for intruding into our domain. They have decided that we must stage some kind of event that will ensure Stingray and her crew are discredited amongst their own kind...."

Noctus thought for a moment. "The prototype fleet project would seem to be ideal for that purpose?"

"The Cooperative suggested as much. With the fleet already nearing completion anyway, the timing has worked out splendidly..." Grupa stroked the green fronds of his beard thoughtfully. "It is, however, not a decision I wholly approve of, Noctus. The more time I spend with these terraineans, the more I find myself... warming to them. Much of what they say has merit."

Noctus wasn't sure he liked what he was hearing. "They are our enemies, Grupa."

"Are they?" Grupa began to walk slowly towards the safety rail at the edge of the catwalk, Noctus keeping in step with him. "Titan is an enemy, of that there is no question. His notion of an alliance by force cannot go unchallenged. But I believe Tempest is sincere when he speaks of peaceful coexistence." He suddenly stopped, turning to face Noctus. "You remember how it was when they imprisoned us?"

Noctus thought back to the two occasions he and Grupa had been incarcerated at Marineville. "We were treated well," he agreed.

"We were indeed, and they had no reason to be so accommodating after we attempted to annihilate them... other than that it appears to be their nature to behave that way."

"I assumed at the time that they were weak for not executing us," Noctus admitted. "Having met them again, despite their eccentricities, I am less sure of that assessment..."

"Precisely!" The two Igneatheans leaned against the safety rail and looked down at the countless rows of hibernating citizens. "You are beginning to learn from spending time with them, seeing their actions for yourself.

These are luxuries denied to the majority of our people. They can only make their decisions based on our reports... and their memories of the past." He sighed. "It is little wonder they make the decisions they do – but must we always treat those who are not our own as our enemies?"

Noctus shrugged. "It is safer."

"But is it *wiser*? Any civilisation that commits itself to a permanent war footing shall only ever know war – and therefore sooner or later it will *have* to know destruction. Is that truly where our great genius is leading us?" He shook his head sadly. "We have skulked down here for far too long, Noctus. If we are to avoid disaster, if we are truly ever to make a new life on the surface, we must begin to think differently. That may involve reaching some kind of accord with the terraineans. Yet how can we, when we are locked into a cycle of counterproductive decisions made by fearful people who can only ever know how things *used* to be, not how they really are *today*?"

Noctus had no answer, but Grupa hadn't really expected one. He patted his subordinate on the shoulder. "Do not worry, old friend... I know better than to go against the wishes of the Cooperative. I shall do my duty."

The two Igneatheans turned and began to walk towards the elevator, Grupa taking a moment to straighten his green and silver tunic before he issued his next order. "Alert technicians to stand by in the command centre; I want remote control units fitted to the prototypes at once, and the fleet ready for deployment within the next thirty marine minutes to carry out the wishes of the Cooperative."

Noctus nodded. "It will be done."

"Excellent! Now – what news of the girl?"

After quietly jumping down from the catwalk overlooking the Igneathean hibernation capsules, Marina had hurried towards one of the tubes vacated by one of the revived workers and climbed inside, lowering the lid until it had almost closed on top of her. Once she was certain any pursuers had lost her trail among the thousands of caskets, she had climbed out again and quickly made her way towards the nearby travel tube she had seen the workers taking earlier.

Breathing a sigh of relief as it instantly carried her back up towards the city, it suddenly occurred to Marina that she had no real plan from this point on. The opportunity to escape had presented itself and she had taken it, but now what? Rescuing Troy and Phones was the priority, but she had no idea how exactly she might achieve that all by herself. Not for the first time she scolded herself for being so impulsive, but resolved to make the best of the decision she had made. It was time to do some snooping around – starting with the sections of the city Grupa and Noctus had *not* shown them during the tour.

An interactive map aboard the travel tube offered her a choice of various destinations and Marina chose an observation level overlooking the vehicle workshops in the engineering plant – reasoning that if Stingray was now under guard there might be other ways of escaping from Igneathea. The travel tube sped on, and less than a minute later she had arrived at her destination.

Disembarking from the travel tube, Marina kept close to the wall as she slowly made her way along the corridor in the direction of a nearby line of observation ports overlooking the workshops. The fact that the majority of the population of Igneathea spent most of their time in hibernation would hopefully make sneaking around the city that much easier, although she was careful not to get too complacent. The noise of the factories below would further serve to conceal her presence, although that noise also meant that she'd have to remain extra vigilant herself in order to keep alert for any Igneathean that may appear in the corridor behind her.

Crouching low as she reached the first of the observation ports, Marina tried to keep herself as inconspicuous as possible as she peered down upon the workshops below. On the bustling factory floor, she could see technicians and engineers examining fragments of the mechanical fish fleet the Igneatheans had wiped out. At first, it seemed somewhat understandable that they would want to analyse the debris... but then, she noticed something curious.

Several larger pieces of mechanical fish debris had been gathered in one corner of the workshop; almost enough material to comprise one single fish, in fact. However, as Marina watched, she noticed that the wreckage wasn't being dismantled – it was being repaired. She watched a crane operator pick up a section of tail fin before lowering it into position near the rear of one of the wrecks, holding it in place while several Igneatheans used welding torches to fuse the broken sections back together again.

They're not just studying the remains, she realised. *They're trying to reconstruct them – or build their own! But why?*

Slipping away from the porthole before she was spotted Marina was about to head back to the travel tube when a sign above an elevator at the far end of the corridor caught her eye. It was marked *'Prototype Harbour – Authorised Personnel Only'*, and as she approached the elevator its transparent double doors swung open to allow her access. After taking a moment to weigh the pros and cons of entering, Marina stepped inside.

Sara would love this place, she thought to herself as the elevator began to descend. *They're even more lax here about security than they are in Marineville! But I suppose they've never had visitors before...*

Marina wasn't sure what she was expecting to see as the elevator reached its destination, but the sight that greeted her when the doors opened was like something out of a dream. A very bad dream indeed.

She was indeed now in a harbour but the vessels that floated in the water ahead of her were clearly not Igneathean. Anything but. With stealth now the farthest thing from her mind, Marina stepped out of the elevator and walked slowly toward the edge of a small pier that overlooked the jetty just a few feet below.

A dozen replica Stingrays, life-size and seemingly perfect down to the last detail, floated in the water below her. As she leaned against a safety rail at the edge of the pier her mind was racing; what were these for? Unlike the replica Stingray that Noctus and Grupa had previously fooled them with during the incident at Professor Cordo's fish farm these Stingrays appeared fully furnished on the *inside* too, but although each one seemed identical Marina could tell at a glance that none of them was the real thing. Not only did she know that the genuine Stingray was back at the airlock they'd entered Igneathea through, these copies lacked her majesty, her spirit. She'd often felt that Stingray was more than mere technology but had a life and soul of her own, just like her crew, and she was almost certain that Troy and Phones felt the same way. That spirit was something that these copies, however perfect they may be technically, just couldn't reproduce. But they'd be enough to fool the untrained eye…

This isn't something they've managed to do just in the short time we've been here, she thought to herself. *This must have been underway long before we even arrived… but why?*

"There she is!"

Marina had been so shocked by the sight of the replica Stingrays that she hadn't even heard the elevator door opening behind her. Without thinking she ran forward, intending to leap onto the safety rail and dive into the water – but a sudden hail of gunfire and the ricochets of bullets around her feet and ankles immediately brought her to a halt. Raising her hands, she turned to face an approaching group of burly Igneathean guards, with the smaller figures of Grupa and Noctus at their head.

"So you've discovered our little secret?" Grupa asked. "Yes, these were another of the Cooperative's ideas. You see, our first encounter with Stingray taught us enough to enable us to build convincing replicas; at least, from the outside. The second encounter gave us the chance to study the interior of your vessel... and create these working duplicates."

Marina's eyes widened at the thought that these duplicate Stingrays could be a match for the real thing. "Oh yes," Grupa assured her, "they are fully functional, down to the last detail. We were intending to use them to defend ourselves in future encounters with your vessel – after all, what better craft to defeat Stingray than a fleet of Stingrays? – but now the Cooperative has had a different idea..."

He raised his radio watch to his lips. "Command centre, this is Grupa. Are the remote control units all in place aboard the prototype fleet?"

"Confirmed. All fitted and functional."

"Then all replica Stingrays in Group A are to be launched immediately. Tell your operators they are to seek and destroy any and all terrainean targets within striking distance!"

"Message received. Engaging startup sequence now."

Seconds later the ratemaster propulsion system on the rear of each of the Stingrays began to rotate, as several Igneatheans hurried to release the vessels from their moorings. In the sudden commotion, Marina decided to attempt another escape – but was immediately grabbed by a guard and held in place.

"We should kill her now, Grupa!" urged Noctus.

"That will not be necessary," Grupa said calmly but firmly. "I gave Captain Tempest my word that he and his crew would come to no harm. We shall honour that agreement by returning her to him intact."

"But she'll tell him what she's seen here!"

"She cannot speak, remember!" Grupa reminded Noctus. "So how can she possibly explain what she has observed? And while they are our prisoners, what does it matter anyway?" He looked out at the replica fleet as the first wave prepared to depart. "By the time Tempest and his friends leave our city, these duplicate Stingrays will have thoroughly discredited Marineville and the World Aquanaut Security Patrol!"

Still struggling in the grip of the Igneathean guard, Marina could only watch helplessly as the first of the replica Stingrays was released from her moorings and slipped under the surface of the water, heading for a launch tunnel that would lead her out of the city and off on her mission of destruction. It was followed by another... and another... and another...

CHAPTER 8

Very Strange Bedfellows

"*Tower from Philippine Station 178! We're under attack!*"
"*Marineville from Rescue Launch Four! Emergency! We're taking fire!*"

"*Come in Marineville! Alert! Stingray's just opened fire on us—*"

The sudden cacophony of chaotic distress calls immediately got the attention of everyone in the Marineville control tower. "What in thunder's going on out there?" demanded Shore. "Come in Station 178! Report your situation!"

"*Marineville, for pity's sake, order Stingray to stand down! Sting missiles will impact in three, two, o —*" The caller's voice had been gradually drowned out by the roar of incoming missiles rapidly closing on their target, before abruptly cutting out completely.

"Stingray?" Shore immediately whirled towards Atlanta. "Contact them immediately Lieutenant, find out what the devil they're playing at!"

"Yes sir!" Atlanta flipped the necessary switch on the console in the centre of the room. "Marineville to Stingray! Come in, Stingray! You are ordered to stand down immediately... come in, Stingray!" Once again, her call was greeted by nothing but static. "Sir, we're not raising them!"

"Then either Troy and Phones aren't on board... or that can't be the real Stingray out there!"

"*Tower from jet squadron commander,*" came a deep voice over the radio. "*Commander, I've just seen Stingray destroy Station 178 while just a mile south of her there's another Stingray going after a freighter en route to Manila Bay. Other wings also reporting Stingray sightings in other sectors. Repeat, we have multiple Stingrays out here!*"

"Stand by, squadron commander!" A plan was needed, and fast, but Shore wasn't sure there was anything in his training to cover a situation like this. "Multiple Stingrays!"

Then it all suddenly fell into place for Atlanta. "Father, that business with Professor Cordo!"

"What about it?"

"Grupa and Noctus tricked Troy and Phones with a fake Stingray, remember? They told me afterwards that from the outside it looked absolutely identical to the real thing. Well, what if it wasn't just a one-off? What if it was the first of many?"

"Say, you're right!" Shore considered the possibility, remembering that Grupa and Noctus had had many hours during that affair to gather additional intelligence on Stingray from the inside to refine their duplicates still further. "Looks like that darn fool Titan's poked some kind of hornet's nest, only now *we're* the ones getting stung!"

"And if that's true, there's no telling how many more Stingrays they might have on the way," Fisher wondered aloud.

"Or how fast they can turn them out," Sara added.

"I don't know what their production rate is, Lieutenant, and I don't care. Right now we have a war zone erupting out there, and we've gotta put a stop to it and fast!" Shore raised his radio mic to his lips and began to bark instructions into it. "Attention all search aircraft and vessels! Now hear this; until you hear orders from me to the contrary, Stingray is to be treated as a hostile vessel. I want all sightings of her relayed to control; rescue launches are advised to steer clear, but if spotted combat vessels and aircraft will engage target immediately. Stingray is to be destroyed on sight!"

"Say again, sir?"

"I repeat; Stingray is to be destroyed on sight!"

"P.W.O.R!"

Atlanta was horrified. "But sir, we can't do that! If Troy and Phones manage to escape in the real Stingray, or even in one of these fakes—"

But Shore was quick to shut her down. "Lieutenant, you know as well as I do that right now we can't afford ourselves the luxury of thinking about three people when hundreds of lives could be at stake!" Then, upon seeing the crestfallen look on his daughter's face, he added softly "Atlanta, honey, right now we don't even know if they're still alive..."

"Which is all the more reason for us to go out there and try to find out, sir!" Sara had been waiting for the ideal moment to push the notion of taking direct action, and now it seemed that moment had arrived. "Our search forces are now going to be split between responding to distress calls caused by these Stingray attacks, and possibly mounting a defence against such attacks themselves. We owe it to Troy, Phones and Marina to have at least one dedicated team still maintaining the search for them, no matter the risk."

Shore barely had time to open his mouth before Atlanta interrupted. "She's right, father!" she said, getting out of her chair and walking towards him. "I've lost count of the number of times Stingray's gone missing and we've just been expected to sit here and wait until she resurfaces again." Shore once again tried to interject, but Atlanta was determined to press her point – and now Sara was right by her side. "Well just for once I think we should be out there on the spot, actually *doing* something rather than just waiting for the problem to solve itself!"

"The problem isn't going to 'solve itself' as you put it Lieutenant," Shore reminded her brusquely. "We got vessels in the area and aircraft in the skies with orders to engage the enemy on sight!"

"But that's not going to get *our* people back!" Sara insisted. "For all we know Troy and the others could be trapped somewhere out there, depending on us to help them!"

"Or they could be perfectly capable of escaping on their own, in which case they'll contact us as soon as they can and we'll warn them to keep clear. But I simply don't believe either of you ladies have the necessary skills to risk sending you out there just now."

"Oh, so that's it?" Atlanta snapped. "It's simply because we're women that you won't let us go out there? You wouldn't dismiss this request from Troy or Phones!"

"Exactly!" Sara concurred. "I have the same thing at Headquarters Atlanta, the guys think they know it all, but when it really comes down to it—"

"*Would you two be quiet a minute and let a fella speak?!!*"

Shore's sudden outburst shocked both Sara and Atlanta into silence. "That's *better*," he growled. "Now, first of all, I don't appreciate being told that I make my decisions based on anyone's gender. Heck, if I were the kind of guy who did that, Marina would be off the Stingray crew so fast it would make your head spin. As far as I'm concerned, picking a team for any assignment is always about selecting the best man for the job, and if the best man for the job is a woman then it's a woman I would send – *providing* she'd had the necessary training."

Both Sara and Atlanta immediately protested, but this time Shore was determined to have his say and he firmly shouted them down. "I know, I'm well aware of your service records and they're both exemplary – but unless either of you have had any aquanaut training that I'm unaware of, you're not qualified to go gallivanting out to the Philippines to take charge of an all-out warzone. Now, are either of you qualified aquanauts?"

Sara bit her lip, frustrated at being forced to admit that technically she wasn't the most suitable for such a mission. "No sir."

Atlanta looked equally disappointed, as she murmured "No sir..."

"So that's that then, end of story." With that rebellion apparently quashed for now Shore hovered away from the two mutineers – before pausing only a foot away from them. "However, I can see I'm not gonna get any work out of either of you until I've let you fly out there to take a look at things for yourself." He suddenly whirled in Fisher's direction. "Lieutenant!"

"Sir?"

"You'll be accompanying Annie Oakley and Calamity Jane here to establish a base of operations out in the danger zone. I'll see about laying on a vessel for you to work from. Find out what's going on, see what you can do about rescuing Troy and the others, and er... try and keep these two out of trouble if possible, will ya?"

"I'll do my best, sir."

"Fine, fine..." Satisfied that they had at last reached some kind of agreement, Shore looked from Fisher, to Sara, to Atlanta, and then back to Fisher, waiting for someone to make a move. "Well don't just sit there grinning man, get on with it!"

Fisher leapt to his feet and headed for the door as Sara stepped forward. "Commander, there is still that 'other matter' that I was—"

Shore was already waving her concerns away. "I will take personal charge of that 'other matter' while you're away Lieutenant, don't worry about that."

"Aye sir!" Sara gave a smart salute before following Fisher to the door. Now Atlanta shuffled forward, looking at her father with obvious guilt in her eyes.

"Commander, before I go I just wanted to apologise…"

Shore had already turned back to the radio map to begin plotting the locations of Stingray sightings. "Oh yeah, what for?"

"Well, for my behaviour just now. I said some things that, well… I-I crossed the line, and—"

Shore rounded on Atlanta, his voice razor-sharp with anger. "You didn't just cross the line Lieutenant, you pole-vaulted over the line and then napalmed it for good measure!"

"Yes sir…" Atlanta's instinct was to look down at the floor, trying not to meet the fire in her father's eyes, but she successfully managed to fight it off. She felt that, for once, she had earned his wrath. She had seen him this angry before, but only on rare occasions – and never with her. Until now. "Respectfully suggest I be subject to disciplinary proceedings when this is all over."

Shore held his very fiercest gaze for as long as he could, but very soon his gruff exterior yielded to the warm smile and loving twinkle in his eyes that only his daughter ever really saw. "It's alright, honey. You go find our people, bring 'em home safe, and I won't press charges."

"Yes sir!" Shore looked back to the map as Atlanta turned to leave – meaning he was unprepared for her to suddenly hug him from behind and give him a big kiss on the cheek. "Thank you, father!"

"Ah, that's enough already!" Shore squirmed under Atlanta's grip, pretending to make a big show of being embarrassed by his daughter's affection – but secretly he cherished every second of it. "Go on, get outta here!"

Shore turned in his hoverchair to watch as Atlanta ran to join Sara and Fisher. She stopped in the doorway just long enough to wave goodbye, and then all three of them were gone. Shore watched the door swing shut behind them – then blinked, wiping away a tear that had somehow appeared in the corner of his left eye.

"Ah, that girl can be so much like her mother at times..." he sighed, before returning all his attention to the current crisis...

"Still no sign of Marina..."

Phones joined his captain at the tiny window of their cell door, which offered only the view of a gleaming metallic – and very empty – corridor outside. "Well, don't worry too much Troy," he said reassuringly. "You know how resourceful she is. Could be she's on her way back with the cavalry at this very moment..."

"Right now I'd settle just for knowing that she's even alive..." Troy sighed.

During their various missions aboard Stingray, Troy and Phones had spent plenty of hours locked in cells by the various adversaries that had held them prisoner. It was something that came with the job, apparently, and something they had had to get used to. The cell they found themselves in currently was certainly in the top rank as far as prison cells went; much like everything in Igneathea it was bright, colourful and functional. They'd definitely seen much worse.

What the pair hadn't bargained on this time though was sharing a cell with two other prisoners. One of those was Titan, still unconscious after his ordeal with the mind sifter. He lay on a metal couch, with his hands and feet still manacled. Troy was grateful for that. He wouldn't soon forget the murderous look on his old enemy's face when they'd encountered each other just a few hours earlier.

Their other cellmate had been sitting on another metal couch directly opposite Titan's since before they had arrived and had yet to speak. In fact, he had yet to do anything at all – until now.

After much deliberation, the Aquaphibian got to his feet, and plodded over to Troy and Phones. Considering their past history with other members of his species this Aquaphibian's body language was oddly non-threatening, and the two men didn't feel in any immediate danger. Nevertheless, it was probably the closest either Troy or Phones had ever been to an Aquaphibian, and they weren't any more attractive up close.

"You... Tempest?" it asked.

Unsure where this was going, Troy did his best to hold eye contact with the Aquaphibian – and ignore the rather pungent aroma of the creature's breath. "Yeah, that's right, friend..."

The Aquaphibian grunted, apparently satisfied for now, before returning to the bench to mull things over further. "What do you make of him, Phones?" Troy asked quietly.

"I dunno, Troy. You notice the way he keeps glancing towards Titan?"

"Yeah. I would have expected an Aquaphibian to wanna keep as close to Titan as possible, but this one looks like he doesn't trust him or something. I reckon something's gone on there. If only we knew what..."

Phones considered the problem for a moment, before a cheery smile appeared on his face. "Well, let's ask him!" Before Troy could stop him Phones had swaggered across the cell to sit down beside the startled Aquaphibian. "Say, Andy – you don't mind if I call you Andy?"

The Aquaphibian shook his head, the confused expression on his face reminding Troy of someone just realising they were sitting next to the crazy man on the bus. "Say Andy, how'd you come to be stuck here with us?"

The Aquaphibian took a moment to consider the question. "I was pilot on Titan's yacht," he began. "Something took control of our ship…"

Phones nodded. "That'd be the guys who've captured us," he explained.

"When that happened, Titan, he… he began to shout. He was very angry…"

Determined to maintain the appearance of being a friend, Phones attempted to make a joke. "Aw shucks, now that's not like him at all!"

But the Aquaphibian continued, his halting words gathering speed as he recalled events that had plunged him into deep trauma. "When he saw our other ships opening fire on each other, he guessed our computers may have been hijacked. He… he took a gun… wanted to free us by destroying the control console… but the Aquaphibian guard aboard our ship accidentally got in the way… Titan didn't mean to hit him… but he did. Titan… the protector of the Aquaphibians… *killed* an Aquaphibian… and he did not care…"

Phones looked towards Troy and a silent nod of understanding passed between the two men. *The dead Aquaphibian Marina and I found on Titan's ship…*

"We serve Titan because he protects us, because he would never harm us," the Aquaphibian continued. "Yet I saw… I *saw*… and he did not care…"

The Aquaphibian's voice trailed off as he became lost in his thoughts once more, mouthing silent words and trying to make sense of what he had seen. After giving the Aquaphibian a friendly reassuring pat on the shoulder, Phones got to his feet and rejoined Troy by the cell door.

"Well, there's our answer," Troy said quietly. "Nice work Phones."

"Heck, I feel kinda sorry for the poor guy," Phones admitted. "Marina's told us that the Aquaphibians look on Titan almost like a god. Seeing him shoot one of them, even if it was only an accident, must have put our boy there into a bit of an existential crisis."

"Yeah... but I wonder if we can use that somehow..."

"How'd you mean, Troy?"

"Well Phones, imagine if he got back to Titanica and told the other Aquaphibians what he saw Titan do to one of them. If they then told it to their friends, word would probably spread pretty fast throughout the entire city..."

"Yeah, but by the time it came out the other end they'd have probably mangled it into something like 'purple monkey dishwasher'..."

Troy almost didn't hear Phones' words; his imagination had been fired by the possibilities that presented themselves. "But think of it, Phones; what if it *did* pay off? What if he fought to get the word out to the other Aquaphibians that this is how their ruler really treats them? Soon they might start refusing his orders, maybe even forming an organised resistance movement. Why, this could be the start of an Aquaphibian revolution that could finally bring down Titanica!"

Phones cast a doubtful gaze in the direction of the Aquaphibian who was currently scratching his armpit and mumbling to himself. "Troy, that's a lot of pressure to lay on our boy there," he said quietly. "I'm not quite sure Andy's the revolutionary type."

Troy also looked across the room, trying to imagine this befuddled-looking creature leading any sort of movement against Titan's regime. "Yeah, maybe not." Then he leaned in a little closer. "*Andy?*" he asked incredulously.

Phones grinned. "Yeah, he reminds me of my brother-in-law," he said, pointing to his chin. "Same jawline."

Before Troy could delve too deeply into Phones' extended family, the door to their cell slid upwards and a guard rushed into the room, pointing her rifle towards the prisoners while a second guard hauled Marina in behind her. She ran to embrace Troy and Phones, giving the guards enough time to retreat from the cell and close the door behind them.

"Marina!" Troy cried. "Gee, it's good to see you! Are you okay?"

Marina nodded but it was obvious she had something else on her mind right now; something of major importance. With a pleading look in her eyes, she mimed writing on a piece of paper, and Troy inwardly cursed himself as he patted his pockets before coming up empty. Having a pen and paper always on him for times like this was something that he always meant to get around to, but somehow never seemed to remember.

But at least he wasn't the only one. "I'm empty too, I'm afraid," Phones added.

"Take it easy Marina," Troy said soothingly. "Let's try to work this out... did something happen to you?"

Marina shook her head. "Then did you see something?" Phones asked.

Marina nodded. "Bad?" Troy asked.

Marina shook her head again. "Very bad?" Again, Marina shook her head, this time making a rising gesture with both hands as if to suggest the scale of the crisis.

"All the bads?" Phones suggested. Marina nodded emphatically, grateful to have gotten the urgency of the situation across to her friends at last. "Well, we got there in the end, Troy," Phones deadpanned. "Sounds bad."

"Well, whatever it is, it makes getting out of here even more imperative," Troy sighed. "We'd better think of something but fast!"

The room was suddenly filled with an evil chuckle, one that instinctively caused Marina to jump towards Troy for protection. "So," a familiar voice muttered scathingly, "the great Troy Tempest is finally defeated by a locked door. Not quite the defeat I had envisioned for you but still somewhat satisfying. It's a pity the traitress Marina cannot tell you what she has seen…"

Titan finally opened his eyes, and turned his head to look at the other occupants of the cell, his eyes filled with malevolent intent.

"…but I think *I* might be able to!"

"There she is!"

Atlanta was the first to spot the small World Navy submarine as it broke the surface of the ocean and began to decelerate. From her seat aboard the W.A.S.P. helijet, she could clearly see the markings on the side of the craft – and her heart sank when she realised who would almost certainly still be in command of World Navy sub two-seven. She resolved there and then not to let that interfere with the reason they needed his help; the safe return of Troy, Phones and Marina.

"Take her down," Fisher ordered the pilot, as he and Sara began to prepare the rope ladder they'd be using to climb down onto the deck of the sub one by one. Atlanta meanwhile had pulled out a radio and opened a channel to Marineville.

"Father, we've just sighted the sub and we're heading on down to her now!"

"*Okay Atlanta,*" came Commander Shore's reply. "*Now listen; some of our craft have been able to get close enough to a few of these replica Stingrays to get a good look at* the control cabin. As far as we can tell, these Stingrays are unmanned."

"Unmanned!" repeated Atlanta in surprise.

"Yeah, guess they're being worked by remote control or somesuch."

"Ready whenever you are!" called the pilot.

"Father, we've got to sign off for now," Atlanta said into the radio. "We'll contact you when we can. I… I love you."

"Love you too, honey, you look after yourselves out there, you hear?"

Atlanta looked to her two colleagues; the second half of the message had clearly been meant for all of them, and right now she was very glad to have Fisher and Sara by her side. "P.W.O.R!"

Closing the channel she pocketed her radio, unfastened her safety harness and let Sara steady her as she climbed onto the rope ladder. The helijet was now hovering only a few feet over the deck of sub two-seven, and in keeping with the bad day she'd been having, Atlanta was disappointed – but not surprised – that Captain Jacques Jordan was waiting below to greet them in person.

"Atlanta, mon chéri!" he purred as she stepped onto the deck. "Ah, it has been too long!"

"Not for me, Jacques," she replied icily, standing aside to allow first Fisher and then Sara to climb down the rope ladder. "Anyway, we've no time to reminisce just now. Troy Phones and Marina are currently missing…"

"So I gathered," Jordan laughed. "Judging by the chaos out here it would seem Tempest finally, how you say, flipped his lid, huh?"

"Jacques, I'm only going to say this once; don't start."

"Atlanta, would I do anything to cause trouble at a time like this?" Jordan asked. "I fear you gravely misunderstand me…"

Coming in at the tail end of the conversation as she stepped from the rope ladder, Sara looked towards Fisher and whispered "I take it there's a bit of history between these two?"

Fisher nodded wearily. "Yeah, you could say that..."

"Pah, *ancient* history!" said Jordan dismissively, pushing his way past Fisher to get to Sara. "Trust me, it is nothing that you need to worry about, my dear," he said smoothly, taking hold of her left hand and raising it to his lips to kiss it. "Charmed, I'm sure."

Momentarily shocked by the captain's unexpected action, Sara quickly freed her hand from his grasp before fixing him with a look that could freeze lava. "And I assure you, *Captain*," she said, "that the feeling is 100 per cent not reciprocated."

With a hollow smile on his face, Jordan raised his hands in a gesture of defeat and watched as Sara moved to one side with Atlanta, who now took out her radio and ordered the helijet pilot to return to base. Leaning in towards Fisher, he asked quietly, "So who's the new girl?"

"That's Lieutenant Coral from World Security Patrol Headquarters," Fisher explained. "Trust me Cap'n, you don't want to get into a fight with her."

"Why?" Jordan scoffed. "What's she going to do?"

Fisher glanced towards Sara, with admiration in his eyes. "Win, I should think." He didn't notice, but his words carried across the deck to Sara's ears – and she couldn't help smiling.

"Alright Captain," asked Atlanta once her call was complete, "what's the latest situation?"

Jordan folded his arms as he began to make his report. "Right now we have at least eight different Stingrays on the loose with sightings reported across approximately one hundred miles of the Manila Bay coastline. But these Stingrays are somewhat erratic in their movements, almost as if whoever's at the controls doesn't fully understand how to work them."

"Which fits with the idea that they're radio-controlled," Fisher mused.

"We're managing to keep them away from any major population centres," Jordan continued, "and so far it appears that these replicas are only attacking surface targets; aircraft and underwater vessels have yet to be targeted."

"So far," Sara repeated. "But that might change if our underwater friends decide to test these duplicates to their limits."

"Not to worry," Jordan laughed. "If these are true replicas of that worthless tub Stingray in all respects, then the Navy is more than up to the task of blowing them all out of the water!"

"Then why haven't you started yet..." Sara muttered to herself.

"As a matter of fact, we have already... oh, mon dieu...!"

The Marineville trio looked in the direction of the ominous sight that had caught Jordan's attention. Less than one hundred feet from the sub a familiar-looking shape was rising fast from the ocean depths, and as it broke the surface the quartet knew they were now in serious trouble. It was a Stingray... and it was turning towards them.

"I think perhaps we ought to get moving!" Jordan almost ran for the hatch, hurrying down the ladder to prepare for their escape. "Stand by for the dive order!"

"Hold it!" Atlanta had grabbed a pair of binoculars and trained them on the new arrival. "It's them!"

Fisher was at her side in a flash. "Troy and Phones?"

"No... Grupa and Noctus!" Sure enough, the two fishmen – or at least, two members of their race – appeared to be seated at the controls of the Stingray that was even now turning in their direction.

"I thought your father said these replicas were unmanned?" Sara asked, as Atlanta passed her the binoculars to take a look for herself.

"Maybe that's their control vessel?" Fisher suggested. "If these Stingrays are remote-controlled, perhaps that control only works over a limited range…"

"Yeah, maybe," Atlanta mused. "Or maybe that's the—"

Suddenly the sub pitched hard to starboard, as if yanked by some invisible force, causing the Marineville officers to lose their balance immediately. Sara staggered backwards from the safety rail lining the side of the deck, then as the craft rolled hard to port she was thrown forward and pitched over the side – but she never hit the water. The quick reflexes of Lieutenant Fisher had seen to that. Lunging forward he had managed to grab hold of Sara's left leg, and as the sub's erratic movement started to ease he slowly began to pull her back aboard.

Seeing what had happened Atlanta also rushed to assist, and soon she and Fisher had hauled Sara to safety. The trio collapsed onto the deck, but Atlanta struggled back to her feet almost immediately. "What does the fool think he's playing at?" she muttered, as she made her way toward the hatch to give Captain Jordan a piece of her mind – leaving Sara and Fisher alone in a heap on the floor.

"Well, you're more than just a pretty face, ainchya?" Sara said warmly, trying to overcome the shock of her experience. "Thanks, Lieutenant. I owe you one."

"You're welcome," Fisher replied. "Any time. And, um, it's John, i-if you were wondering…"

He was blushing, and Sara could tell Fisher wasn't someone who had had much experience with women. But then, Sara hadn't had much experience with men either; her dedication to her work seldom gave her any opportunity for romance, and it wasn't something she'd ever actively sought after. Most men who did show any interest in her usually displayed it in the same crass style as Captain Jordan... but Fisher was different. There was something about this quiet young man that she found very endearing. Maybe there was something here, maybe not... but for a moment or two, Sara began to think it might just be worth trying to find out. "Thank you, *John*..."

Suddenly the sub reeled wildly again, sending the two officers sliding back towards the edge of the deck – but this time they each managed to grab hold of the safety rail in time to prevent disaster.

Atlanta's head appeared at the hatch. "You two had better get below, we've got trouble down here!"

Helping each other to their feet, Sara and Fisher made their way quickly to the hatch and clambered down the ladder onto the sub's wheelhouse, Fisher sealing the hatch for safety once they were inside. "What happened, Captain?" Sara asked. "I almost went overboard back there, what the blazes are you playing at?"

But Jordan appeared to be wrestling with the sub's controls, struggling to keep her on an even course. "It was not my doing, mes amis!" he protested.

As if to prove the point the sub once again lurched violently to starboard, slamming everyone aboard against the bulkhead. No one was hurt, but it gave them all a chance to see why Jordan had been struggling. The sub's controls appeared to be operating themselves; levers moving of their own accord, instrument dials adjusting themselves... and the ship's wheel spinning like a roulette wheel.

"She's out of control!" Jordan cried, as he staggered back to the control panel and resumed wrestling with the wheel. "She's out of my control!"

CHAPTER 9

Death From Above

"An armada of Stingrays? Titan, that's crazy!"

"It is true, Tempest!" In the cell he currently shared with the Stingray crew the defeated despot was now sitting upright on his bunk, his eyes gleaming with manic energy as he revelled in knowing something his old enemies did not. "You see, their mind sifter operates on a more unusual principle than most others I have seen. It uses the strength of the collective unconscious brain power of the hibernating Igneatheans to reach deeper into the subject's mind than any other such probe could go. I was only able to resist for so long because I have learned to hone my mental defences over the years... and so, as they forced themselves deeper into my mind, I saw images from theirs!"

Titan shook his head, remembering the kaleidoscope of imagery that had assaulted his senses some hours earlier. "Ah, the visions were going by so fast, many of them were foggy, indistinct... but I saw an image of their engineers working on a fleet of replicas of your accursed Stingray, as clearly as I see all of you now!" He jabbed an accusing finger in Marina's direction. "Listen to the traitress Marina! She knows I speak the truth..."

Reluctant to agree with her former captor, but unable to deny what she had seen, Marina's eyes met Troy's and she nodded sadly. "And these duplicates... they've launched them, haven't they?" Marina blinked in surprise at Troy's guess, but again she nodded.

"We already know that they can build a pretty convincing mock-up of Stingray," Phones pointed out. "I suppose it's not too much of a stretch to imagine they could build full working replicas... especially after they spent all that time aboard her."

"Yeah, I guess so Phones... but why would they want a fleet of replica Stingrays?"

"Let's face it, there could be any number of reasons... none of them good for us."

From his bunk on the other side of the cell, Titan began to chuckle once more. "But potentially very good for me..." he murmured, before laying on his back once again.

"Which makes getting out of here even more of a priority," Troy muttered. "Heaven knows what chaos they're causing with those duplicates." He turned his attention to the cell door – but only for a few seconds. Marina was already tapping him on the back, and as he looked at her again she made a cross with her fingers. "You mean there's more?"

"I'm not sure I can take much more..." muttered Phones, much less cheerfully than he intended to sound. The long hours of incarceration were now beginning to take a toll even on his usual good spirits.

Marina took a moment to consider how best to explain what else she had seen. Resorting to mime, she made a slithering snakelike motion with her right hand, hoping desperately that Troy would understand her meaning. "Fish?" he guessed. Marina nodded, then pointed to her jaw and made a show of slowly opening her mouth as wide as it would go – before using her index fingers to simulate the firing of a mechanical fish torpedo from it. "Mechanical fish... you mean to say they're building mechanical fish down here too?"

Titan now sat bolt upright again. "What?"

Marina was nodding frantically again. "How many?" Troy asked. Marina held up a single finger... but the look in her eyes made it clear that number was only temporary. "One... but more being built, is that right?"

Marina nodded, then after a moment she sighed and buried her face against Troy's arm, relieved to have finally gotten everything she had seen across to her friends. "You did very well, Marina," Troy told her quietly. "Now we know exactly what we're up against..."

But Titan clearly felt otherwise. "She lies!" he roared. "This is a trick to get me to help you!"

Marina suddenly glared at Titan, and Troy immediately came to her defence. "You were quick enough to say she was telling the truth when she first told us about the replica Stingrays!" he snapped angrily. "And now, thanks to you, they have a whole pile of mechanical fish debris on their doorstep to study. You really think they'd find out you were planning to attack them, and not retaliate at all?"

Titan was shaking his head, not wanting to accept the truth of Troy's words. "No... no, I–I don't believe it..."

"Believe it, boy," Phones replied. "Sounds like when they're finished whatever they've got planned for us, they're coming after you next."

"They wouldn't dare be so foolish!" Titan sneered. "We would annihilate them!"

"Stop being so proud for just a moment and think about this, Titan!" Troy urged. "If they plan to use replicas of your own vessels to get past Titanica's defences, you might not be able to retaliate until it was too late!"

"And at least with Stingray everyone knows that there is only one," Phones pointed out. "A load of duplicates suddenly turn up, folks are gonna know they're not the genuine article. But who in Titanica's gonna be able to tell a fake mechanical fish from the real thing – until they start taking potshots at you?"

"I could," Titan growled. "I could tell at a thousand leagues!"

"But you're the only one who knows that there are fakes, and if you don't help us escape you won't be there to sound the alarm!" Troy pointed out. "Titan, it's in all our interests to get out of here now. Why not work with us to find a way?"

"Help you, Tempest?" Titan laughed. "You must be mad…"

"I'm asking you to help *yourself*, Titan!" Troy cried. "And if you won't do it for yourself, do it for the people of Titanica! Without you there to coordinate a defence the city will be wide open to an attack from the Igneatheans. Help us so you can prevent the pointless massacre of your people!"

But Titan was still shaking his head. "No, Tempest. No, if seeing you die at the hands of these creatures means that I have to sacrifice every last living being in Titanica… then it is a sacrifice I am very willing to make." Unnoticed by Titan, the Aquaphibian pilot's eyes widened in alarm and he looked away from his leader in shock, as if wondering how he had ever once followed this man.

Troy however *had* noticed the Aquaphibian's reaction and decided to make some use of it. "You know something Titan?" he said, slowly advancing on his old enemy while also feeling rather like a lion tamer in the zoo. "The more I see of you, the less I like you."

Titan scoffed. "I assure you the feeling is fully reciprocated, Tempest," he sneered.

Troy continued, almost as if he hadn't heard Titan's words. "But until now, whenever I thought of you, I took you to be an intelligent man, albeit a man for whom power is everything. Power over his territories, power over his people, power over anything he can acquire. Now the intelligent man I believed you to be would understand that clinging on to some pointless vendetta can only end in the destruction of all those things he has fought so hard to acquire. So I don't believe a word you just said about letting Titanica be destroyed. They're just the desperate words of a frightened animal."

Troy shrugged, and turned away from Titan. "But hey, maybe that's all you really are deep down – so if my first impression of you was incorrect then Titanica will soon fall to the Igneatheans... and your name will forever be associated with one word."

While Troy had been speaking, Titan's demeanour had changed. He had leaned forward on his bunk, listening to every word out of his old enemy's mouth. It *almost* seemed to be sinking in. "And what word would that be?" he asked quietly.

Troy turned and looked Titan in the eye once more. "Defeated," he said coldly. It was only a three-syllable word, but Troy somehow managed to make it ring like a great bell in Titan's ears. "And if that's the legacy you plan to leave for yourself, that's fine with me. But it's not an epitaph I plan to share with you. *We're* getting out of here. You can either help us... or stay here to rot."

For a moment, Troy almost allowed himself to believe that he was actually getting through to Titan. Much of what he'd said had been true; he *did* take Titan for an intelligent man... and surely any intelligent man could see the wisdom in cooperation at a time like this?

But apparently not Titan. The thwarted dictator suddenly hurled himself towards Troy, not caring that his manacled feet wouldn't let him get far. The same murderous expression that had so shocked Troy earlier was once again etched across his old enemy's face – but once again someone was there to prevent Titan from harming him. This time, however, it wasn't an Igneathean.

The Aquaphibian was suddenly between Troy and Titan, facing his master with a look of utter contempt. "Out of my way, fool!" Titan growled. When the Aquaphibian didn't move, he added, "You would dare to question the orders of the great Titan?"

But now the scales had finally fallen from the Aquaphibian's eyes. "You... you are not great," it growled, shoving Titan back onto his bunk so forcefully that everyone in the cell heard his head strike the wall. "Tempest speaks the truth. You *are* a small weak stupid man!"

Struggling to sit up, Titan rubbed the back of his aching head as best he could with his hands manacled. "You imbecile..." he moaned through his pain. "Tempest... is our enemy..."

"No... *you* are our enemy! You would leave our people to die! I heard those words from your own lips! But we will not follow you anymore! I will show them what you *really* are!"

With that announcement hanging in the air, the Aquaphibian plodded back to his bunk and sat down once more. "*I* will help to save Titanica," he said to no one in particular, before shooting a hateful glare towards Titan. "Even if *you* will not..."

Titan looked like he had much more to say but a combination of exhaustion and the blow to his head finally got the better of him. His eyes fluttered closed and he slid sideways as he passed out again.

"Well, maybe that's for the best," Phones mused. "For now you're just pounding your head against a brick wall with Titan, Troy. No pun intended. When he comes to, why not leave the guy to stew for a bit?"

"Not much else we can do, is there?" Troy sighed. "But whatever happens, he's coming back to Marineville with us whether he wants to or not. Phones, this is the best chance we've ever had to bring him in!"

"I'm glad you think we're getting back to Marineville," Phones replied, pressing his fist hard against the locked cell door. "This thing's not budging until one of those Igneathean guard gals opens it from outside."

Troy peered through the bars in the door, out onto the corridor where two of the large Igneathean females were talking to each other quietly. "Yeah, but we need to give them a reason to come in here…"

"I wonder how many prisoners they actually get to guard down here…" Phones mumbled thoughtfully. "Could be we might not have to get too creative in our thinking…"

"Got an idea?"

"Well, it's not gonna win any points for originality. But like I said, maybe it won't have to…" He gestured towards their Aquaphibian cellmate, whose vacant-eyed face once again wore an expression of deep confusion. "Though it all depends on our buddy Andy over there…"

Troy watched as a smiling Marina cautiously sat down next to the Aquaphibian, who appeared somewhat reassured by her presence. "Phones, as crazy as it sounds, I think we've finally found an ally down here…"

Chaos reigned aboard navy sub two-seven. Every time it seemed as though the vessel was finally holding a steady course she would suddenly lurch onto a new one, continuing to abruptly change speed so often that her crew barely had enough time to get to their feet before they were thrown to the floor again.

"She's never done this before!" Jordan cried out. "What is happening?"

"Isn't it obvious?" Atlanta yelled back. "It's those two outside! If they're controlling the Stingrays on remote, then it figures that maybe they can do the same to us."

"You think they've tapped into the control console directly?" Sara asked.

"I don't know. Why, does it make a difference?"

"It might," Sara replied, drawing her pistol as she struggled to her feet once more. "Let's find out!"

Another sudden change of course slammed Sara hard into the bulkhead, but she recovered after a few seconds and aimed her gun towards the main control console. "Everyone keep your heads down!" she ordered, and then took the shot. Her aim was good, and the console erupted in flame and sparks.

Almost immediately, everybody aboard could tell that Sara's desperate action had affected the entire vessel; navy sub two-seven had been released from enemy control and was now only moving through the water by her own inertia.

Fisher helped Atlanta to her feet, then nodded to Sara. "Nice work," he said admiringly.

Sara shrugged. "I'm sure you guys would have thought of it sooner or later," she teased.

"Zut alores, my poor ship!" moaned Jordan as he surveyed the smouldering ruin of the control console. "Even those accursed Aquaphibians never did this much damage to her..."

"But Jacques, it worked!" Atlanta pointed out. "With no controls to hijack, those guys out there can't control this sub anymore! Listen, the engines are out, and we're slowing down..."

"But with no instruments, we've got no way of knowing what's going on outside!"

"At least we've still got the periscope," Fisher observed, as he peered into the lower end of the viewing tube. "Say, that got their attention right enough! Looks like they're coming in alongside..."

"Probably wondering what's gone wrong," Sara murmured.

"Or moving in for the kill!" Jordan squeaked.

"No Jacques, if they wanted us destroyed, they could have done that any time," Atlanta noted. "Sara's right, this was an experiment... and now they wanna find out what went wrong." She smiled, as a wicked thought suddenly occurred to her. "Who'd like to go up there and welcome them aboard?"

Despite his misgivings about the attack on the terraineans, Grupa had nevertheless decided to make use of the opportunity to test another of the latest inventions from the Igneathean technical section. While the Stingray replicas were currently being remotely controlled from Igneathea, just as Titan's mechanical fish fleet had been taken over, a smaller portable remote-control device had taken slightly longer to produce. After some months of engineering work a prototype had recently been constructed – and the replica Stingray attacks on the terraineans provided a useful cover for giving the device its first test.

Taking the real Stingray from her berth in the airlock, Grupa and Noctus had travelled from Igneathea to the ocean surface, and to the coast of the landmass known to the terraineans as Luzon. Along a one-hundred-mile stretch around Manila Bay, the replica Stingrays had clearly caused the chaos and destruction the Cooperative had hoped for. From Stingray's cabin the two Igneatheans could see columns of smoke rising from burning buildings all along the coast, while local news reports they'd picked up over the radio confirmed that several vessels had been successfully attacked and sunk.

Upon hearing that news Grupa felt a small pang of regret at the loss of life that those attacks almost certainly meant, but tamped it down by reminding himself that this was being done on the orders of the Cooperative. His conscience had no place here. Besides, the terraineans had put up a fair fight; while just over half of the replica

Stingrays were still operational several had already been destroyed, and he did not doubt that the rest would join them in the next few hours.

Again, it didn't matter. They'd served their purpose, and could be easily replaced in a very short time. Certainly enough damage had been done to strike a significant blow to the reputation of the W.A.S.P.s – providing that the involvement of the Igneatheans never became public knowledge – but the point of the exercise wasn't to reign down mass destruction upon the terraineans. That was to be saved for the residents of Titanica.

Eager to give the portable remote-control unit its first trial run, Grupa had selected a small submarine that he calculated would not pose a threat to Stingray should the test be a failure. Activating the device, he had sent a signal to the sub that had taken control of its major systems, allowing Grupa to navigate the vessel from his chair aboard Stingray. Although the small remote offered little more than rudimentary control over the sub's course and speed, it was still an encouraging result that suggested larger more powerful terrainean vessels might also be just as susceptible as this one was. He could only imagine the panic aboard the sub as he set it careering on random courses across the surface of the water.

But when the submarine had suddenly come to a halt, despite all indicators on the control device showing that he should still have remote access, Grupa had felt he had to investigate in person. Something unexpected had occurred here. Either the remote-control device had malfunctioned in some way (which he considered doubtful since after all it was Igneathean technology), or the terraineans aboard the sub had hastily devised some elaborate means of blocking its signals... which was even more doubtful.

Borrowing one of Stingray's monocopters, he had travelled the short distance to the disabled sub in just a few seconds. Taking a moment to relish the feeling of the sun on his skin – a sensation most Igneatheans hadn't felt in centuries – he quickly found the main access hatch and began to open it, intending to listen in on the terraineans to ascertain how they had overcome his control of their vessel.

The position of Stingray relative to the sub meant that right now Grupa was out of sight of Noctus, and that his colleague had no way of seeing what he was now seeing. As his hand touched the hatch door it was suddenly thrown open from the other side – revealing a dark-skinned terrainean pointing a gun at him. "Gotchya!" she hissed with a grin of satisfaction.

Before Grupa could turn to flee, he felt a pistol jab at the base of his spine. "I wouldn't," Fisher told him. "How many more of you are there on that Stingray?"

Grupa raised his hands in a gesture of surrender. "Just one other…"

"Call him up," Fisher ordered. "Tell him whatever you have to to get him away from the controls for a spell. Long enough to give us all time to get aboard."

Grupa considered his options for a moment, before slowly reaching for his radio and activating it. "Noctus," he began, choosing his words very carefully. "Prepare the other monocopter. I've just taken some more prisoners…"

From her observation post at the top of the ladder leading to the access hatch, Sara looked down at Atlanta and grinned. "We got one!" she whispered, before scrambling up onto the deck of the sub.

Atlanta moved to follow her, then stopped as she realised Jordan wasn't moving. "Jacques, are you coming?"

But the Captain didn't seem to hear her, so upset was he by the sight of the ruined control console that had rendered his vessel immobile. "This is absolutely, categorically, without a doubt, the last time I ever help the W.A.S.P.s!" he cried.

"I'm sure it can all be fixed," Atlanta said, forcing sympathy into her voice that she wasn't really feeling as she grabbed his arm and pulled him towards the ladder. "But right now, we have to go!"

"Go?" Jordan was shocked at the very idea of abandoning ship. "You mean... oh no... no, I cannot leave. It would be the death of my career to abandon ship during battle. Think of my reputation!"

"I'm thinking," Atlanta snapped, "of your *life*, and all our lives, plus the lives of our friends. They're worth a great deal more than this one little ship and your vast ego!" But even as she spoke the words, the prospect of being lumbered with Jordan complaining and panicking for the remainder of their mission made her wonder if they stood any chance at all with him along. The stakes were already high enough without adding another random element into the mix. If they were going to take that Stingray, she couldn't waste the element of surprise her friends had just managed to seize.

"Atlanta, let's go!" called Sara from the hatch. Realising she had no more time to lose, Atlanta moved to leave.

"But what about me?" Jordan asked desperately. "You can't just leave me here undefended!"

But Atlanta knew there was no more time for subtlety. "Oh Jacques, you know I'd love to help you out," she said semi-sincerely as she took hold of the ladder leading up to the hatch. "For old times' sake, and all that. But I also know how you feel about that 'old tub' Stingray... and besides, you've got an old naval tradition to observe..."

Jordan's face paled. "Tradition?"

"Yes, you know... the one about the captain going down with his ship?" With that, Atlanta began to climb towards the hatch.

"Sacre bleu!" Jordan spluttered, moving to call up the ladder after her. "Even you would not be cruel! Atlanta! Atlanta, come back!"

On the deck, Sara watched as Atlanta clambered out of the sub and slammed the hatch shut behind her. "You're not actually gonna leave him out here to fend for himself, are you?" she asked. "Right now this sub is something of a prime target, powerless in the middle of a war zone..."

"Oh, don't tempt me!" Atlanta grinned. "No, he's got the lifeboats if he can stop thinking about himself for long enough to remember them, though I wouldn't give much for their chances out here just now." She passed Sara her radio. "Call up the helijet that dropped us. Ask them to swing back around to pick Jacques and his crew up, then you join us aboard Stingray. Nobody else dies today, Sara... not if we can help it!"

With that, Atlanta moved to join Fisher, who still held Grupa at gunpoint, and Sara watched as the pair discussed a strategy for getting aboard Stingray undetected. It felt so good to see her instincts about these two being proved so very correct; both clearly had an aptitude for field work that their duties in the Marineville control tower simply didn't offer. Despite his quiet, calm and (to Sara's eyes) undeniably handsome exterior Fisher obviously knew how to handle himself in a scrap, while Atlanta seemed to have leadership qualities that Sara planned to suggest to Commander Shore he considered refining as a matter of priority.

Sara had seldom worked in a group like this before, most often flying solo on her various missions and having no backup on the spot to call on. She'd worked that way for so long that it had become the norm, to the extent where she'd have baulked at the notion that she might work well in a team... but she smiled as she realised she might be open to doing so again in the future – providing she had two such dependable teammates as John Fisher and Atlanta Shore to rely on.

"Yes ma'am!" she said to herself quietly, before making the call to the helijet...

Back aboard Stingray, Noctus was busy carrying out Grupa's instructions, although he wasn't really sure why his comrade was bothering to take any more prisoners. After all, they already had two terraineans incarcerated back in Igneathea, along with representatives of three other underwater races. How many more of these strange and disruptive creatures did they really need to collect?

However, it wasn't his place to question Grupa's orders, and he had dutifully left the controls of Stingray to retrieve the other two monocopters from the storage area near the airlock hatch in the nose of the craft. He didn't hear the several pairs of approaching footsteps slowly coming down the access ladder from the airlock itself – until it was too late.

"Hands where we can see them! Okay... turn around nice and slowly..."

Noctus obeyed the instructions of the unfamiliar voice, slowly turning around with his arms raised to see two uniformed terraineans – one male and one female – pointing guns in his direction. Grupa stood behind them, a wry smile on his face, and as he made eye contact with his comrade Noctus found himself smiling too. That smile quickly became a laugh that soon both Igneatheans were enjoying loudly and heartily. It clearly wasn't the reaction the two confused terraineans had been expecting.

"What's so funny?" asked Atlanta.

"Your guns," Noctus chuckled. "They won't work in here!"

Fisher and Atlanta looked at each other in shock, before each pointed their pistols towards the floor and fired. Nothing happened.

"Yes, your friends had the misfortune to discover that earlier too," Grupa observed in an amused tone of voice. "You see, we have studied every inch of this vessel. There is nothing about its operation that we do not know – and that includes the working of your Marineville pistols. When we captured Stingray earlier we installed a device that effectively disables the firing mechanism connected to the trigger – which I only just realised I neglected to deactivate after we captured your friends. My apologies."

Noctus suddenly produced an Igneathean rifle. "This gun on the other hand works perfectly," he announced, waving it in their direction.

Grupa gestured towards the door leading from the airlock to Stingray's cabin. "Now move, up to the command deck," he told them, leading the way as the two Marineville operatives followed with Noctus bringing up the rear.

Slowly climbing the stairs to Stingray's control deck the two Igneatheans quickly positioned themselves between their prisoners and the submarine's controls, backing Atlanta and Fisher towards the standby lounge at the rear of the cabin.

"What happens to us now?" Fisher asked.

"I must admit I'm not entirely certain," Grupa began. "Dear me, so much blood has been spilt already today that I'm reluctant to add to it."

"Two more bodies would make very little difference at this point, Grupa," Noctus pointed out.

"True," Grupa agreed. "But you forget Noctus, you and I have both spent two quite pleasant spells in the Marineville jail. Since these two are clearly also W.A.S.P. officers, perhaps it is only fitting that we treat them the way they treated us," he suggested. "It will at least give you a chance to meet your friends again."

"Troy!" Atlanta cried. "Then he and the others *are* alive..."

"Of course. We are not savages." He nodded to himself, apparently content with the decision. "Yes, you may as well join your friends for now. After all, I hardly think we have anything to fear from two such... oh dear me, now what is that terrainean expression? Ah yes; sheep in wolves' clothing." He gave a quiet chuckle. "Just like everyone at Marineville..."

But seconds later the smile abruptly vanished from Grupa's face as he suddenly felt the cold touch of metal pressing hard against his left temple. "These two, perhaps, but what about me?" asked Sara as she entered his field of view from behind, having climbed the staircase to Stingray's upper deck unnoticed and in absolute silence. Before Noctus could react, Sara quickly disarmed him, before tossing his rifle over to Fisher.

"Ah, yes, you again. A–and you would be?"

"Lieutenant Sara Coral, World Security Patrol Headquarters. Where we're issued different firearms to those at Marineville... which means whatever you're using to negate their weapons isn't going to work on mine."

Grupa chuckled nervously. "Would you care to put that statement to the test?"

Sara pressed the gun harder against Grupa's head. "Would you?"

The smile faded once more from Grupa's face, and Sara knew that she'd rattled him. "I thought not. Now, we want to know where you're holding the Stingray crew, we want them released, and we want these replica Stingrays of yours ordered to stand down immediately."

Grupa and Noctus shot each other a look of concern. "Only a coward would negotiate from brute force!" hissed Noctus.

"Ah, I think you misunderstand your situation," Sara replied, her voice now colder than ice. "You are not currently prisoners of the W.A.S.P.s, you are prisoners of the World Security Patrol. As an agent of such I am fully authorised to use any means necessary to extract information from you. This is not a negotiation. This is an interrogation. And I am accountable to no one in this matter. Absolutely no-one. Do you understand?"

There was now panic in Grupa's voice and on his face, as he looked towards Fisher and Atlanta for help. "A–and the two of you will allow her to do this? You would stand there and permit this blunt instrument to do harm to our persons?"

"Like I said," Sara reminded him, "'accountable to no one'. It covers a wide remit. You called John and Atlanta and the others at Marineville sheep pretending to be wolves just now. Well, that may be so... but the thing about us wolves is that we can be very unpredictable. Some wolves do what we do to *protect* the sheep, we make the hard choices so that the sheep can sleep soundly in their beds at night." Sara now leaned in close to whisper directly into Grupa's ear. "And we don't take kindly to other predators who decide to mess with our flock. Do you understand?"

"It is a trick, Grupa!" Noctus hissed. "They would not allow any prisoners to be mistreated! This female is trying to frighten you! Tell them nothing!"

"Oh, are you volunteering to go first?" Sara asked, suddenly whirling on Noctus. "I'd be just as happy to start with you. Cos right now, this big bad wolf is feeling very *very* hungry..."

Noctus immediately cowered from Sara's glare, raising his hands in terror, and she turned her attention back to Grupa. "Perhaps you'd like me to start with him anyway?" she asked, gripping his arm tightly with her free hand. "It'll give you a chance to get used to the techniques I'll be using on you..."

The air of smug superiority that had pervaded Grupa from the moment he and Noctus had taken Atlanta and Fisher prisoner had now entirely evaporated; in fact, Sara was almost certain she could feel him trembling in her grip. "Your friends are being held in our city, Igneathea," he said finally, in a quiet voice heavy with defeat.

Sara loosened her grip on his arm. "You'll take us there and get them released?" Grupa nodded. "Alright, now we're making progress. And the replica Stingrays?" When Grupa didn't reply to her question right away, Sara shot a questioning look towards Noctus, who buckled instantly.

"Are also controlled by the city," he stammered. "But we're out of radio contact with them from here."

"Then it sounds like we'll be paying a visit to this city of yours after all," Atlanta chirped. "Only with you guys as *our* prisoners. Well, Lieutenant, you're the aquanaut on our little team; think you can handle Stingray okay?"

"Sure, no sweat," Fisher replied, managing not to let his excitement at the thought of taking command of Stingray show in his voice. "Only I'll need a navigator."

"Oh, I think our friend here would serve quite nicely," Atlanta suggested, nudging Noctus towards Phones' chair. Noctus looked from the chair to Grupa, as if awaiting instructions – then practically leapt into it as Sara loudly cleared her throat.

"Yes, well... y–you heard the lady, Noctus," said Grupa in the most dignified voice he could muster. "Best speed to Igneathea, if you please."

"It better be quicker than that!" Atlanta cried, pointing towards the sky. "Look!"

From the cabin window all five occupants of Stingray could see the need for urgency. Flying directly at them from out of the Sun was a W.A.S.P. bomber – and as they watched in horror, they spotted multiple vapour trails streak out from the belly of the aircraft as it opened fire on their position. When her father had ordered that any Stingray was to be attacked on sight, Atlanta had been the first to protest for fear of the order signing a death sentence for Troy, Phones and Marina.

She had never imagined that it might mean the end of her, Fisher and Sara instead...

CHAPTER 10

Power Mad

"Tower from Stingray, do you read me?"

Despite the ongoing reports of chaos in the waters around Manila Bay, the sound of his daughter's voice over the radio speaker somehow made everything seem a little bit brighter to Commander Shore. "Atlanta, is that you?" he asked. "Gee, it's good to—"

"Father, listen! A W.A.S.P. bomber has just opened fire on a Stingray!"

Shore nodded, turning to face the radio map on the wall behind him. "Yeah honey, we just had a report on that. It's in area—"

"Father, that's the real Stingray, and I'm aboard her right now!"

"What?" Shore quickly overcame his shock, wasting no time in changing frequency on his radio mic. "Tower to jet squadron commander! Urgent!"

"Go ahead, Commander."

"Confirm you've just opened fire on that Stingray you sighted?"

"That's right, sir. Impact in ten—"

"Destroy those missiles by remote, immediately!

"Say again, Commander?"

"You heard me! Destruct, man! Destruct!"

"P.W.O.R.!"

The next few seconds passed agonisingly slowly for Commander Shore, until finally the pilot's voice broke the silence. *"Missile detonation confirmed at twelve feet over target, sir."*

"...and Stingray?"

"No sign of debris...heck, no sign of anything now the ocean's all churned up," came the pilot's voice. *"I'm sorry sir, I —"*

But Shore had no time to listen to the pilot's apology when the lives of three brave young people were hanging in the balance... including that of the one person who meant the most to him in the whole world.

"Stingray from Tower, do you read me?" he called desperately into his mic. "Come in Stingray!" But there was no reply.

Shore had been trained to handle crisis situations; it was all part of being a W.A.S.P. officer, and even more so since he'd taken command of Marineville... except right now he wasn't thinking as the commander of Marineville. Right now, he could only think as a father. A million possibilities were running through his mind... and all of them were scenarios he'd hoped he'd never live to endure.

"Atlanta..."

But Stingray was intact – just. Fisher had ordered a crash dive seconds after the bomber had opened fire on them, but it was touch and go whether even Stingray could move fast enough to outrun disaster. No sooner had the sub fully submerged than the bomber's payload had detonated over the ocean, and the vessel had been buffeted by the shockwave of the resulting explosion. Although Fisher and

Noctus were relatively safe in their seats at the front of the cabin, the rest of Stingray's passengers hadn't fared as well.

Atlanta, Sara and Grupa had all been thrown to the deck by the force of the blast, with Atlanta having also tumbled down the staircase to the lower deck – and by the time Sara had noticed where she'd landed Grupa was already moving down the stairs towards her. Aware that he might use this turn of events to his advantage, Sara drew her pistol and slipped underneath the safety rail lining the top deck to get to her colleague first. "Don't try anything!" she warned the startled Igneathean as she landed in front of him.

Grupa froze, but then Sara saw that he wasn't trying to hurt Atlanta at all. He *was* leaning down towards her, but his arm was extended to offer a helping hand. "It's alright, Sara," Atlanta said, accepting Grupa's aid and allowing him to help her stand on shaky legs. "I'm okay..."

"You're sure?"

"Yeah, yeah, I'm fine... well, we're all still in one piece then?"

The trio made their way back up to the upper level, where Noctus was ready with a report. "Missiles exploded just thirty-two feet over our present position," he announced flatly. "In case anyone was wondering."

Fisher hated to admit it but he'd been quite impressed by Noctus' skill in handling Stingray. He had given the flood Q dive order so instinctively that it had temporarily slipped his mind that his co-pilot wasn't a W.A.S.P. officer, or even human come to that. Nevertheless, Noctus had understood the command instantly and worked Stingray's controls like an expert, as aware as any of them that time was of the essence.

"Any damage?" Fisher asked him.

"Checking," Noctus replied, quickly surveying the instruments for any indication of trouble. After a moment, he shook his head. "Negative. We were lucky."

"*Atlanta? Atlanta, sweetheart, talk to me! Please honey, tell me you're—*"

Atlanta grabbed her radio watch from the floor where it had landed when she'd fallen. "Yes father, I'm here!" she said, unable to keep the emotion from her voice. "We're all okay, we're safe! I say again, we're all okay!"

"*Oh, thank heaven!*" Hearing the relief in her father's voice, Atlanta found herself blinking back tears as she realised just how close they'd come to destruction. "*When we lost contact back there, I... I thought—*"

"I know, father, I know," Atlanta said soothingly, not wanting to put him through any further pain. She could only imagine the thoughts that must have been running through his mind in the last couple of minutes. "But I'm fine, really. We're all fine."

"*I'm so glad to hear that... if anything happened to you, I'd—*"

Deciding to spare the commander from embarrassing himself in front of four witnesses, no matter how much she wanted to hear his voice right now, Atlanta quickly switched the topic of conversation back to business. "Listen father, we've retaken Stingray. The *real* Stingray. We've also captured Noctus and Grupa, and we're now heading on to their city to rescue Troy and the others."

"*You want some backup? I'd feel happier if you had a full assault team going in with you...*"

"No father!" Atlanta was keen to prevent this from turning into a full-scale invasion; that might only lead to greater loss of life. "If you can spare a patrol vessel or two then have them stand by near where we lost contact with the mechanical fish fleet, just in case, but don't send anyone else in until we signal, okay?"

"Okay honey," Shore agreed, albeit with some reluctance in his voice. "I'll be waiting to hear from you. I... I love you."

Atlanta beamed at his words, not caring who noticed. "I love you too, father! Over and out!" With that, she ended the call and looked around at her four travelling companions. "Well if we're going, let's go!"

"Aye aye, Atlanta!" As Fisher and Noctus worked the controls between them Stingray suddenly came to life again, banking sharply to port before accelerating away into the murky ocean depths.

"How long will it take us to get there?" Atlanta asked.

"About thirty marine minutes present speed, I should think," replied Grupa.

"Fine. Now, I don't know why all of Stingray's furniture has ended up in a heap downstairs, but while we travel to your city you are going to tidy this place up."

Sara couldn't help smiling at the sight of Atlanta talking to Grupa like he was a naughty boy with a messy bedroom, and at Grupa's visible look of disappointment. "And while you work," she added, "I want to know exactly what you've been doing to our friends since they went missing. And if you people have harmed so much as one hair on any of their heads—"

"I know, I know," Grupa grumbled. "You'll turn me over to Lieutenant Coral here."

"Oh no," Atlanta said, in a calm steely tone Sara had never heard her use before. "I'll deal with you myself." Grupa's eyes widened in alarm; it hadn't escaped his notice that in the confusion, and despite her fall, Atlanta had somehow managed to acquire Noctus' rifle. "Let's go..."

Sara watched the pair head downstairs then leaned over the back of Fisher's chair, gesturing her head in the direction of Noctus. "Think you can handle him?" she asked.

Fisher glanced at his temporary co-pilot, who was presently keeping his gaze firmly on the waters ahead. "Well, he seems to know what he's doing. First sign of trouble, I'll give you a yell."

"Fine, fine..." An awkward silence fell over the pair, made even more uncomfortable by the incongruous presence of Noctus. Sara was the first to think of something to say. "Thanks again for the save back on the sub," she whispered, patting Fisher on the arm. "I won't forget that."

"O–oh, my pleasure..." Fisher replied, suddenly finding himself blushing. Being taken hostage, facing enemy attack, captaining a submarine about to be blown out of the water – Fisher had taken all of these things in stride. They were part of the career he had chosen, after all. How come it was only now, when all he had to do was make conversation with an attractive woman who clearly liked him too, that he suddenly felt totally out of his depth?

"And thanks for getting us out of there, and saving our bacon here when our guns failed," he added. "Getting them to cooperate with us, I mean. That was, er, some bluff you pulled off..."

Sara tapped her chin thoughtfully with the butt of her pistol. "Who said I was bluffing?" she asked in a hard deep voice, rolling her eyes towards the ceiling in an attempt to look coldly disinterested in the notion of actually carrying out her threats. Fisher looked at her in shock – but then he realised that he too had just fallen for another of her bluffs, as a twinkle of mischief appeared in her eyes. "Eyes on the road, 'Captain'," she purred, pointing towards the cabin window, forcing him to return his attention to piloting Stingray. "It'd be nice to get where we're going in one piece..."

With that, Sara moved downstairs to assist Atlanta in her questioning of Grupa. Fisher sighed as he watched her go, then suddenly found himself making eye contact with Noctus, who appeared to be regarding him with a sympathetic look.

"You have my pity, terrainean," he said mournfully.

"Oh?" Fisher asked curiously. "Why's that?"

"Our females are also terrifying creatures. You are clearly doomed to a horrible fate." With that, Noctus returned his attention to navigating Stingray, while Fisher took a moment to enjoy something he had been dreaming of ever since he was first assigned to Marineville – sitting in the captain's chair aboard Stingray during an actual mission. Yet for all the sense of fulfilment that came with the moment, he couldn't shake the image of Sara's perfect smile from his mind.

On the contrary, he thought to himself. *I've never felt so blessed in all my life.*

"Stay back! He's gone berserk!"

"Troy, look out!"

"Watch it, Marina! He's armed!"

"Kill Tempest! *Kill Tempest!*"

The sudden cacophony of frantic voices from the other side of the cell door startled the two Igneathean guards as they arrived with the evening meal for their prisoners. Peering through the observation window in the door they could see the three members of the Stingray crew cowering in fear from their Aquaphibian cellmate, who was standing in the middle of the room waving a jagged chunk of a broken plate in their direction.

Setting the trays of food down one guard immediately grabbed a passcard from her belt, slamming it to the electronic security lock while the other unshouldered her rifle and raised it. As the door swung open she rushed into the room – but was unprepared for the Aquaphibian's change of tactic.

Grabbing hold of the end of her rifle he swung her across the room, using her own momentum against her and slamming her hard into the far wall. Rather than close the door and sound the alarm the second guard rushed forward to assist her unconscious colleague, and that's when Troy and Phones jumped her. That was also the moment when they made an important discovery; not only were Igneathean females a whole head taller than human males, they were also quite a bit stronger too.

Immediately throwing the two men off with a roar, the guard balled her fists as she prepared to retaliate – only to find the Aquaphibian on her back. She spun around, attempting to dislodge him, but he clung to her like a limpet until finally she jabbed her elbow into his hip. He fell, down but not yet out.

Meanwhile, Troy and Phones had pulled a mattress from one of the cell's bunks and now shoved it towards her, but she immediately grabbed it and hurled it back at them as if it weighed nothing. As the two W.A.S.P. men fell to the floor, Andy retaliated by tearing the bunk itself away from the wall and throwing it as hard as he could towards her. Incredibly the guard moved as if to catch it – only to trip on the body of her unconscious comrade. She fell over backwards, and the bunk landed noisily on top of both guards a second later. Muffled moans now came from beneath the bunk, suggesting at least one of the guards was only semi-conscious – but it didn't sound like that would last for long.

It was at the height of the action that Titan had decided to make his move. Having been pretending up until now to still be unconscious he had suddenly leapt to his manacled feet and began to hop, slowly and steadily, across to the open cell door. Having their hands full dealing with the guards Troy, Phones and Andy were in no position to do anything to stop him – but one person was.

As Titan approached the cell door Marina slid along the floor and stuck one leg out across his path. With a cry born more from frustration than pain Titan crashed to the ground, slithering his way out into the corridor in a desperate attempt to escape.

Grabbing one of the guards' fallen rifles Marina followed, leaping over Titan and pointing the weapon directly at him. He halted his slow advance, and looked up at his former slave with contempt. "You... you wouldn't..." he sneered. "It would take courage and fortitude... two qualities you have always lacked!"

Marina shook her head. It was true that she would never fire a weapon in anger; in fact she'd rarely even held any much less fired one, although even so, she doubted she would be able to miss Titan at such close range. Looking down at the man who had caused so much pain in the past, not only to her and her father but also to members of so many other underwater races, she realised that she was in a position many of them had probably dreamed about. She now held his life in her hands... and was very relieved to realise that the thought gave her no sense of power or satisfaction. Just pity for this sad man who had chosen to dedicate his life to ruining those of others.

"No, she wouldn't ever do it," Phones agreed, as he appeared by her side. "As for the other things you said; that's just a loada hooey." Smiling gratefully Marina handed the rifle off to Phones, clearly glad to be rid of it, before giving him a questioning look – which was answered a second later as the Aquaphibian hurried from the cell, followed finally by Troy, who slammed the door shut behind him.

"Everyone okay?" he asked breathlessly, clutching another stolen rifle between his hands.

Phones did a quick visual check of their party. "Yeah, looks like it Troy."

"I think I've broken my ankle," Titan moaned, clutching his leg and shooting an accusing look at Marina. "Your pet Pacifican here is a monster!"

Troy didn't even bother to reply to Titan. Instead, he turned his attention to Andy. "You did good, friend," he said, patting the Aquaphibian on the arm. "You still wanna stick with us?"

The Aquaphibian spent a few long seconds considering the matter. "If I help you escape, you will let me warn my people that they are in danger?"

"If we get out of this we'll run you straight to Titanica and let you out there," Troy assured him. "That's a promise."

"Then... I help you."

"Fool..." Titan mumbled from the floor. "*Traitor...*" If the Aquaphibian heard his words, they certainly didn't wipe the proud smile off his face. It was so much nicer to be around people who valued his contribution than people who just shouted at him all the time.

"So what's the plan, Troy?" Phones asked. "I reckon once those little ladies in the cell come to, they'll probably kick the door down between them. Maybe we shouldn't be here when they do?"

"Right. Well, now we've got weapons, and between us we should be able to work out the route back to Stingray," Troy decided. "I say we take it."

"That's the first place they'd look for us, ain't it?" Phones asked. "Might we be better taking one of their own ships instead?"

"You know how to handle those things?"

"Well, no..."

"And we can't take the time to learn if they choose to send more after us and we end up with a fight on our hands." Troy was adamant that there was only one way out of the city now. "No, for my money it's Stingray or nothing. They may put up a fight, but it's a chance we'll have to take

– always assuming we can get the controls to work for us, that is. You two with me?"

Marina nodded her agreement enthusiastically, while Phones just smiled. "You know you can count on us all the way, skipper. And I guess it'd be a shame to leave the old girl behind after she brought us here in the first place."

"It would at that..."

"What can I do?" Andy asked, clearly hungry for more action. Troy was reluctant to hand over one of their newly appropriated weapons to the Aquaphibian, more out of concern over his skill in a firefight rather than any lingering trust issues. Still, it seemed a shame not to take advantage of that brute strength of his and, as something moved just out of the corner of his eye, Troy knew exactly what use Andy could be put to.

"Bring him," he ordered, pointing to the crumpled form of Titan on the floor before taking a moment to scout the way ahead. Happy to obey his new master Andy advanced on his former master, bending down to scoop him up from the floor and throwing him over his shoulder as if he were a sack of flour.

Phones and Marina were having trouble keeping a straight face. "I suppose you all think this is funny?" Titan snarled at them, despite facing in the opposite direction.

"Well, yeah, kinda!" Phones admitted, as Marina mimed taking a photograph of the moment, causing him to burst out laughing.

"The way to the travel tube's clear Phones," said Troy, back from his brief reconnaissance. "Let's move!"

"Right behind you, Troy!"

And with that, the group set off for the travel tube, their attempt at stealth only being let down somewhat by Titan's loud protests echoing along the corridor.

"Put me down, do you hear? Put me down this *instant*...!"

Aboard Stingray, Sara was dividing her time between watching Noctus at the controls and keeping an eye on Grupa as he helped Atlanta tidy up the mess on the lower deck – where, it transpired, the Stingray crew had used the sub's furniture and fittings to build a barricade in an ill-fated attempt to keep the ship from being taken by Grupa and his people.

Sara found some irony in the sight of Grupa himself being made to dismantle the very same barricade, and as she watched him sullenly dump an inexplicably soggy book into a waste basket it was hard to believe that this dejected little creature was capable of being a threat to anybody. With that in mind, she decided to pull Atlanta into one corner of the navigation bay and ask her something that had been on her mind ever since they'd taken this ship.

"I know those two say it is," she began, "but we are absolutely sure that this is the *real* Stingray and not another duplicate, aren't we?"

"Oh yes. No question."

"How can you be so certain?"

Atlanta smiled, then reached for a framed photograph on the desk beside her. The glass had become cracked at some point during the day's action, but not enough to obscure the picture inside. It was a group photo, obviously taken during some sort of party back at Marineville, and featured Commander Shore, Marina and her father Aphony sitting in the centre of the picture, while around them stood Troy Tempest, Phones, Atlanta and Fisher. Except for Aphony the men were all in tan dinner jackets, the two women wore elegant dresses, and everyone was smiling. Even Oink, Marina's faithful pet seal cub whom Sara had met at dinner last night, had donned a bow tie for the occasion.

"That was only taken a couple of months ago, on Marina's birthday," Atlanta explained. "*After* Noctus and Grupa made off with Stingray the first time."

"Even so, they could have duplicated this since grabbing Troy and the others," Sara suggested. "They do seem to be quite thorough when it comes to the details."

Taking the picture from Sara, Atlanta turned it over and eased the photograph out of the frame. "Read the back," she suggested.

Sara took the photograph from Atlanta, discovering an elegantly handwritten inscription on the reverse side. *"To my dearest friend Marina... with love on your birthday and every day. Thank you for being you and brightening all our days, Atlanta."*

"She'd been asking for a photo of us all together to keep aboard Stingray for a while," Atlanta explained. "A way to remember us when she's away from Marineville on missions." Taking the photo back from Sara she looked down at it, rubbing her fingers over this memento of a lovely evening with the people who mattered most to her. "Call it a hunch, call it intuition, but I just *know* that this is the same photo I gave her."

"That's a very nice thing to do for her," Sara commented, more than happy now to believe that they really were aboard the genuine Stingray. "You must care for her a great deal."

Atlanta nodded. "Well, you've probably noticed that there aren't too many female W.A.S.P. officers in Marineville," she explained, "and most of the few that are there are quite a bit older than I am. When Marina came along... well, I was a bit suspicious of her at first, but once I got past that we bonded very quickly. She's like the sister I always wanted but never had, and somehow, everything's been better since she arrived." She looked down at the photo again, and sighed quietly.

"We'll get her back," Sara promised. "We'll get all three of them back."

Atlanta looked at Sara and nodded, but an air of sadness pervaded her hazel eyes. Sara understood exactly what it meant, because she was thinking the same; *easier said than done.*

"Oh, enjoy these days Atlanta," Sara sighed, gesturing to the photograph again. "Because *this*... this sense of family that you guys at Marineville have is not the norm in most of the security services. I only wish it were. You're very lucky to have such good friends..."

There it was again, Atlanta thought. That palpable undercurrent of regret that Sara exuded whenever any discussion of anyone's personal life came up. Having read Sara's file Atlanta knew that this wasn't a woman who made friends easily, most likely due to the nature of her job... but it was also desperately obvious that she regretted not having the time or opportunity to do something about it. Aside from the people she'd met at Marineville in the last couple of days, was there anyone out there who would truly mourn Sara Coral if the worst should happen? Atlanta hoped so – but she wouldn't have wanted to put money on it.

"Yes, I think I am lucky to have the friends I've got," Atlanta replied brightly – before taking Sara's hand and squeezing it tightly. "And just as lucky that new friends still come along from time to time."

Sara seemed somewhat startled by the gesture, as if the idea of anyone reaching out to her in friendship was almost an alien concept, which made Atlanta decide to take it one step further. Setting the photo down on the table, she reached out her arms in a hug – which to her relief Sara gratefully accepted.

"You are always welcome at Marineville, Sara," Atlanta said quietly. "*Always.*"

Sara didn't reply – but Atlanta felt her grip on her tighten slightly in that instant. When they ended the hug moments later, there were tears visible in Sara's eyes that she very quickly attempted to dab away.

"So, still think we're all insane?" Atlanta asked.

Sara grinned. "Oh, now that I've seen you all in action, I'm more convinced of it than ever," she replied playfully, looking up as an obviously bored Grupa slowly pushed a broom past them. "But then if this is the kind of thing you have to deal with every day, I'm really not surprised..."

The Stingray crew had fared well on their journey across Igneathea. Just as it had done for Marina, the fact that the majority of the population were in hibernation had greatly reduced their chances of being discovered. They proceeded with caution, not wanting to tempt fate, but on the rare occasions they saw or heard an Igneathean approaching them they were always able to duck out of sight until the danger had passed. They'd had to change travel tubes several times to connect to the line leading to the airlocks, but even that hadn't been too difficult. No barriers impeded their progress, no alarms sounded their escape. Even better still, Titan had eventually stopped complaining.

Everything seemed to be smooth sailing as they approached the door leading to the airlock where they'd been forced to leave Stingray, but upon reaching it Troy peered through the door's observation porthole – and frowned. "Phones... we've got a problem."

"Shucks, and my day had been just dandy up 'til now. What's up?"

Troy pointed to the door. "No Stingray."

Phones peered through the porthole, and tutted. Sure enough, the berth where they had last seen Stingray was now empty, aside from water and a few guards on the quayside. "Well, are we certain this is the airlock we came in through?"

"As sure as we can be," Troy replied. "I guess it wouldn't hurt to backtrack a little and see if we took a wrong turn somewhere. If not, we might have to fall back on your suggestion of stealing one of their ships..."

Before Phones could reply Marina hurried forward, gesturing frantically. "What is it, Marina?" Troy asked. But it only took him a moment to realise what she'd been trying to draw to their attention. "Say, where's Titan?"

The three members of the Stingray crew all looked towards Andy, who seemed just as surprised as they were that his former master had vanished. Looking behind him, he suddenly realised that *he* had been the one carrying Titan, and thus really should know where he was now. With panic in his eyes, he attempted to come up with a convincing explanation. "I, I, I... I do not know."

"Well, how long has it been since you realised he wasn't on your shoulder anymore?" Phones asked. "Five minutes? Ten? Two?"

"I, I, I... I do not know..." Andy considered the matter carefully, replaying the events of the last few minutes in his mind. "I remember! I set him down just before we boarded the last travel tube... he is heavy... but I do not remember picking him up again."

Phones sighed. "You wanna split up and search for him, Troy?"

Troy waved a dismissive hand. "Nah, leave him be Phones."

"But I thought you said—"

"About bringing him in. Yeah, I know I did, but right now the most important thing is to get out of here. We can come back for Titan later." He grinned.

"Besides, how far can he possibly get on his own?"

For the first time in his life, Titan found he could actually relate to a terrainean. Not a real one, of course – that would be crazy – but a fictional one. He had never ever felt so enraged before, had never experienced so overwhelming a desire to have his revenge as he was feeling now... and as he wrestled with that anger his thoughts turned to the human Ahab and his quest for vengeance upon the whale that had taken his leg.

"'As if his chest had been a mortar,'" he quoted to himself, "'he burst his hot heart's shell upon it...'" While the words may have originally been written by a terrainean to express the feelings of a fictional terrainean there was nevertheless great wisdom in them, an understanding of the nature of pure vengeance itself that Titan couldn't help admiring. That was the kind of anger he was feeling right now; the kind of anger that simply had to be channelled into massive devastating action, no matter the cost. The Igneatheans had earned the wrath of Titan, and they would come to regret it very soon.

Of course, they'd brought it all upon themselves. Why couldn't they see the wonderful opportunity that he had presented to them? Wasn't it an honour to have even been considered to serve anywhere in Titan's grand alliance of underwater races, never mind be chosen as one of the first recruits?

And yet how had the people of Igneathea responded when he had arrived to make this offer? With nothing but arrogance and hostility. The destruction of his mechanical fish fleet had been a setback. Subjecting him to interrogation had been humiliating. Throwing him in a cell with the accursed Troy Tempest and his clan had just been insulting. But to follow all those indignities up with plans to attack Titanica itself... well, that was the moment they'd signed their own death warrant. They now had to be utterly exterminated. And there was the germ of an idea forming in Titan's mind as to how that could be accomplished...

His half-hearted pretence of a broken ankle had eventually paid off, albeit not exactly how he'd planned.

Titan had finally managed to escape from Tempest and the others when the traitorous Aquaphibian had briefly put him down to scratch while the terraineans were examining the travel tube map and discussing what route to take. He'd quietly fallen to the rear of the group at that point, and then simply stayed behind when they had finally moved on. The W.A.S.P.s had been too busy hatching plans to notice he hadn't followed them, while the Aquaphibian was occupied trying to further ingratiate himself with them. They'd probably noticed that he was missing by now, but with so many travel tube routes and terminals throughout Igneathea he knew the chances of them finding him now were very slim indeed. They had no way to know that he'd taken a travel tube to the engineering plant.

With his wrists and ankles still manacled it had seemed a long and humiliating journey from the travel tube station, hopping down the corridor leading to the gallery overlooking the vehicle workshops in the engineering plant, but he had to see if the despicable Marina had been correct. There he saw it for himself; not only did the Igneatheans have one mechanical fish already constructed, but three more were almost complete too. He wanted to slam his fists against the window in frustration, but the manacles made it impossible. Before he moved on to the matter of revenge, it was time to solve that little problem.

Finding a laser bandsaw in one of the nearby workshops he had made short work of the manacles, finally regaining full use of his limbs for the first time in hours and leaving him free to wreak vengeance on these pathetic inhabitants of this city. He had been intending to attempt to hijack one of their own submarines to use against them – until he spotted two words on the travel tube map that had made him change his plans…

Power plant.

Like everywhere in Igneathea, access to the power plant did not appear to be off-limits – at least, that's what Titan assumed as he disembarked from its travel tube terminal and marched purposefully along the single corridor that appeared to lead to it. Turning a corner at the end of the corridor, however, he ducked back out of sight when he noticed a single Igneathean soldier standing guard in front of the door to the power plant. When no alarm or footsteps reached his ears, meaning he hadn't been detected, he smiled deviously.

Reaching into a pouch on the side of his right boot, he now retrieved one of his most prized possessions; an antique hunting knife that had once belonged to his father. It was the only memento he still had of his youth in the city of Hydroma, and it had served him well over the years in everything from battles to treaty negotiations. In fact, he'd been hoping to use it on that fool Tempest back in the cell, but the manacles had thwarted that ambition. For Tempest, another day of reckoning would come. But this guard's life expectancy could now be measured in seconds.

Peering into the corridor as much as he dared, Titan chose his moment well, waiting until the guard got bored and turned her back to him – before quickly stepping into the corridor and taking careful aim. Once the guard was in the best position for him to strike, the blade spun silently through the air and plunged into her back with the same precision as if he'd delivered the blow at point-blank range. She gave a grunt of pain, then crashed heavily to the floor.

Scurrying along the corridor to where she had fallen, Titan knelt down beside her to retrieve his knife from between her shoulder blades, sliding it back into his boot before turning away from the body to locate the guard's rifle...

But suddenly the guard had snapped back to consciousness and was now clawing at his feet, snarling with fury as she attempted to snatch the knife from his boot.

Surprised by her formidable strength, and genuinely fearful for his life now, Titan eventually succeeded in grabbing her rifle – and then slammed the butt of it hard into her chin. The guard's head snapped backwards, her arms went limp, her eyes closed, and she lay very still.

Titan didn't bother to check her pulse. If she wasn't dead now, he thought, she soon would be. Along with the rest of her accursed race. Still, at least this one had admirably attempted to put up a good fight. He vowed to remember her for that.

Reaching down to the belt around her waist he grabbed a keycard, of the same kind he'd seen other guards using to gain entry to and from the prison cell over the last few hours. Slapping it against the reader on the door he cursed as nothing appeared to happen – but then after a moment the reader flashed green and the door to the power plant slid open. Inside, he could see three male Igneathean technicians at work within the large industrial complex, moving between the three massive atomic reactors in the centre of the room and occasionally checking the displays on various instruments and computer banks.

This time, Titan did not even consider employing subtlety. Instead, he marched into the power plant quite openly, immediately aiming his stolen rifle at the nearest technician and shooting him down before the unfortunate man even knew he was there.

The second Igneathean whirled around, his eyes widening with fear as he saw Titan approaching, then lunged towards what appeared to be an alarm on the wall – but he never made it. Titan's stolen rifle cracked once more, and the technician pitched over a nearby handrail before crashing to the floor.

The third technician, standing beside what a strange sense of déjà vu told Titan must be the main control console, raised his hands as Titan approached. Titan smiled, imagining what it must be like to live in a world where such a gesture was expected to mean something.

"Now then, my good man," Titan told him, "you are going to answer my questions. Any hesitation will mean instant death." He nodded to the control console. "You control power to the entire city from here, correct?"

"Y–yes… the atomic reactors supply the entire city…"

"I thought as much…" It now began to make sense to Titan why this room seemed somehow familiar; this was somewhere else he had seen while under the assault of the mind sifter. It was obviously of great importance to the Igneatheans for thoughts of it to constantly be at the forefront of their group consciousness… which meant it was very appropriate to use this place to launch his ultimate revenge upon them.

"I wish to set these reactors to overload," he said in the same tone of voice he might use when inspecting a potential purchase in a submersible showroom. "How soon could this be accomplished?"

"W–well, we can boost the power from all three reactors from this console," the technician explained reluctantly. "If not resolved, the increased energy flow would set up a critical feedback loop in the city's power supply grid within fifteen marine minutes, which could feed back to the reactors within thirty, but…"

"But…?"

"But it would be the end of us!" the technician cried. "At that thirty-minute point it would be impossible to reverse the overload – and that would mean the destruction of the entire city!"

"Oh!" Now employing his most sarcastic tone of voice Titan threw his free hand over his lips, making a great show of pretending to look surprised. "Oh, I had no idea! Why, that almost sounds like a very bad and deeply foolish thing to even *consider* doing…"

He shouldered the rifle, allowing himself to enjoy the slight look of relief that now appeared on the face of the technician – before it abruptly returned to panic as Titan instead reached down to his boot and produced the knife, still slick with metallic green blood. He advanced on the technician, backing him up into a wall.

"As you can see, I've already used this to spill the blood of one of your kind today," he explained in a gleefully sadistic tone as he turned the knife over in his hands – before pointing the tip of its blade towards the technician's throat. "Do you wish to become the second? No? Then carry out my instructions! Set the reactors to overload, immediately!"

Terrified at the thought of what this clearly unhinged individual might do to him if he refused, the technician turned to the console and reluctantly obeyed the order. Titan watched as he took hold of the first of three large red levers on the control console in front of him, moving each one in turn from a position in the centre of a circular mount up as high as they would go – into the danger point. Almost immediately, dials and readouts on the consoles above began to fluctuate wildly, as the power from the reactors inexorably began to build.

By the time he began moving the third lever the technician's hands were trembling, and he turned to plead with Titan – only to find the knife close to his throat once more. "Do it!" came the order.

The technician obeyed, sliding the third and final lever into the danger zone. When that was done, he looked back to Titan in horror – as an ominous warning alarm suddenly sounded from behind him. "It'll mean total annihilation..." he gulped. "The end of the Igneathean civilisation itself..."

The two men turned to the monitors mounted over the reactor controls, as their dials and readouts reported imminent disaster all across the board. Several of the displays began to flash a red alert, casting an increasingly hellish glow across Titan's twisted features. "Excellent," he chuckled as he watched the results of his handiwork. "Excellent!"

He spun around as the sound of running footsteps caught his attention. The technician had suddenly bolted, sprinting for the exit as though his life depended on it. Grabbing the rifle Titan attempted to shoot him down – but even as he fired he knew he hadn't had time to take perfect aim. The technician cried out as a bullet struck him in the left shoulder but he managed to keep running, and before Titan could get off another shot he was out of the power room and into the corridor beyond.

Titan let him go. What could a race made up of such weak cowardly men do against the might of the great Titan? With only one door in and out of the power room he could easily defend against invaders if the fool sounded the alarm, although he didn't plan to be here long. A small emergency escape elevator in one corner of the room offered a way out, and he would allow himself plenty of time for that before the reactors blew – but first, he had to make absolutely certain that nothing could be done to prevent the city's destruction before he left.

"Defy the might of Titan, will they?" he muttered to himself as he watched the readings and gauges climb further into the red. "Well, I'll teach them the price of defiance! I'll see Marineville in flames yet... and the ruins of Igneathea will serve as a lesson to anyone foolish enough to stand in the way of me and my ultimate goal!"

CHAPTER 11

An Unlikely Hero

Grupa had a feeling something was wrong the moment Stingray returned to Igneathea. As the water around the sub was pumped out of the airlock, leaving her once again floating next to the dockside, it was clear that no preparations had been made for their arrival. The connecting bridge that had linked the sub to the dockside previously had not been set in place, and so the quintet had to make use of Stingray's monocopters to disembark the sub.

"What the blazes is going on here?" asked Grupa once they were all safely across. "Someone should have been here to greet us..."

"I don't like this, Grupa," said Noctus. "Where are all the guards?"

"I don't know," replied Grupa, looking around warily. "I just don't know..."

"If this is some kind of trap..." Fisher warned him.

"No tricks, Lieutenant. No, something's wrong here. We must find out what, at once..."

"Just remember I'm watching you," Sara reminded him. "You go where we say, you do what we want."

"And what we want is to find our friends," Atlanta added, gently but firmly.

"And you can have them with my blessing," Grupa grumbled, as he led the group towards the large door connecting the airlock to the rest of the city. "The sooner you all leave Igneathea the better I'll like it. We weren't planning to hold them for much longer anyway."

Pressing his pass card to the electronic lock, the door slid open vertically almost instantly. The last thing any of the group expected to see immediately on the other side of it was one of Titan's soldiers standing in the corridor beyond with a startled expression on his face.

"An Aquaphibian!" cried Fisher, raising the Igneathean rifle and quickly taking aim. His reflexes were fast – but Marina's were faster. With almost imperceptible speed she seemed to appear out of nowhere and placed herself between Andy and Fisher's rifle, waving frantically to her colleague to hold his fire.

"Marina!" Atlanta gasped as she ran forward to embrace her friend. "Gee, it's so good to see you!" She gestured to the Aquaphibian. "Is... is he with you?"

Marina nodded, and Andy nervously peered over her shoulder to confirm it. "Friend," he said quietly.

Fisher lowered the rifle. "Sorry about that," he said. "Gee, that could have been—"

"Messy," finished Sara, now also receiving a welcoming hug from Marina.

"How did they escape from their cell?" whispered Noctus to Grupa.

Grupa shook his head. "It would appear," he replied quietly, "that the terraineans are more resourceful than we gave them credit for."

"Troy and Phones," Atlanta asked. "Are they—"

"Atlanta!"

Atlanta's face lit up at the sound of her friend's voice at the far end of the corridor, where Troy and Phones had been consulting a travel tube map on the wall. "Oh Troy!"

The pair ran into each other's arms, and it was all Atlanta could do to keep herself from kissing him.

"How'd you get here?" Troy asked.

"Stingray!"

"Stingray?" Phones asked. "You mean, the real thing?"

Atlanta nodded. "The one and only!" she confirmed. "Along with some other old friends of yours..."

"Yes, forgive me for interrupting this happy reunion," Grupa said loudly as he walked up to them. "But perhaps you could explain what's been going on in this city during our absence?"

It didn't take long for them to find out. When Grupa called in to the control room to order the replica Stingrays still out at sea to self-destruct, he was informed of the sabotage in the power room – and the subsequent panic as news of it spread across the city.

It wasn't until they arrived in the power room themselves, along with the Stingray crew, that the full extent of the disaster facing them became apparent. Hurrying to the reactor control console Grupa was able to see for himself on the monitors that the three main reactors were rapidly approaching a point of critical overload.

Noctus was quick to point the finger of blame at their former prisoners. "Tempest, if this was your doing—"

"It wasn't them, Grupa!" The technician that Titan had threatened earlier staggered up to them, his arm now in a sling. "It was another alien! He burst in, murdered the others, and... and forced me to set an overload in the reactors..."

"Titan..." Grupa growled quietly.

"Yeah, Titan," Troy confirmed. "He escaped from our cell when we did, and we didn't exactly have a chance to lock him up again. We – well, I – wanted to take him back to Marineville, but he sort of got away from us..."

"And the emergency escape elevator has been taken," Grupa noted gravely. "He could be anywhere in the city by now!"

"Not him," said Phones. "If he's set this place to blow, the only place he's heading is the exit to get as far away as possible. He'll be wanting the fastest ship you've got."

"Is all this as bad as it sounds?" Atlanta asked, gesturing to the reactors.

Grupa shook his head. "Worse," he said gravely. "We're looking at all three reactors going critical just under twenty minutes from now..."

"I don't understand," Atlanta said. "Can't we just shut them down before they reach that point?"

Grupa gestured to the levers on the console. "Try," he said, stepping aside to allow her access.

After glancing at Troy for reassurance Atlanta stepped forward and attempted to lower one of the levers out of the danger point. When it proved too difficult to move it with one hand she tried again with both, but still made no progress. "I can't," she said finally. "It won't even budge..."

"What you're feeling," Grupa explained, "is the power feedback loop that Titan has created across all three reactors. A buildup of energy that even now continues to grow."

"That energy can't simply be absorbed back into the reactors," Noctus added. "It has to go somewhere."

"Can't we syphon it off somehow?" Fisher asked.

"The only place it could go is into the city's main power supply grid," Grupa explained. "But there's so much energy built up in the reactors now that to do so would almost certainly overload the entire grid."

"Which is why you feel such strong resistance in the control levers," Noctus added. "It's to prevent that much energy from being dumped into the grid at once. If that were to happen the damage to Igneathea would be incalculable…"

"It is just feasible that it *could* be done," Grupa confirmed. "But it would mean someone still being here at the controls lowering the levers as the power grid overloads. It's either that, or allow the reactors to go critical…"

"How many ships do you have available?" Troy asked.

"Ships? A dozen battlecruisers, several unarmed support craft – about twenty, I should think. Why?"

"Is that enough to hold everyone currently in the city?"

Grupa had a horrible feeling that he knew exactly where this conversation was heading. "Yes, just about…"

"Then you've got to order an immediate evacuation of Igneathea," Troy urged him. "Get all of your people onto those ships and get them out of here. We'll take any overflow in Stingray."

"And what about the Chamber of the Cooperative?" Noctus asked incredulously. "Grupa, you can't agree to this! We can't just leave them all down there!"

"And just how do you suggest that we relocate one hundred and sixty thousand people in the short time we have left?" Grupa snapped. "We'll barely have enough time to get the city evacuated!"

"Grupa, we are responsible—"

"I *know* that, Noctus! Better than you could ever understand. But there is nothing we can do for them now." Alarmed at his outburst, Grupa patted his protégé on the shoulder, before more calmly adding "They're far enough below the city and there's enough power stored in the underground batteries that they… they may yet survive, at least until an alternate power supply can be established."

"You guys don't have time to argue about this," Sara said firmly. "If this city is gonna be completely evacuated in the next fifteen minutes, we've all got to move fast to get it done."

"We?"

"Sure feller, we're all in this together now," Phones said cheerfully. "After all, what's the alternative?" A murmur of agreement rippled amongst the other W.A.S.P. operatives.

Grupa nodded to his subordinate. "Noctus, get to the control room," he said firmly. "Order an immediate evacuation of Igneathea."

For a moment it looked like Noctus wanted to protest still further, but one look at the readouts over the reactor controls changed his mind. They would be racing against time to save even a few people now. "Understood, Grupa..."

"We can help you organise that," Atlanta offered, and as Noctus hurried from the room he had Atlanta, Fisher, Sara and Marina hot on his heels. As he watched them go, Troy heard Grupa straining behind him. Turning, he saw the city administrator attempting to lower one of the reactor control levers out of the danger level.

"What are you doing?" Troy asked.

"As I said," Grupa explained in a pained voice, "it is not inconceivable that the reactor overload could be averted if these levers can be lowered out of the danger point. As leader of the Igneathean people, it is my duty to remain here and attempt to save our city..."

But even as he said the words, Troy could tell that Grupa had no chance of achieving his goal. He may have possessed a genius for engineering, strategy and leadership – but he clearly lacked the physical strength necessary to move even one of these levers, let alone all three, out of the danger zone before time ran out.

"Phones," Troy said quietly, "get to Stingray and get her prepped for launch. If I'm not back in time, go without me."

"Troy, you're not thinking what I think you're thinking... are you?"

Troy turned to face his old friend. "Phones, we're partly responsible for this. We let Titan get away, this is on us."

"Aww Troy, nobody can blame us for what Titan did..."

"Maybe not," Troy replied, shooting a look back towards the flashing red danger symbols on the reactor controls and Grupa straining in vain with the levers. "But you saw how many people are down there in that cave. We can't just abandon them to their fate..."

Turning back to face Phones, he held out his hand. "Wait as long as you can, but if I'm not back in time... well, look after them all for me, will you?"

"You know it, Troy..." Phones wasn't an overly sentimental man – at least, he'd never seemed that way to Troy – but as his friend gripped his hand firmly Troy could see in his eyes a reflection of the admiration and respect that their long years of comradeship had brought. "Don't leave it too late, alright?"

Troy smiled fondly. "Just you keep my seat warm," he said.

"Always," Phones replied with a grin. Then he turned and bounded from the power room, and Troy approached Grupa.

"I don't think there's much you can do here," he said, easing the smaller man away from the controls. "And your people, however many of them survive, are still going to need a leader when all this is through. I'll take over here."

Grupa watched in astonishment as Troy took hold of the lever he had been grappling with, and, taking hold of it with both hands, pulled down on it firmly. It still didn't move, but as Grupa watched his old enemy attempting to save their city he could see that Troy had more of the physical strength required to achieve the task than he himself did.

"Why?" Grupa asked. "After all we've done to you, why would you help us?"

As he strained against the force of the power feedback forcing the lever to stubbornly remain where it was, Troy took a moment to consider Grupa's question. After trying and failing to come up with something profound – since these might after all be the last words he'd ever say to anybody – he realised that there was only one answer he could give; the truth.

"Because that's the only way we're ever going to have peace between your world and mine," he said. "Andy, take him to Stingray."

The Aquaphibian grunted in acknowledgement, then grabbed Grupa by the arm and followed Phones. Troy watched them go... then redoubled his efforts to avert disaster...

"Attention all citizens. This is a mandatory evacuation order. Please make your way immediately to the nearest travel tube and report to the docking bays for evacuation vessel assignments. I repeat..."

Halfway across the city, Titan ducked out of sight as a group of approaching Igneatheans hurried past him, on their way towards the docking bay to board one of the submarines about to depart the city. Exactly where he had been trying to get to.

He seethed with frustration. Maybe he could have snuck aboard undetected before the evacuation order had been given, but he'd never get out of the city aboard one of their vessels now. He'd stick out like a sore thumb amid the panicking throng.

Which left only one escape route open to him.

The irony of it was not lost on Titan, but he didn't have any time to find an alternative. With the Igneathean vessels now off limits, and the mechanical fish replicas still drydocked in the workshop, there was only one kind of vessel that could get him away from the city in time.

Swallowing his pride, Titan slipped quietly through the door marked 'Prototype Harbour'...

Back at the airlock, the Stingray crew were standing on the sub's hull waiting anxiously for Troy's return. At the sound of approaching footsteps they braced themselves for his arrival... but it was only Noctus returning with the Igneatheans from the control centre.

"The evacuation's well underway," he told them as they helped usher the Igneatheans aboard. "Ships have already begun to depart and all personnel are being checked aboard. Anyone there's no room for will be redirected here."

"Troy's cutting it fine," Fisher said grimly, glancing at his watch.

"He knows how long he's got," Atlanta said nervously. "He'll be back in time. He... he must be!" Beside her, she felt Marina rubbing her arm in sympathy.

Sara noticed the gesture and suddenly felt oddly out of place among such a close-knit group. The idea of Troy risking his life when he so clearly belonged here with his friends didn't sit well with her – so, as she often did when something felt wrong, she decided to do something about it.

"I'll go see what's taking him so long," Sara volunteered, pushing her way past the others and leaping onto the quayside.

"Hold it!" Phones cried. "We shouldn't go splitting up. Troy'll want us all together when he gets back."

"And we will be," Sara promised. "There's still eight minutes left, we've plenty of time!" And with that, she sprinted away, leaving the W.A.S.P.s to watch helplessly as she disappeared out of sight.

Now they had two friends to worry about.

Grupa had insisted on making sure that all the evacuation ships got away from the city before he did, which meant that he had had to persuade Andy to make a detour to see the last vessel depart before they headed on to Stingray. He had no intention of attempting to board one himself to elude the justice of the terraineans, but as the leader of Igneathea the responsibility he felt for its citizens demanded he ensure they all got away safely.

Even so, there were just slightly more people than they had ships for, so now he and Andy were escorting a group of a dozen Igneatheans back to Stingray. As they approached the corridor leading to the airlock where the sub was moored, they were just in time to see Lieutenant Coral running towards them. She didn't stop to tell them where she was going, and they didn't ask – but the sight of her running past suddenly caused Grupa to realise a possible solution to all their problems. "Of course!" he cried. "Why didn't I think of that before?"

The Aquaphibian stared at him blankly. "Er…"

"Our females! Only one of them might have the physical strength necessary to bring these reactor levers back to normal levels." Checking around their group, he noticed that all of the Igneatheans walking with them were male. "Ah, but they'll all be aboard the evacuation ships by now…" He quickened his pace. "When we reach Stingray I shall have one stopped and one of the guards ordered to return to the power room immediately…"

Grupa had led his party all the way back to Stingray before he realised that the Aquaphibian was no longer by his side…

"Captain, we've done all we can here. I think it's time to go!"

Troy didn't look up as he heard Sara approaching. Every muscle in his arms ached with the strain of attempting to force the lever to move. "It's budging…" he groaned, forcing his full weight against it. "Only another inch or so… and we'll have this one below the danger line…"

Sara glanced at the monitor. "Troy, there's only six minutes left. If we're gonna get out of here in time, we *have* to leave now."

But Troy shook his head. "Sara, beneath this city there's a vast chamber full of Igneatheans in hibernation. If these reactors blow, it'll mean the deaths of hundreds of thousands of people." The pain of his efforts was all too visible on Troy's face, but he went on. "Sure, they may technically be our enemies... they may even have plotted to destroy us... but it doesn't mean that they don't deserve a chance to live...!"

And this is why none of them can imagine life without him, Sara thought to herself. "I never thought for a moment that it did," she replied in a quiet voice heavy with admiration, as she moved to add her strength to his.

"Less than five minutes to go..."

The quiet calm in Fisher's voice was entirely at odds with the increasingly bleak mood among the W.A.S.P. officers standing on Stingray's hull. Fisher looked up from his watch as Phones stepped towards him, and he could tell that his colleague was thinking exactly the same thing as he was. *They're not going to be back in time...*

"Lieutenant," Phones said with an uncharacteristic seriousness, "get to the controls. Start her up."

This was one order Fisher would have given anything not to have to obey, but he understood what needed to be done. He nodded, then climbed down into Stingray and headed for the control cabin to prepare the sub for departure.

"We're not leaving!" Atlanta cried. "Phones, we can't!"

"Atlanta, we've gotta be ready. If Troy and Sara don't make it back—"

"Then we stay until they do," she said firmly, as beside her Marina nodded in furious agreement. "And if we don't get out in time, then—"

"Honey, it's not just us. We got a whole heaping helping of refugees aboard Stingray to think about now too." Putting his arms around Atlanta and Marina, he added gravely "You think Troy'd thank us for throwing away all their lives...?"

"No," Atlanta replied quietly, drying her eyes with the back of her hand. "No, of course he wouldn't..." Marina was also shaking her head in solemn agreement.

"We'll give them every second," he assured them both, "but when I say it's time to go – we are going, no matter what..."

In the power room, Troy and Sara were trying desperately to wring every last ounce of strength out of their exhausted muscles in order to shift the reactor lever. They'd made some progress; it was now teetering above the danger line, but even their combined strength wasn't enough to lower it beyond that point. And with only four minutes left, and two more reactors to deal with after this one, only a miracle could save them now.

"Troy, you go," Sara gasped. "Go on, get out of here. They're waiting for you..."

"You choose a heck of a time for a noble gesture..."

Sara shook her head. "It's not being noble, it's just common sense. You have a whole family back at Marineville, people who depend on you. Me, I... well, let's just say that I'm not gonna be missed—"

Troy looked her firmly in the eyes. "Sara, even if I believed that, there is no way I am going to just bail on you. We get this done together – or not at all..."

Sara smiled at him grimly. "I guess that's fair enough. I really couldn't face Atlanta and the others if I came out of this and you didn't..."

Before Troy could reply, the sound of heavy approaching footsteps caught the attention of both officers. "Friend Tempest!"

"Andy?"

The Aquaphibian bounded over to them with a purposeful look on his face. "I am strong," he announced proudly, gently pushing them aside and taking hold of the lever with both hands. Summoning all his strength, Andy pulled down on it – and it slowly began to lower past the danger level.

"I don't believe it..." Sara gasped. "He's doing it. He's actually doing it!"

"Yeah – but it still might not be enough," Troy noted gravely. "He's gonna be fighting against that power loop all the way."

"I heard what you said..." Andy grunted as he continued to pull the lever slowly down.

"About what?" Troy asked.

"About Titan. Titan got away... because I did not pay attention. You did not tell them that."

"Well, it hardly seemed the right time to debate blame..."

"And Titan caused this," Andy gurgled. "So... I am responsible... I must make amends... and I shall..."

As if to prove the point, he gave a great heave on the lever and pulled it all the way to the bottom – and one of the three flashing red lights on the console above them abruptly disappeared. Reactor number one had been successfully shut down – but the display on the console still showed that two and three were going to blow in less than three minutes. Andy took hold of the second lever, and began the process all over again.

Troy felt Sara's hand on his shoulder. "Troy, there's nothing we can do here now..."

"Yeah..." Troy knew she was right, and yet he hated to leave Andy behind. Looking into the face of a being whose species he had never known as anything other than an enemy, Troy wondered what the Aquaphibian's life might have been like if he had ever known anything other than servitude to Titan.

"Thank you," he said quietly, placing a grateful hand on Andy's shoulder.

Now fully concentrating on his vital task, the Aquaphibian still managed to grunt a grateful acknowledgement. "Titan bad. Tempest... friend..."

"Come on, Captain!" called Sara from the power room door.

Troy took one last regretful look back at Andy, still consumed with his mission at the reactor controls... and then followed her.

Inside Stingray it was standing room only as Troy and Sara fought their way past a throng of Igneatheans to get to the upper level. "All set to go, Phones?" Troy asked as he leapt into the captain's chair.

"Just about," Phones confirmed. "The last Igneathean subs are away and all our people are here on Stingray. Well, all except..." He looked around, trying to pick one unique face out of the crowd of passengers. "... say, where's Andy?"

"Buying us some time," Troy said bluntly. "So let's not waste it. Get us out of here Phones, fast as we can."

"Aye aye!"

"Everyone hold on tight!" Troy called out to Stingray's passengers. "This could get bumpy."

The airlock seemed to take an eternity to flood, but once it was full and the outer door to the outside world

200

opened Stingray raced away from Igneathea at Rate Six, heading for the tunnel that would lead them from the city's subterranean sea and back up towards the ocean door protecting it.

"Phones, prep a recon buoy and launch when ready," Troy ordered. "We can monitor the city on the video link."

"Right, Troy." Phones operated the necessary control on his console. "Recon buoy away." He smiled, spotting the open ocean door ahead of them. "And there's our light at the end of the tunnel..."

Seconds later Stingray had finally left the tunnel and was back in open sea. Around them the Igneathean evacuation fleet of battlecruisers and support craft closed up in a tight formation, as if aware that their leader was aboard the terrainean vessel and might require protection.

But Grupa was too preoccupied to consider his own safety right now. He was sitting with Noctus in front of one of the portside consoles, watching the video feed from the relay buoy on the monitor. As Troy and Phones approached him, he looked up at them with dread in his eyes.

"One minute until the reactors are due to go critical..." he said quietly.

"Or until we find out if Andy got them back below the danger level," Troy replied.

Grupa nodded, his wide eyes unable to look away from the screen. "Even if he does, the feedback loop will still dump all that energy into Igneathea's power supply grid and devastate the city... I just hope it will not be irreparably so."

"And if he doesn't do it?"

"Then the reactors go critical and Igneathea will be blown out of the water," Grupa said mournfully. "And it will certainly mean the end of our people underground..."

"When I left he'd already shut down one of the reactors," Troy confirmed, remembering his last glimpse of

Andy working at the controls. "As for the last two... well, we'll know soon enough."

"Any moment now," Grupa agreed. "Five, four, three..."

"Everybody find something to hold on to," Troy announced loudly. "Just in case...!"

"..."zero."

All aboard Stingray braced themselves for an atomic shockwave that never came. On the monitor, they watched as the massive egg-like structure that was the city of Igneathea seemed to ripple with a series of wild electrical discharges that grew in intensity with each passing second.

"He's done it," Grupa said quietly. "That's the power supply grid overloading..."

They watched the monitor as jagged forks of energy lashed out into the waters around Igneathea – before quickly arcing back into the city itself, slashing through the outer defences of the enormous structure as if they weren't even there. As the walls of the city were breached massive air pockets billowed into the surrounding water as the sea rushed into Igneathea, surging through almost all sections of the city. The city's lights flickered and then went dark, and several dozen small explosions erupted from various rooms across the surface of the superstructure – but soon the energy had dissipated, the water had settled, and the explosions had ceased. The total destruction of Igneathea had been successfully averted – but with so much damage still done, it was a hollow victory indeed.

Aboard Stingray, the Igneatheans watched in horror as the only home they had stood dark, deserted and devastated. "The city is in ruins," Noctus said quietly.

"But it still stands," Grupa reminded him. "We must be grateful for that. We can rebuild. The damage will no doubt be extensive but it *can* be salvaged."

"And the Chamber of the Cooperative?"

Grupa patted Noctus on the arm. "We shall see." Turning to Troy, he added "Your friend was a very brave man."

"He..." Troy fell silent. He had been about to say that Andy hadn't really been their friend but then he imagined the look of disappointment on the Aquaphibian's face if he'd still been around to hear that, and couldn't bring himself to say those words. "Yeah," he said finally. "He sure was."

"Cap'n!" called Fisher from the pilot's chair. "Hate to bother you skipper, but we've got company; seven mechanical fish, closing fast!"

Rushing to the front of the cabin Troy and Phones slid into their chairs the instant Fisher and Marina vacated them. "That must be Titan's reinforcement fleet," Troy announced. "And their missiles'll be fitted with Professor Burgoyne's strengthened nosecones!"

"Now he tells me!" sighed Phones, looking over his shoulder at Grupa. "This'd be a real good time for that little gizmo of yours to do its stuff."

"Giz... mo?"

"Y'know, that little remote-control thingy of yours. If you took control of their ships, you could end this fight before it started..."

"Ah yes!" Grupa felt about his person for the device, only to come up empty-handed. "I, um, must have left it back in the city..."

"Why are things never straightforward?" sighed Phones.

"May I use your radio?"

Troy gestured to the microphone as Grupa leaned forward to speak into it. "Attention Igneathean fleet, this is Grupa," he began. "The approaching mechanical fish are *not* under our control. I say again, they are hostile. Engage at will. Stingray and our own unarmed vessels must be protected at all costs. Repeat, top priority to defending Stingray and our non-combat vessels. Out."

Troy and Phones looked at Grupa in surprise, but he shrugged it off. "You did not abandon us in our hour of need. It is only right that we not abandon you," he explained, now looking a little self-conscious. "Besides, I happen to have a personal stake in not seeing Stingray destroyed..."

"Heads-up, Troy," cried Phones. "Here they come!"

Unnoticed by anyone aboard Stingray or the Igneathean fleet, a second Stingray now slipped from the tunnel leading from the subterranean sea. At the controls of the duplicate, Titan took in the scene at a glance and smiled at the arrival of his own mechanical fish reinforcements, realising that perhaps it was still possible to salvage something from this disaster.

"Titan to mechanical fish fleet!" he yelled triumphantly into the radio. "You see before you the accursed Stingray, along with the survivors of our bitter enemies the Igneatheans! Attack immediately, and destroy them all!"

Four of the fish immediately moved to engage the Igneathean battlecruisers, but the other three had a different target in their sights; him. He watched as they slowly turned to face him, the jaws of each craft slowly lowering as they prepared to fire. Titan only just had time to take evasive action as their first salvo of missiles tore past him, detonating among some rocks to the aft of his Stingray.

"The fools!" he cried, before yelling at the radio. "Attention mechanical fish fleet! This is Titan, aboard the replica Stingray you have just opened fire on! Call off your attack immediately! You're supposed to destroy Tempest's Stingray, not mine!"

It suddenly occurred to Titan that he didn't know enough about the workings of Stingray to be sure that anyone was even receiving his message. Taking a moment to peer down at the radio, Titan found himself wishing this ridiculous vessel came with some sort of instruction manual – only to grab the controls and hang on for dear life as another nearby explosion shook the entire craft.

"Not this Stingray!" he yelled. "The *other* Stingray!"

But it was no use. It was beginning to dawn on him that piloting Stingray was a two-person job, and right now he was very much alone. Still, how hard could it be? After all, he was Titan, and surely he could handle any terrainean contraption – couldn't he?

A sudden explosion from the rear of Stingray suggested otherwise. The sub pitched into a downward spiral, her cabin lights flashing intermittently as the vessel lost main power, and despite Titan's best efforts to control her the replica Stingray crashed seconds later, eventually coming to rest upside down on the seabed.

Titan barely had time to recover from being thrown out of his chair and landing awkwardly on what used to be the ceiling, before he realised that his face was wet. He looked up, noticing water spraying into the cabin from a small crack in a nearby porthole – which, as he watched, quickly developed into a larger and far more dangerous one.

"Curses! Not again!" he cried, before leaping to his feet and stumbling towards the stairs…

Even with the Burgoyne missiles aboard, the mechanical fish that had decided to engage the Igneathean battlecruisers stood almost no chance. They may have had an advantage in weaponry – but with the devastation of their home the Igneatheans were out for vengeance, and they were merciless in pursuing and destroying the aggressors. One by one the mechanical fish were isolated from the rest of their patrol and overwhelmed – without getting anywhere close to firing range of the real Stingray.

"Troy, the other three seem to be retreating," Phones observed. "Looks like they're heading back to Titanica."

"Ah, let 'em go Phones. There's been enough life lost today." Relinquishing his chair to Fisher once again, Troy now returned to Grupa and Noctus, who were both still staring at the monitor displaying the image of the ruined Igneathea. He reached over their heads to turn it off, and they turned to face him.

"I trust you realise that we can't let the two of you go," Troy said quietly. "You're both under arrest, once again, for crimes against the World Aquanaut Security Patrol."

Noctus jumped to his feet, an indignant look on his face. "You can't do that!" he insisted. "Our people have just lost everything, their home, their history – perhaps even their brothers and sisters underground. They *need* Grupa's leadership, to…"

He fell silent as he felt Grupa's hand squeeze his arm. "He is right, Noctus. We must return with them to Marineville to atone for what we have done."

"Then let it be I alone that faces the punishment! You are needed here."

But Grupa shook his head. "Unacceptable. I will contact the other ships and appoint a temporary leader to take charge of things here."

Realising his friend could not be persuaded otherwise, Noctus sank back into his chair with a defeated look on his face. "Are these others your prisoners too, terrainean?" he asked, gesturing to the other Igneatheans aboard the cramped Stingray.

"Not at all," Troy replied, "but they can hardly stay here. For now we'll take them back to Marineville with us and fix 'em up with temporary accommodation until there's room for them to return to your people."

"Commander Shore might even agree to bring a ship out here for them to live in until you get your city repaired," Phones suggested. "Since we'll have to bring your people on those ships supplies for the short term anyhoo…"

Noctus looked to his mentor. "And you agree to this, Grupa?"

"I do."

"Why?"

Although Grupa's words were directed at Noctus, he was now looking at Troy, remembering the captain's bravery in his attempt to save Igneathea from disaster. "Because that's the only way we're ever going to have peace between their world and ours," he replied, extending a hand in friendship. Smiling, Troy wasted no time in reaching out and shaking that hand warmly.

It was good to see that his words had touched the heart of more than one underwater creature today.

The designers and engineers who had between them devised the aquasprites, the mini-submarines attached to Stingray, would have congratulated themselves if they could have seen the way a perfect duplicate of one of their creations was currently banking and weaving from its pursuers. But, if any of them had been within Titan's reach right now, he would have strangled them for creating such a slow and rather cramped vessel.

After abandoning the replica Stingray in one of her aquasprites, Titan had attempted to flee the scene of battle unnoticed. Unfortunately, things hadn't gone to plan. Quite the contrary; the three surviving mechanical fish had completely forgotten their attack on the Igneatheans and were now chasing his small aquasprite relentlessly as he attempted to make his escape. As they took turns firing missiles in his direction it was taking all of Titan's piloting skill to keep the small craft from being blown to pieces – and with no weapons aboard the short-range craft, he'd have to rely on his wits alone to outmanoeuvre his pursuers all the way home. Considering the limited speed and manoeuvrability of the aquasprite, and the relative stupidity of the Aquaphibians, it was probably an even match –

which meant it was going to be a long and uncomfortable journey back to Titanica.

"Curse those foolish Aquaphibians!" he cried, as another missile detonated less than fifty yards from the aquasprite. "Curse those wretched Igneatheans! And a thousand curses on Troy Tempest and Stingray!"

CHAPTER 12

Fool's Bargain

A few days later, in the conference room of the Marineville control tower, all eyes were on Grupa as he stepped forward to sign a document that lay on the long table in the centre of the room. Also in attendance were all those who had been involved with the Igneathea incident, including Noctus, the Stingray crew and control tower staff, as well as several of Commander Shore's superiors from World Security Patrol Headquarters in Washington.

"As representatives of the Igneathean Cooperative," Grupa began, "we officially agree to an end to hostilities between the Igneatheans and the terrainean peoples... and we most gratefully accept the assistance of the World Government in the rebuilding of our city."

Some work had already been done on that front. Upon returning to Marineville the Stingray crew had stressed the urgency of determining the fates of the Igneatheans residing underground, and had returned the following day with a team of scientists and engineers in order to do just that. Despite the massive damage to the city, which would be the work of many months to repair, the underground chamber many miles beneath it had suffered only minimal damage.

Thanks to the sacrifice of one brave Aquaphibian, the power supply to the life support capsules had not been interrupted even when the power grid in the city had been destroyed, meaning that the hibernating Igneatheans were still sleeping as soundly as if nothing had ever happened. Some who had escaped from the city had even volunteered to go back into suspended animation, easing the burden of resources on the small fleet of ships that even now still guarded the ocean door leading to Igneathea against reprisal attacks from Titan.

"Thank you, Grupa," said Commander Shore. "And now it is my duty to inform you of your sentence, as decreed by the World Government Supreme Court."

Taking a deep breath, he began to recite the list of charges. "Grupa, you have been found guilty of plotting and carrying out terrorist attacks against the surface peoples of the Earth, including the devastation and destruction of multiple civilian and military vessels and installations around the area of Manila Bay, with loss of life calculated at some forty-seven men and women. You have been sentenced to forty years hard labour at a World Government Maximum Security prison facility in the Netherlands, at the end of which time your case will be assessed once more."

If Grupa was unhappy with the verdict, it didn't show on his face. He merely nodded in acknowledgement of the sentence, not expecting to be let off lightly after everything he had carried out in the name of the Igneathean Cooperative.

Shore then turned to address Grupa's long-time associate. "Noctus, you have been found guilty of conspiring to aid and abet these attacks against the surface world. You have been sentenced to a thirty-year prison sentence at the same facility. That sentence is hereby suspended, and you are remanded to the custody of the World Security Patrol Engineering Corps, to assist first in the rebuilding of the surface installations destroyed by your duplicate Stingrays, and then in the reconstruction of the city of Igneathea. Once those tasks are accomplished, you will be free to rejoin your people."

Noctus' eyes widened in surprise at the verdict. He looked towards Grupa, who appeared to be smiling.

"Unless there are any other questions?" Shore asked. "Okay, that's it. This meeting is dismissed."

As the assembled delegates began to file out of the room, Shore fell in alongside one of his superiors. "George, if you can spare a moment, I need to call in a favour..."

Noctus meanwhile was still trying to comprehend the verdict that had just been handed down to him. "I do not understand, Grupa," he said, as the security guards they were handcuffed to started to usher the two Igneatheans towards the door. "I was with you almost every moment of the attack on the terraineans. I carried out the orders of the Cooperative just as you did. Yet you receive the harsher penalty?"

But Grupa was still smiling. "Things are as I would have them be. I led, you followed faithfully, as you have always done. It is right that you not escape punishment entirely. But a new Igneathea requires a new leader, and I believe that only one who has seen the destruction our warlike thinking brought upon us can take on that role. You my friend are the bridge between the old and the new, so your task is the harder; convincing the Cooperative that our future lies in cooperation with outsiders as well as ourselves. You *must* make sure that they understand it was our own hubris as much as Titan's treachery that led to our downfall!"

"I will ensure that the change you speak of begins today," Noctus promised. "We will make the new Igneathea one of the true wonders of the underwater world. It will be as though the original had never fallen!"

"Of that I have no doubt, my friend," Grupa replied proudly. "Just make sure that it doesn't follow the original in every detail. It is true there is value in preserving our history and heritage – but it would not do to get lost in our past and ignore our future. We *must* have a future, and with the aid of the terraineans, we shall."

"I understand, Grupa." Noctus stopped at the door, raising his free hand and extending his palm towards Grupa. Grupa matched the gesture, pressing his hand firmly against Noctus'.

"Until we meet again, Noctus."

"Farewell, Grupa."

And with that, the two security guards led the Igneatheans away into the corridor – albeit in separate directions.

Troy watched them go, and then realised that he was now almost totally alone in the conference room. One man however was still sitting at the table, staring into space apparently deep in thought.

"Something wrong, Phones?" Troy asked as he approached him.

"Yeah," Phones admitted quietly. "Just thinking about Andy. All these debriefings, conferences and hearings since we got back, and the poor guy's not been mentioned once."

Troy thought about that for a moment, then smiled. "Seems to me that he has been mentioned, several times," he said, sitting down in the chair next to Phones. "You heard the report from the Engineering Corps. If those reactors had gone critical it would have not only obliterated the city, but also buried the hibernation chamber beyond anybody's ability to reach it. As it is, that last working reactor is now supplying the power that's keeping them alive. Those one hundred and sixty thousand Igneatheans down there would have died if not for him."

"That's a lotta people alright," Phones agreed. "Too bad not one of them knows what he did for them."

"Yeah... well, maybe you could suggest to the new Igneathean ambassador that once they've rebuilt their city they erect some kind of statue or monument in his memory?"

That brought a smile to Phones' face. "Yeah," he agreed excitedly. "Yeah, maybe I will..."

"Come on," Troy said, giving his friend a gentle pat on the arm, "Commander Shore's got something important he wants us all in the control tower for..."

"So we still don't know for sure whether or not Titan made it out of Igneathea before the city exploded?"

"No Commander," Troy replied. "But I wouldn't wanna bet against it."

"Yeah, me neither," Phones added. "That creep's got more lives than a catfish."

"Well, if he did get away, I hope this experience left such a bitter taste in his mouth that it'll have nipped this whole 'alliance' idea in the bud," Shore replied. "Though something tells me the Harmonians and the Igneatheans were only the beginning..."

"Yeah," Troy sighed. "If only we'd been able to recover those stolen documents we might at least have been able to slow him down on that front."

"Well, we may have caught a break there Troy," Shore told him, before nodding to Sara. "Okay, Lieutenant Coral, let's have him in here."

"Sir." Sara moved to the door and gestured to Sergeant Waterman waiting in the corridor outside. Stepping aside to let him into the control room, Troy and Phones were surprised to discover that Waterman was handcuffed to a prisoner; a diminutive underwater being that Phones didn't recognise and Troy had only ever caught a brief glimpse of.

"Gentlemen, this is Sculpin," explained Shore. "Incredible as it sounds, he's the diabolical mastermind who carried out the theft of the Stingray records from our archive."

"How did he get here?" Phones asked.

"Would you believe he turned himself in?" Shore asked. "Yep. Chugged into Marineville in a mechanical fish while you were all trying to get out of Igneathea."

"Well, this beats me, Commander," admitted Troy. "What kind of spy decides to turn himself in to the enemy?"

"The kind in fear for his life!" Sculpin explained. "Thanks to you Tempest, I failed Titan once before – and he almost had me put to death! I knew that if his latest plan... um, which I may have played a small part in formulating... also failed, I'd be the one to take the blame again – and this time he wouldn't be so merciful."

"What made you so sure that Titan's plan would fail?" Phones asked.

"Because when they involve the W.A.S.P.s, *all* of Titan's plans fail," Sculpin explained simply. "So I figured that the best way to ensure my own survival was to go along with this latest scheme, while also taking the opportunity to prepare an escape route for myself. It didn't matter to me where I ended up, just so long as I got away from Titan." He clapped his hands in excitement. "And I did!"

"Turns out the trash can he used to leave Marineville wasn't the one he arrived in," Shore explained. "Lieutenant Coral here discovered that one during her investigation..."

"Which Sculpin had kitted out to serve as a communications relay between Titanica and Marineville," added Sara. "He made contact with us through that shortly before we came out to rescue you, and the Commander took over the negotiations after we left."

"You kept quiet about that!" Atlanta noted.

Sara grinned, and tapped her nose. "I wanted to surprise you," she replied.

"What negotiations would these be?" Phones asked.

"Well, while you were all away, Mr Sculpin and I struck a bargain," Shore explained. "We'd give him sanctuary from Titan, in exchange for getting those documents back."

"A nice quiet life as a W.A.S.P. prisoner of war in a nice quiet jail somewhere far away from Titanica," Sculpin sighed happily. "That's all I really want..."

"And you agreed to this, sir?" Troy asked Shore incredulously.

Shore shrugged. "Look Troy, he had us over a barrel on this one. I don't much care what happens to this guy, just so long as we get those papers away from Titan." Shore held out his hand to Sculpin. "So, Mr Sculpin – our stolen documents, if you please?"

The smile suddenly fell from Sculpin's face. "Ah, yes, the papers, well... um... you see, I tried, I really did try! But I, um... I couldn't get them..."

"You couldn't get them, I see..." Shore's voice was quiet and matter-of-fact, but everyone in the control room knew him well enough to understand that he was about to explode. Everyone, that is, apart from Sculpin, who almost fainted when Shore suddenly rounded on him and roared, "So what in thunder makes you think that I won't just drop you in the middle of the ocean and call up Titan to come and collect you?"

Sculpin's heart sank as he felt his carefully detailed plan falling apart before his eyes. "But... but you *can't* do that! Please! You promised me sanctuary if I—"

"*If* you returned the documents you stole from our archive, I know!" Shore reminded him. "*Are* you in a position to do so at this very moment?"

In desperation Sculpin patted himself all over with his free hand, finally locating a single crumpled piece of paper in his pocket. "Yes, er... here you go! I–it's the page containing the formula for the Burgoyne metal."

Shore took the paper from Sculpin, and frowned at it. "Huh. One down. That only leaves... how many more was it, Lieutenant?"

"Four hundred and fourteen, sir," Sara replied instantly.

"In other words, Mr Sculpin, the way I figure it you haven't quite met the conditions of our bargain," Shore went on, much to Sculpin's horror. "Which means that until you do, I can't offer you sanctuary, asylum or even a bed for the night."

"But surely you have a cell!?" pleaded Sculpin. "Or even an empty cupboard somewhere? I–I really don't take up that much space!"

"Lieutenant Coral?"

Sara shook her head firmly. "No can do, sir. We're full to the brim providing temporary shelter for the Igneathean refugees that came back with us."

"That's what I figured," Shore replied, turning back to the increasingly panic-stricken Sculpin. "However, if you *were* able to retrieve those documents for us, I might – just *might* – be willing to reconsider your case. Until then, your request for asylum is denied." He nodded to Sara. "Okay Lieutenant, get him out of here."

"Sergeant." At Sara's command, Waterman marched the heartbroken Sculpin away. "You know where to take him…" she said ominously, as they walked past her and out into the corridor.

"Well, how do you like the nerve of that guy?" Troy asked in amazement as the door swung shut behind them. "He robs our archive, then expects *us* to give *him* a break!"

"Kinda feel for him though," Phones replied. "After what I saw of Titan up close I know that if I lived in Titanica I wouldn't wanna work for him either!"

As laughter rang out in the control tower Sara also smiled, realising how much she loved the easy camaraderie the Marineville personnel enjoyed – which only made her next task all the more difficult. It was time to say her farewells. "Well, with the guy who broke into your records archive identified and apprehended – sort of – I guess it's time for me to be on my way," she said reluctantly. "It's been one of the greatest honours of my life serving with you all, and—"

"Hold on there, Lieutenant," Shore interrupted gruffly. "Now just where do you think you're going?"

Sara blinked in surprise. "Well, I–I rather thought my assignment here was over... um, sir."

"Oh, you did, did you?" She fell silent as Shore fixed her with a stern look that reminded her of more than one instructor from her academy days. "Now listen here Lieutenant, I'm in charge of Marineville and I decide when an assignment is over, is that understood?"

Sara instinctively snapped to attention. "Sir, yes sir!"

"That's *better.*" Shore began to pace up and down the control room in his hoverchair. "Now, since you've returned to Marineville, I have personally received reports from no less than *five* members of the W.A.S.P.s – who shall remain nameless! – regarding your performance during Stingray's last mission. And some quite startling allegations have been made against you!"

"Allegations?" Sara was horrified. "Sir, I can't imagine—"

Shore rounded on Sara. "For heaven's sake, will you be *quiet* Lieutenant?" he snapped, before resuming his hover-pacing once he was satisfied she wouldn't interrupt again. "Now, these allegations range from conspicuous dedication to duty and meticulous attention to detail, to notable prowess in combat and even, on more than one occasion, risking your life to save others."

Sara felt the mood in the control tower beginning to lighten considerably, and as her new friends gathered around her she began to realise what was happening. They were giving her the one thing she wanted more than anything else; a place where she belonged.

"All this tells me that you're an exemplary officer and I'd be a fool to let you go so easily," Commander Shore continued. "Particularly, now that Sculpin has failed to live up to his end of our bargain, since we have this increased threat from Titan to worry about." He now turned to face Sara with a proud smile on his face.

"So, until further notice, and with the full blessing of your superiors at World Security Patrol Headquarters, I'm officially placing you in command of the Marineville police." He held out his hand, and she shook it eagerly. "Congratulations, Lieutenant. You made enough noise about 'em not being up to scratch – well, here's your chance to whip 'em into shape."

"Thank you, sir!"

"But before all that, you're the guest of honour at an official 'Welcome to Marineville' party at Marina's house tonight," Atlanta added cheerfully.

"I don't know what to say!" Sara gasped as Marina almost knocked her off her feet in her haste to give her neighbour a hug. "Well, you all know how to make a girl feel welcome, and... and I'm more grateful than I can say. Thank you, all of you."

"It's us who should be thanking you," Troy replied.

"Yeah," Phones agreed. "If you hadn't come to our rescue we could still be locked in a cell with Titan right now..."

Sara was now blushing, a problem that only increased as Fisher hesitantly stepped forward. "Lieutenant," he asked nervously, "I–I've never done anything like this before, but... well, would you know what to say if I suggested drinks tomorrow night at the Blue Lagoon?"

Sara's big brown eyes sparkled with excitement. "You mean... just the two of us?"

"That's what I was thinking... b–but only if you really w–"

But the rest of Fisher's words were cut short as Sara leapt towards him and pressed her lips firmly against his.

Totally unprepared for the kiss, Fisher soon found himself returning it, and when it was over there was a smile of true contentment on Sara's beautiful dark face. "That's what I say to that," she replied happily.

"Great! Well, shall I pick you up at eight?" Another kiss followed, much to Atlanta and Marina's amusement. "...s–seven?"

"Ain't there some rule about officers kissing other officers in the control tower?" Phones asked.

"Well, if there isn't now there soon will be if they keep that up," Shore snapped. "Okay you two, knock it off already!"

As Phones, Atlanta, Fisher and Marina crowded around Sara, asking her what her plans were for her new job, talking about places around Marineville they wanted to show her and people they wanted her to meet, she could only stand there and drink it all in. She was feeling truly happy for the first time in her life. Finally, she was home.

Away from the rest of their colleagues, Troy addressed Commander Shore. "Well, aside from Titan, his alliance and those documents, that seems to wrap everything up nicely Commander," he noted. "Except for one little thing – what are you planning to do about Sculpin?"

But Shore just chuckled, in a way that told Troy he'd already decided *exactly* what to do. "Yeah... what *are* we going to do about Sculpin?"

EPILOGUE

Tea For Three

"**M**ore seaweed tea, great Titan?"

Titan barely noticed as X-20 poured him another steaming mug of his favourite beverage from the antique teapot on the dining table before them. Since his return to Titanica several days ago he had barely spoken to X-20, or indeed to anyone. The events of Igneathea were too painful, too humiliating, to be shared.

When his stolen aquasprite had finally reached Titanica after more than a day's journey back from Igneathea, it had arrived burned, battered and holed in several places – most notably the cabin. After exiting the craft Titan's first order of business had been to identify the Aquaphibians who had been shooting at him all the way home – only to realise for the first time that one Aquaphibian looked much the same as another. He did briefly consider having the entire species exterminated for all the trouble they had caused him during this affair but that would only cause more problems than it solved – and it would certainly spoil the homecoming banquet they'd decided to throw in his honour.

"Perhaps it would help to talk about what happened to you while you were away?" X-20 suggested. "They do say a problem shared is a problem... um..." He trailed off, as Titan's angry glare made him realise just how little he'd actually missed his master during his absence.

"X-20," Titan began, "believe me, your attempts to lift my spirits are not unappreciated. But if you utter one more syllable I shall have you destroyed."

X-20 nodded, and helped himself to a barnacle biscuit from the tea tray. The two men sat in silence, sipping at their tea, until finally Titan looked around the room in slight confusion. "And just where is Sculpin hiding himself?" he asked.

X-20 opened his mouth to reply, then quickly shut it again. Titan rolled his eyes. "You may speak," he sighed.

"Sculpin has not returned, majesty," X-20 explained. "He volunteered – er, I mean, I ordered him to take charge of the reinforcement fleet, but he was not aboard any of the mechanical fish that, ah, 'escorted' you back to Titanica."

"Then the fool must have perished in the battle at Igneathea!" Titan fumed. "A pity. His scheme to infiltrate Marineville proved surprisingly successful. I was anticipating great things from him…"

Before X-20 could reply, a loud crash reverberated around the throne room, causing the two men to jump to their feet and sending Teufel into a tizzy in his tank. "What is happening?" Titan cried. He'd already had more than enough drama for one week.

"Look, Titan!" X-20 was pointing towards the ocean window, where a small projectile was slowly drifting towards the seabed, having apparently struck the reinforced glass just seconds earlier.

"A missile! We must be under attack!" Cautiously, Titan and X-20 approached the window, scanning the surrounding sea for any sign of potential aggressors but finding none.

"Not just any missile, Titan," observed X-20. "I believe that one comes from one of our own mechanical fish!"

Titan squinted at the projectile, then nodded. "You are correct, X-20! It *is* one of ours." He rubbed his chin thoughtfully, watching as the missile finally came to rest nose-first on the seabed outside. "But the question is; who fired it at us? And why?"

"Perhaps the more important question we should be asking ourselves," suggested X-20 as he began to back nervously away from the window, "is why hasn't it gone off yet?"

Suddenly the missile belched a flurry of bubbles, as a hatch almost as tall as a man opened on one side – revealing that there was indeed a man inside. Titan and X-20 both tilted their heads to get a better look at the small, green-skinned figure waving at them from the interior of the missile. Even upside down, he looked very familiar.

"Get him in here!"

Sculpin wanted to cry. He'd come so close to escaping from Titan forever. His plan had been foolproof but for that one moment in the lab when X-20 had accidentally ruined it all for him by showing up when he had. By now Sculpin could have been safely installed in some terrainean prison facility somewhere, forever safe from the wrath of Titan and eventually free to start a new life elsewhere in the underwater world. All he truly wanted was somewhere quiet and trouble-free to live out his remaining marine years, without the constant fear that came with life in Titanica.

Instead, he now found himself *back* in Titanica, standing before the throne of the one man he feared more than anyone else in the world – and in the position of having to make up a credible story for how he had got here.

"As you know, great Titan, *I* was in command of the reinforcements that were sent to rescue you," he explained, desperately punctuating his story with dramatic gestures to give it more credibility. "There I was, valiantly leading the charge against the Igneathean battlecruisers and the accursed Stingray—"

Titan leaned forward on his throne. "*Which* Stingray?"

Sculpin suddenly had a horrible feeling he was skirting around the edge of a very sensitive subject. "I–I was aware of only one…"

Titan nodded and leaned back. "That's alright then. Continue."

"Anywhere, there I was, in the centre of a long and fierce battle indeed but despite the bravery of our loyal Aquaphibians and the tactical genius of my good self, we were soon overwhelmed by superior firepower. My fish was eventually the last one standing, but soon even we were hit by enemy fire. I was doomed!"

It may have been hysteria brought on by fear but Sculpin found he was starting to become caught up in the drama of his own fiction. It wasn't often he got to imagine himself as a hero. "Those cowardly Aquaphibians abandoned ship, but thinking fast, I managed to remove the warhead from one of our missiles, climbed inside, and reprogrammed the guidance system to bring me safely to Titanica – before launching myself away from the doomed fish!"

He shook his head at the memory of his fictional ordeal – at least the next part of his story was somewhat true. "Oh, the journey was an arduous one, but I had no fear, for I knew that my faith in the great Titan would deliver me safely home." He only hoped it sounded more credible than the truth; that he'd attempted to defect to the W.A.S.P.s and that the infuriating Commander Shore had rewarded his failure to return the stolen documents by stuffing him into a missile casing and having him fired from his own mechanical fish back into Titanica as punishment.

Titan was now inspecting his fingernails in a disinterested manner. "And I trust you spent your journey home devising another plan to rid me of Troy Tempest and Stingray?" he asked. "That is, if you don't want a one-way trip back to Aquatraz?"

"A p–plan? Oh, yes, naturally, I thought of little else..."

"Then share this great plan, so that I may pass judgement on it."

Sculpin's heart skipped a beat. Why did life hate him so much? He'd just spent four hours locked inside a missile and now here was Titan demanding a world-beating plan. Straining to think of one, Sculpin said the first words that came into his head. "Giant... robot... er, sea snails?" he stammered. Behind him, X-20 buried his face in his hands.

"Giant... robot... sea snails..." Titan repeated slowly. Sculpin nodded, not really caring whether he lived or died anymore. The stony look on Titan's face more than suggested that the latter was a definite possibility, and right now that was fine with him.

Then Titan suddenly jumped to his feet. "Yes," he cried. "I like it! It's the last thing the W.A.S.P.s would ever expect! It has superb potential! The possibilities are endless!" He pointed directly at Sculpin, who instinctively ducked. "You may begin at once!"

Amazed that his hastily conceived notion had actually passed the scrutiny of Titan, but just desperate to leave the room at this point, Sculpin nodded in frantic agreement. "Oh, er, yes. Yes, great Titan! At once, yes..." Against all odds, he'd found another lifeline. Now all he had to do was make it work...

X-20 watched Sculpin with suspicion as he hurried from the throne room. Something about the story of his dramatic escape didn't ring true but until he could more precisely identify what it was that didn't add up here he decided to keep quiet. At least, about Sculpin.

"This notion of forming an alliance to destroy Marineville, Titan," he began hesitantly. "Perhaps it might be worth calling a halt to that plan for the time being?"

"A halt?" asked Titan incredulously.

"Yes, Titan," said X-20, determined to get his point across gently but firmly. "It would be fair to say, would it not, that the Igneatheans did not prove themselves to be worthy of an alliance with the great Titan..."

"That is true," Titan agreed, as he began to slowly descend the stairs from his throne. "Those cringing fools were a great disappointment to me..."

"Therefore, perhaps a period of careful deliberation and reflection is called for," X-20 advised. "A quiet lull in which to consider all possibilities and strategies, with a view to perhaps relaunching the plan at a later date – once we have located potential allies who truly *deserve* to share in the glory of your triumph."

Even as X-20 spoke those calm well-chosen words, he knew that they were all in vain. The same maniacal look that had first sent Titan tearing off on his ill-fated trip to Igneathea had come over his master's face once more, and X-20 knew that events were about to take another needlessly convoluted turn.

"Oh no, X-20," Titan chuckled. "Not when the W.A.S.P.s now know of my plan. They will undoubtedly now begin to seek allies of their own, to defend against our might. Therefore, we must make haste, redouble our efforts to find new recruits for our cause – and forge the greatest and most powerful alliance of underwater nations in history!"

X-20 watched as Titan began to walk over to Teufel's tank, where the large fish barely reacted to his approach. It didn't matter to Titan though; he needed an audience, and his pet god provided a captive one. And as he made eye contact with Teufel, he felt his strength returning, his determination becoming absolute.

"Tremble in fear, terraineans!" he announced as if addressing the whole of humanity. "Let the word go forth to every corner of creation that the mighty Titan, ruler of the underwater city of Titanica, will not rest until Marineville lies burning at his feet! Let Troy Tempest and his wretched flock know that their days are numbered, and let all others who would oppose me be swept aside by the tide of time... because this was only the beginning!"

As Titan's words finally gave way to maniacal laughter, X-20 nodded supportively. It was the only thing he could do, because he didn't dare voice what he was thinking inside.

That's what I was afraid of...

OTHER GREAT TITLES
BY ANDERSON ENTERTAINMENT

STINGRAY

Stingray: Operation Icecap
by John Theydon

The Stingray crew discover an ancient diving bell that leads them on an expeditionary voyage through the freezing waters of Antarctica to the land of a lost civilisation.

Close on the heels of Troy Tempest and the pride of the World Aquanaut Security Patrol is the evil undersea ruler Titan. Ahead of them are strange creatures who inhabit underground waterways and an otherworldly force with hidden powers strong enough to overwhelm even Stingray's defences.

Stingray: Monster from the Deep
by John Theydon

Commander Shore's old enemy, Conrad Hagen, is out of prison and back on the loose with his beautiful but devious daughter, Helga. When they hijack a World Aquanaut Security Patrol vessel and kidnap Atlanta, it's up to Captain Troy Tempest and the crew of Stingray to save her.

But first they will have to uncover the mystery of the treasure of Sanito Cathedral and escape the fury of the monster from the deep.

A GERRY ANDERSON PRODUCTION

Five Star Five: John Lovell and the Zargon Threat

by Richard James

THE TIME: THE FUTURE
THE PLACE: THE UNIVERSE

The peaceful planet of Kestra is under threat. The evil Zargon forces are preparing to launch a devastating attack from an asteroid fortress. With the whole Kestran system in the Zargons' sights, Colonel Zana looks to one man to save them. Except one man isn't enough.

Gathering a crack team around him including a talking chimpanzee, a marauding robot and a mystic monk, John Lovell must infiltrate the enemy base and save Kestra from the Zargons!

Five Star Five: The Doomsday Device

by Richard James

THE TIME: THE FUTURE
THE PLACE: THE UNIVERSE

The Zargon home world is dying. With their nemesis in prison on trumped up charges, they have developed a brand-new weapon of awesome power.

As the Zargons plot another attempt on the planet Kestra, a group of friends must band together and rescue their only hope for survival – John Lovell!

Five Star Five: The Battle for Kestra
by Richard James
THE TIME: THE FUTURE
THE PLACE: THE UNIVERSE

As the Zargons prepare their last, desperate attempt to invade their enemy planet, John Lovell and his gang of misfits stand accused of acts of terror on Kestran soil.

With a new President in place, the 'Five Star Five' are forced underground before they can confront the enemy within and thwart the Zargons' plans.

Thunderbirds: Terror from the Stars
by John Theydon

Thunderbird Five is attacked by an unknown enemy with uncanny powers. An unidentified object is tracked landing in the Gobi desert, but what's the connection? Scott Tracy races to the scene in the incredible Thunderbird One, but he cannot begin to imagine the terrible danger he is about to encounter.

Alone in the barren wilderness, he is possessed by a malevolent intelligence and assigned a fiendish mission – one which, if successful, will have the most terrifying consequences for the entire world.

International Rescue are about to face their most astounding adventure yet!

Thunderbirds: Peril in Peru
by John Theydon

An early warning of disaster brings International Rescue to Peru to assist in relief efforts following a series of earth tremors – and sends the Thunderbirds in search of an ancient Inca treasure trove hidden beneath a long-lost temple deep in the South American jungle!

When Lady Penelope is kidnapped by sinister treasure hunters, Scott Tracy and Parker are soon hot on their trail.

Along the way they'll have to solve a centuries-old mystery, brave the inhospitable wilderness of the jungle and even tangle with a lost tribe – with the evil Hood close behind them all the way...

Thunderbirds: Operation Asteroids
by John Theydon

What starts out as a simple rescue mission to save a trapped miner on the Moon, soon turns out to be one of International Rescue's greatest catastrophes. After the Hood takes members of International Rescue hostage during the rescue, a chase across space and an altercation among the asteroids only worsens the situation.

With the Hood hijacking Thunderbird Three along with Brains, Lady Penelope and Tin-Tin, it is up to the Tracy brothers to stage a daring rescue in the mountain tops of his hidden lair.

But can they rescue Brains before his engineering genius is used for the destructive forces of evil?

SPACE: 1999 Maybe There –
The Lost Stories from SPACE: 1999
by David Hirsch & Robert E. Wood

Strap into your Moon Ship and prepare for a trip to an alternate universe!

Gathered here for the first time are the original stories written in the early days of production on the internationally acclaimed television series SPACE: 1999. Uncover the differences between Gerry and Sylvia Anderson's original story Zero G, George Bellak's first draft of The Void Ahead and Christopher Penfold's uncredited shooting script Turning Point. Each of these tales shows the evolution of the pilot episode with scenes and characters that never made it to the screen.

Wonder at a tale that was NEVER filmed where the Alpha People, desperate to migrate to a new home, instigate a conflict between two alien races. Also included are Christopher Penfold's original storylines for Guardian of Piri and Dragon's Domain, an adaption of Keith Miles's early draft for All That Glisters and read how Art Wallace (Dark Shadows) originally envisioned the episode that became Matter of Life and Death.

Discover how SPACE: 1999 might have been had they gone 'Maybe There?'

The Armageddon Engine
by James Swallow

Adrift in deep space, Commander John Koenig and the people of Moonbase Alpha face an uncertain fate when a planet-killing alien weapon at the heart of a sinister cloud diverts their lost Moon on to a fatal trajectory.

As each moment brings the Moon closer to total obliteration, Koenig leads a desperate mission into the unknown to save all life on Alpha. Does hope lie among a rag-tag colony of refugees hiding in the shadow of devastation? Or can the Alphans find a path into the heart of the war machine and end its destructive rampage? With time running out, the answer will mean the difference between survival... or annihilation.

Intergalactic Rescue 4: Stellar Patrol
by Richard James

It is the 22nd century. The League of Planets has tasked Jason Stone, Anne Warran and their two robots, Alpha and Zeta to explore the galaxy, bringing hope to those in need of rescue.

On board Intergalactic Rescue 4, they travel to ice moons and jungle planets in 10 exciting adventures that see them journey further across the stars than anyone before.

But what are the secret transmissions that Anne discovers?

And why do their rescues seem to be taking them on a predetermined course?

Soon, Anne discovers that her co-pilot, Jason, might be on a quest of his own...:

Damaged Goods
by Richard James

First Action Bureau exists to protect the Earth from criminal elements before they get the chance to act. Using decades of 'big data' and globally connected quantum artificial intelligence, First Action Bureau is able to predict criminal activity before it occurs...

Nero Jones has led a troubled life, but things are about to get a whole lot worse... Press-ganged into joining First Action Bureau, a shadowy organisation set up to counter terrorist threats, Nero finds herself thrown into a range of increasingly more exciting missions under the guidance of the mysterious Nathan Drake.

As she learns more about the Bureau, she's haunted by half-forgotten memories that lead her to question everything she knows. Just what is real and what is fake? As she delves deeper into the Bureau's history, she comes to a startling conclusion; nothing is true!

Shadow Play
by James Swallow

The last line of defence in a clandestine war, SHADO is all that stands between humanity and a force of alien invaders – and leading that fight is the uncompromising Ed Straker, commanding Earth's defenders around the clock. But what happens when the man at the top is pushed too far?

After an experiment goes wrong, Straker awakens from a coma with missing memories and strange hallucinations that threaten his grip on reality – but is it the result of alien interference, or has the commander's iron will finally cracked?

Facing danger from within and without, Straker must find the truth... even if it kills him.

available from
shop.gerryanderson.com